罗衣

著

在 中 间

In
Between

上海文艺出版社

推荐序
朱砂

我蛮早知道罗衣,看她妈妈的微信,知道她写作,也画画,做模特,生得好看聪明念书好,就是那种别人家的孩子,于是别人家妈妈当然高兴了,谈起来总是喜气洋洋的。再后来拍 vlog,我猜跟今天这本书有直接的关系,读起来像是她拍摄里的独白。

罗衣的独白当然都是第一人称的,是因为她念法国学校吗?如果我悍然猜想的话,会是因为读萨洛特的自述,读佩雷克的《W》,乃至更远的传统吗?今天的口语写作肯定不再是问题了,写作的形式,内容和传播方法被一次次地拓展再拓展,于是基于口述和日常经验的描述四处可见。接着是影像制作的大面积普及,书写的权利更进一步的下放。于是重要的不再是制作方式,而是新的观看和阅读关系。对影像的观看,阅读和即时回应形成了一次次的补充和再书写。日常生活的价值被重估了,在旧日可能会被认为是流水的记录,就会变成今天鲜活的细节。作者也不再藏身于自己家中，而是仿佛与读者们同在。文字与画面还有观众的评论形成一种复杂的生产关系，继而形成新的生产资料，在手机和电脑里，作者与读者是同构的。

我们大概还会肯定上个世纪小说与群治之关系里的想象，继而肯定新文学与新民的关系。那么视频会是新的形式继而带来更新的新民吗？无论如何，影像俨然成为普遍的阅读形式。于是罗衣的描写构成了这样的新旧对比。在更为广阔的文化图景里，一个涉及更多人参与，形成连接与价值的恰恰是这样的组合关系，一个新的事实。而我总是滞后的，自惭形秽地慢个半拍，在暗处无力地揣度和猜想。那么阅读罗衣或许会是一个更好的开始。

目录

001　我是谁

003　总是在迁徙
005　被不同的语言分裂
007　混血的文化
008　我是谁
011　真正的应该和被告知的应该
013　一切生命的感受都是美丽的
014　开始整洁的房间
016　美好是需要自控的
018　笛卡尔的蜡
021　安静可以是一种力量
025　每个人只有一条属于她自己的道路
027　我不喜欢分享

029　白日梦

- 031　脑海里的小饼干
- 032　白日梦
- 035　在"朦胧地带"旅行
- 037　森林的光芒
- 039　空虚之子,便是无聊
- 041　哭泣的艺术
- 042　一些断章
- 043　如果时间是永恒的
- 044　马龙·白兰度们
- 046　情绪和壁柜
- 047　思乡病
- 048　再见房间 2B-315
- 050　羽毛下的藏匿

051　存在与消失

- 053　存在与消失
- 055　我与我若即若离的记忆
- 058　关于孤独的对话

060　与痛苦同行的幸福

062　从旧金山开往上海的地铁

064　风筝的高度

066　被再定义的假期

069　仪式是生活的盐

071　松鼠仍然在树枝间跳跃

074　我们会留下活过的痕迹

075　日常琐事

077　秋天的快乐

078　白色波士顿

080　早上好,陌生人!

082　历史的一个词就是我们全部的一生

085　一个特殊的时期开始了

088　温柔的抚慰

090　一个人的房间

092　此时的孤岛

094　十四天,回家等待中的日记

107　一切都是未知的

109　女性 & 爱情

111　两个人
113　两个人的日常
115　最终都会成霜
116　金属蛇
117　成为一个女人
118　美是有差异的
122　女性的两难
123　一个黑人妈妈
127　精神才是不凋谢的花朵
129　衣服的社会标签
132　我的身体是一颗行星

133　世界 & 城市

135　共享并保持个人边界
136　巴黎街头
138　纽约的一次聊天
145　笔直的纽约和更高的上海
147　心灵天文馆

149	印象派的暴风雪
151	在海滩上
153	被唐人街安慰
155	不被看到的城市阴影
159	如果风景是有感知的
161	一切都是时间问题
163	我和我的花园

165 艺术与美

167	美是一种思想
169	爱上法国新浪潮电影
173	与世界共享一支笔
175	伟大的正午
176	科学并不是绝对客观的
180	在马德里邂逅毕加索
182	人是艺术的核心
184	作品后面的思想者
185	两种工匠
187	主观的景象
190	消费主义的僵尸

192	少就是多
194	因为缺乏被教育而自由
196	音乐是种过滤器
198	一个仰慕者

201　下一个路口

253　Chloé Chloe Chluoyi LuoYi

255	Unrooted
257	Linguistic Schizophrenia
260	True Ought, Told Ought
262	My Love Mine All Mine
263	Cat the Bat

265　Daydreaming

267	Cookie Jar
268	The Twilight Zone
270	Son of Void, He is Boredom
271	Fragments
272	If Time is Eternal
273	Marlon Brandos
275	Closeted

276	Homesick
277	Farewell 2B-215

279   Existence and Disappearance

281	Existence and Disappearance
283	Horses and Cows
285	Happy New Year
287	San Francisco–Shanghai Express
289	To be a Kite
291	Vacant Vacations

293   Life Itself

295	Autumn is a Second Spring
297	Morning, Stranger!
299	A Word in History is an Entire Life
301	Isolation Island

303   Womanhood

305	All Will Form A Common Frost
306	Womanly

309   Around the World

311	Anatomy of a Subway
312	Psychic Planetarium

313	An Impressionist Blizzard
315	On the Beach

319   Art and Aesthetics

321	Art and Beauty
323	Midday Thought
325	Picasso in Madrid
328	A Subjective Scene
330	Less is More
332	If You Don't Understand the Rules, Then There Are No Rules
334	Music is a Filter

337   The Next Crossroad

我是谁

总是在迁徙

生活让我不断地在各个城市中迁徙，如同一棵树的根散落在了各地。

当我还是一棵幼苗时，我经常想象自己能长成一棵百年橡树，根深到地球的基岩，树干比一个人的拥抱还粗。结果却是，我长得越来越像野草，不断被移植，不断地迁徙。

每当我的根想植入一片土壤、学会吸收地下的物质和液体，并与当地的生物偎依在一起时，我就会被连根拔起，被栽到另一片土地上去。我刚刚熟悉的过去的土壤会有一些残存物依附在我的根上，但也就仅此而已——旧泥土迟早会被新的泥土吞没。

于是，我只好再次学习适应新的泥土，在新的土地里吸收不熟悉的物质和液体，和新的生物朋友连接在一起。很多次这样的重复循环之后，我会忍不住问自己，除了在地上留下一个即将被另一株植物填满的洞外，我是否还给旧土壤留下了些什么？

我希望是的。

也许，野草不是个合适的比喻，我更像覆盆子树、葡萄藤或任何攀缘植物。我的根会一直深深地扎入泥土里，长出更宽更大的枝干和树叶，四处蔓延，一直延伸到陌生的土地上。

我在延伸的过程中也会结出果实，而当果实成熟时，它们会落到地上，腐烂，最后渗入树下的土壤中。最后这些果实是长成了独立的植物，还是变成了滋养其他根系的营养物，我无法预料，但我知道，我的一部分留在我走过的地方，我的经历是有价值的，这就足够欣慰了。

被不同的语言分裂

当我刚开始读萨尔曼·鲁西迪的《撒旦诗篇》时,我对他的一些用词感到有些困惑——不是因为它们有多粗野,更多是因为它们的拼写。"米国。""咸心。"鲁西迪是按照人物的发音来拼写单词的。他把他们的口音印在了纸上。

语音拼写是赋予角色深度和个性的可靠方法,类似于在人物对话中使用口语化语言。但不知怎的,这种写作方式会让我觉得尴尬。因为如果我要把我的语言以语音拼写方式写下来,我不清楚有多少词会是标准的美国式拼写,有多少词会是中法混合口音的拼写?

如果是五年前,我敢肯定从我口里出来的80%的单词都会拼写得很奇怪。"girls"会被拼写为"gueurelz","world"会被拼写为"weureld",这是英文的法国口音读法。但今天,我的英文已经熟练到了这样一种状态:听起来像美国人,足以让"亻仑享夊"(鲁西迪会这么写)的英国人以为我来自美国,让美国人以为我来自加州,至少来自加拿大。

然而,尽管我的英文发音和本地人差不多,我还是会觉得说英语很尴尬。这不是因为我的舌头和喉咙发出的声音,而是因为我说英语的方式,是用英语单词说法语,在语音后面,那个思考的大脑是被法语训练出来的。虽然在美国,我学会了要对"what's up"回答"not much",但是很美国化的句式并不能改变句式后面的语言逻辑。当我需要写下自己的思考时,我仍然会使用法语的思考方式,喜欢使用冗长的句子,这不得不感谢波德莱尔和福楼拜。

现在,英语已经开始取代法语越来越多地占据我的日常表达,但我不认为我能摆脱我原本的思维方式,植根于我大学以前的法语教育,形成了我的思想基础。

人在不同语言的系统中,也会有很不相同的思考问题的方式,而我,被分裂在好几种语言之中,如同有好几个不同的化身。

混血的文化

上海最让我惊叹的是它具有新与旧、东方与西方、喧嚣与宁静的和谐融合。拿武康路的武康庭来说，虽然建筑物外壳是过去的老洋房，但它们的核心已经完全转化，以符合时尚的现代人群的需求。霓虹灯、现代画廊和时尚商店延长了这些建筑的寿命，否则它们就会可悲地变得无关紧要。

这是我的城市，我在这里出生和长大，在这座城市里认识了自己。我的母亲是中国人，父亲是法国人，我有着西方教育的背景，同时又有强烈的东方价值观。这座城市是不同文化、时代和节奏的交汇点，是无限可能和创新的摇篮，这个城市，给了我多维度看待世界的眼光。

两年前，当我最后一次回家的时候，外国人仍然期望中国人说英语，但今天，6岁的俄罗斯孩子们跑来跑去说普通话，仿佛这是他们的母语。

这个城市和我一样，都是混血文化的结合。

我是谁

上一次去纽约时，我才 12 岁。那时，我和我的父母在一起，没有任何担忧，不用负任何责任。现在我 18 岁，快 18 岁了，这也是我第一次独自旅行，老实说，我很害怕。

我在纽约待了一个周末。离开纽约的前一天，我和茱莉亚音乐学院的朋友一起去看了场日场歌剧：《玛尼》。歌剧的主角玛尼说了一些让我印象深刻的话，她哭诉她如何在不断地变换人格，好像她从来不是同一个人。

她的哭诉触动了我。常常，我也很好奇这一刻的"我"是不是一秒前的"我"，或是一秒后的"我"，我想知道和我妈妈在一起的那个"我"是不是与独处时的"我"或与朋友在一起时的"我"是同一个"我"。

同样，在纽约的"我"并不是在波士顿或是在上海的"我"，也不是在中央公园、第六大道、哥伦布大道或另外任何地方的我。

我像玛尼和其他任何人一样,一直在不断地生长,如同河流永不停歇。但是,不管我之前是谁或现在是谁,在纽约和朋友看日场歌剧的我和深夜觅食的我,都是一个快乐的我。

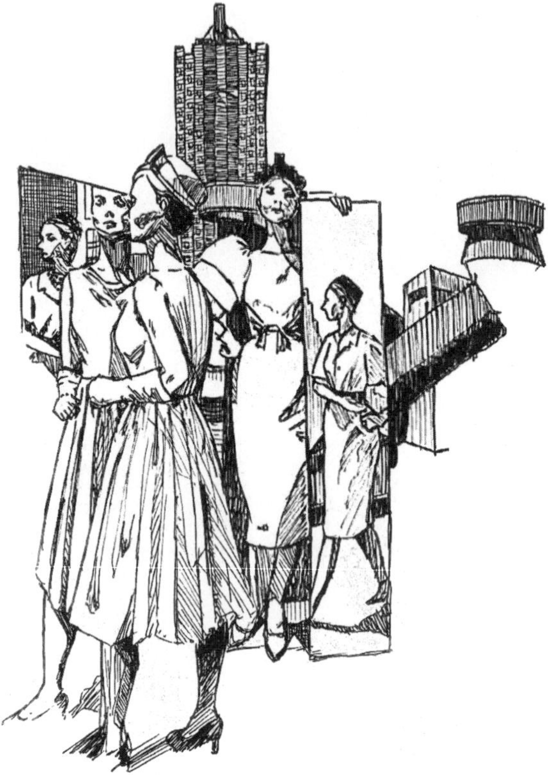

真正的应该和被告知的应该

旅行多少都是为了逃避一些事情：太熟悉的环境，无法忍受的人，开始变得相同的日子，以及让我们不堪负荷的责任。同时，旅行也给我们提供了一个审视我们的行为和决定的机会，它拉开了我们与过于熟悉的生活的距离，给我们一个另外的视角，让我们能够重新评估我们的状态。

观察生活习惯与你不一样的人是一种很好的提示，能够让人反思自己，意识到生活没有什么是确定的，我们的行为和感受中哪些元素是后天养成的品味，哪些是本能和天生的。

在美国，尤其是年轻群体里，很多人平衡生活的方式就是一天狂欢豪饮，第二天又去参加高强度的动感单车课程。而瑞典人就不一定是从一个极端走向另一个极端，他们喜欢把平衡感维持在一个黄金分配范围内。每天骑车上班，下班后和同事一起喝杯酒，聊聊天，不过分，但是更容易持续，相对于极致的刺激，他们更倾向简单的快乐。

想想我们平日里相信和遵循的一切所谓应该的事，哪些是真正应该的？哪些是因为觉得应该而去构建的？那么，这一切有多少是必要？为什么是必要的？有多少东西占用了你大量的时间和精力，但实际上却没有那么重要？

我还没有弄明白的问题是：当你清除了一切你所学的无价值的思想与行为以后，除了作为一个孤立的原子化个体，还能如何和别人生活在一起？

一切生命的感受都是美丽的

生命中有些让我感受到疼的东西,它们潜伏在我的身体里,我能看到它们。但是我不惧怕。

一切存在都是真实的,它们是我的经历,是的,我确实经历过一些什么。我,不是我的父亲,不是我的哥哥,不是我的朋友,而只是我,所有的经历和感情铸成了现在的这个我。

万种感觉在我的身体中升华,而这些所有的感觉都属于我,我有我的悲伤,我随心所欲地修饰它们。我有我的感知,即使丑陋,它们也是我的,是美丽的。

开始整洁的房间

"有组织的混乱",这是我在十几岁的时候,父母让我收拾房间时,我用来形容我的房间的词语。

青少年的房间通常都很乱,而随着年龄的增长,人们变得越来越整洁,对杂乱的无法容忍在中年之后更是达到极限。我想这是因为整理一个人的房间就像整理一个人的心灵一样。换句话说,一个人的环境是一个人思想的投射,由于额叶皮质不成熟,青少年的行为举止比成年人更加冲动和非理性,这也解释了为什么他们的房间如此混乱。

我想我的额叶皮质在过去的两年里成熟了一些,这次回家是我第一次意识到我的房间是多么的杂乱。与现在的生活习惯相比,我几年前的生活习惯简直一团糟。当时的我习惯晚睡,每天只睡4个小时,不注意营养,缺乏生活的组织性。而现在,我每天准时在午夜到来前睡觉,避免吃过度加工的食物,并有自己打死也不会破的纪律。

我学会了把自己看作是我身体和思想的设计者,我要为我的身体在它存在的所有场域里的状态负责,这就是长大了吧。

美好是需要自控的

我注意到人的内在和外在是相互影响的。

干净的饮食习惯能够让我们的皮肤更好。阅读——无论是小说还是课本——会扩大我们的知识基础，会让我们的眼睛里闪着火花。这些是影响外部状态的内部变化。

在忧郁的时候强迫自己微笑也会让自己心态变得好一些，有一个良好的日常护肤习惯也会滋养身体体内的细胞，外貌的美好会带来一个人的自信，这些是影响内在状态的外在变化。

然而，内在改变似乎没有外在变化那么显而易见。只是，外在变化可以在需要更少努力、更少时间的情况下提供更多的即时满足。改变发型是一件马上就能注意到的事情，但学会感恩，找到内心平衡，这些变化却不会立即透露出来。

也许，如果想改变内在，从改变外在开始会更容易。因为养成一个立刻见效的好习惯会激励促成另一个过程更加缓慢的好习惯。

当我们似乎无法控制内心的混乱时,我们必须记住,外在部分是可塑的、可控制的,而能够控制看得见的东西,必定就能控制看不见的东西。

笛卡尔的蜡

人的思维真是有趣，可以把无限大的东西在想象中缩小到无限小，也可以把无限小的东西放大成无限大。像这样，在某些时候，我可以通过我的思维方式来调整我所处的环境。当我面对的事情变得太压抑和沉闷时，我会通过想象那些更远、更高、更长久的东西来换换气。

对我来说，重要的是如何适应所有的情况，也就是能够将所有情况都视为正常态。这就像穿了一套适合所有场合的装束，比如一件适合开会、聚会、郊游或宅家的小黑裙。这种能让人融入所有场景的能力会使我们的生活流动和谐起来，使人可以在没有太多情绪起伏的情况下把握生活状态。这种能力有助于避免身处陌生人之间时的尴尬和孤独，让我们即使和这些说话、穿着和行为方式不同的人在一起也能够处于舒适放松的状态。

但这不意味着必须一直妥协，以至于忘记自己是谁，自己想要什么。其实，每个人都有自己坚实的价值观，很难被改变。与其说我们应该为了对应一个环境而不断对自己剪枝、除根，还不如鼓励自己这棵树好好生长，朝着更多的方向蔓生出枝叶来。

事实上，我们很像笛卡尔所写的那块蜡。一块蜡通过它独特的气味、颜色、大小、硬度、声音以及所有这些出现在我们面前的东西来影响我们对它的认知。但是如果你把这块蜡靠近热源，它的特性就会改变，我们也会得到全新的感受。

然而，无论这块蜡有着怎样的变化，蜡还是蜡，就如同无论我们如何适应我们的环境，我们仍然是我们。

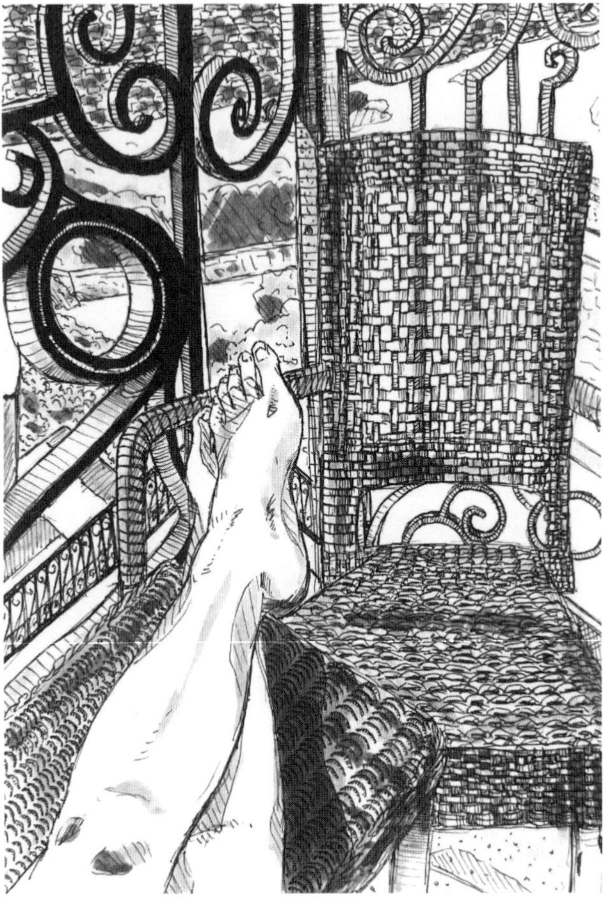

安静可以是一种力量

我对公开演讲的恐惧超过了我对学数学的恐惧。

一周前,我开启了我在美国读书的第二个学期。当我看到我的新课程表时,整个人都僵硬了。"周二周四,每早八点,公开演讲课,富里德教授",课表上赫然写着。战斗还是逃跑?我的第一本能反应是如何把这门必修课给推了,推到越迟越好。然而,我内心深处又有一个声音提醒我说,学好这堂课将会对我有很大的帮助。

我是一个生性羞涩而安静的人。从上幼儿园开始,我就永远是那个独自静静地在角落里玩娃娃玩得很开心的小姑娘。我从来不会主动去找其他小朋友玩,更别说在课上举手答题了。一直到小学,我的老师们每学期都把我的父母叫到学校开家长会。在学校,我没有欺负同学,作业也按时写,功课也算优异,我唯一的错误,永远的错误,就是太安静了,安静到孤僻,安静到老师们担心我有自闭症,甚至建议我父母带我去看心理医生。但事实上，我只是喜欢安安静静地当一个小透明。幸运的是我的父母坚信安静就是我的个性，坚信我只是单纯地不需要那么多的交流，否则谁知道我会不会被迫吃各种药、接受许多不必要的治疗。这么多年过去了，我仍然如此。当我的朋友们热衷于在周末的晚上一起出去蹦迪喝酒时，我宁愿舒舒服服地待在家里画画、看书、和我妈妈看美食纪录片。

人们经常因为我话少而觉得我又酷又高冷，这让一些人觉得我有神秘感。但实际上，我说话少的最大原因是我不知道该如何与他人打交道。当别人和我说话时，我往往第一时间不知道该怎么反应，我不知道我是否要迎合他们的想法，我不知道他们期待得到的回答是什么，我更不知道如何去找闲聊的话题。

自从去年秋天来了美国后，我发现我并没有见过任何一个内向社恐的美国人。这里，每个人都充满活力、善于社交。这使我很纳闷：难道这里就没有内向的人吗？！所以，一天晚上，在我和我的美国男朋友通话时，我向他提出了这个问题。"[外向]只是美国文化的一部分"，他说。我看到的美国人，似乎都擅长言辞和沟通，在美国，人们偏爱

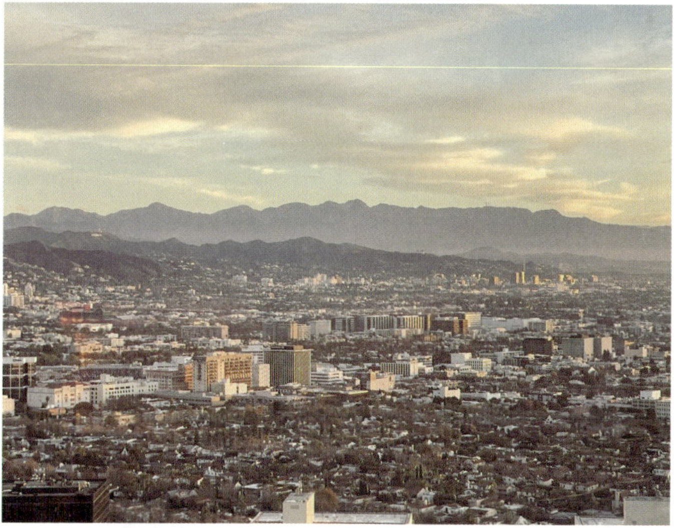

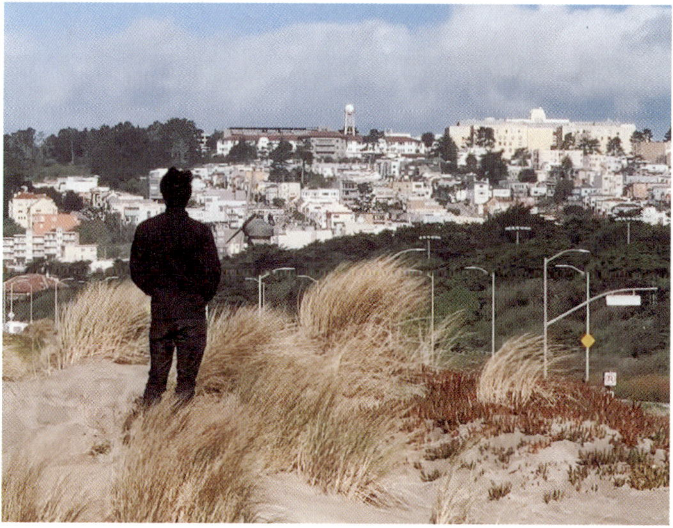

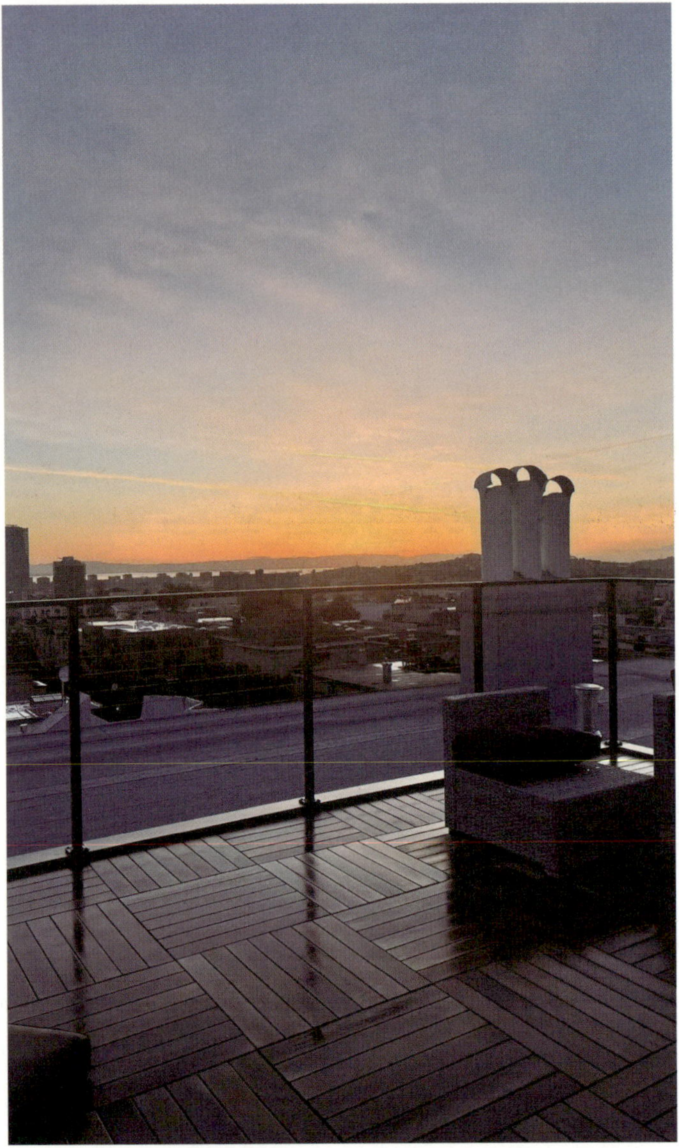

有行动力的人，这是一种美国大众价值。

根据作家苏珊·凯恩的观点，从二十世纪时开始，美国流行一种新的文化，一种被历史学家称作"个性"的文化。那时，美国迅速地从一个农业经济体发展成了一个大的商业经济国家。人们突然开始搬迁，从小城镇搬向城市，并且完全改变了他们之前和所熟识的人们一起工作的方式。这些搬去城市的人在一群陌生人中有必要证明自己，因此，领袖气质和个人魅力这样的品质突然间似乎变得极为重要。从那时开始，所有励志的书也开始强调这些品质，如戴尔·卡耐基所著的《如何赢得朋友和影响他人》。活在这么一个环境下，大多数性格内向者都会逼迫自己去扮演外向者的角色。即使他们实际上只想待在家里读书，但他们始终还是会为了证明自己而和朋友去拥挤吵闹的酒吧，来掩盖自己的孤独和脆弱，在别人面前扮演一个受欢迎的公众角色。

我曾经尝试过像其他人一样，在社交场合努力表现所谓的活泼和热情，但是每一次都会把自己搞到筋疲力尽。我不断地问自己，我是否必须和他人一样，以一种社会价值来衡量自己的存在？我是否需要强制改变自己以迎合别人的喜好，成为一个在社交中受欢迎的人？

坦率地说，不擅长社交带给我的并非只有坏处，我也因此获得了大量的时间，对外的封闭激发了我的想象力，我内心的张力。我最具有创造力与思维能力的时候，是我安静独处的时候，在一个人的环境中，我沉浸在自己的创作工作中，那是一个属于我的无边界的世界，在那里，我很自由。

上帝关了一扇门，又打开了一扇窗，谁知道哪一个更好？

对我来说，安静才是真正的力量。

每个人只有一条属于她自己的道路

我注意到,我的思想和态度变化从来不是特别的激进,这些变化总是一点一点地出现,就像"天"慢慢长出尾巴,从"天"变成"夫"。这是一个谨慎而温和的过程,以至于当改变发生时,它们甚至不像改变。我想这和很多其他事情是一样的:亲密的关系不是一夜之间培养起来的,油画不会立即变干,水果的生长也需要时间,除非是杰克和豆茎,或转基因食品,但科学还没有到那一步。

有时候这也让我有点沮丧。我是在速度中长大的,我习惯了快节奏的生活,甚至可能有点沉迷于不断变化带来的肾上腺素。斯宾诺莎说过,除了欲望,我们什么都不是。任何改变,任何行动都是为了实现这些欲望。那么,这是否意味着我对改变上瘾,因为我渴望太多?

我确实意识到,渴望太多,过于分散,最终什么也得不到。无法发生实质性的改变,是因为你把所有的精力都花在了一堆建筑基础上,而这些基础往上生长需要更多的东西以及更长的时间。太多的欲望，最终留下的只能是一个个未完工的建筑工地，它们被我们扔在角落里，积满灰尘。

我唯一能做的就是选择我最强烈的愿望所在，做我喜欢的事情并有所成就。这需要我把所有的努力和精力都集中在这个愿望之上。我不能完成的其他的美好愿望，我会在别人身上发现，我只需要仰慕他们。这就是遇到不同背景的人的奇妙之处，我会在他们身上看到那些不属于我自己的道路的成果，并给"如果当初我——"这个疑问找到一些答案。

每个人，都只能走好一条属于她自己的道路。

我不喜欢分享

以前,我是唯一的 Chloé
Chloe 有很多,但 Chloé 只有我一个
可是,你看,我的宿舍居然来了一个
难道一个 Chloé 不够吗?
现在,锐音符不再是我的了
我得与另外一个人分享它
她个子更小,头发更卷曲,皮肤也更白
我把音符分成两半,一半给她,一半给我
我不喜欢这样做,但她是一个好女孩
我没啥可抱怨的

白日梦

脑海里的小饼干

我的脑海里，有许多小饼干。巧克力味的，苦瓜味的，肥皂泡味的，日落味的，大的，小的，光滑的，什么样的都有。

不知从何时起，这些小饼干填满了我的脑袋，它们挤来挤去，每一个都要得到我的重视，可是慢慢地，它们变得越来越多，我的脑子都要装不下了！

没办法，新来的小饼干只能压碎那些有年头的旧饼干，使它们成为我脑袋里积的一层灰。被压碎的饼干们虽然失去了最初的形状，但是它们的味道没有变。只要把这层五颜六色的灰揉一揉，捏一捏，就能捏出我最初的模样。

白日梦

嘀,嗒!嘀,嗒!

"这就是肝脏的作用……"教授的话语在墙上回荡,并且在时间的轨迹里消失。除了暖气震耳欲聋的嗡嗡声和笔在纸上的摩擦声外,从他嘴里滔滔不绝地冒出来的话语是唯一的声音。

话语是什么?利用话语,我们能够创造也能够摧毁,我们能够被安放也能够被激荡,我们能够靠近也能够疏远。对于我,话语能让我远走高飞。

"我离这里很远;我远离课堂,远离学校,远离波士顿令人作呕的寒冷,远离这些人群。"只是想着这些话,我就身在他方。

我在一个暖和的地方,正好在阳光下。这个地方没有名字。它没有出现在任何地图上,但是包含了使生活更加美好的所有元素。我的哥哥和我在一起,我的父母也在身边。我们走在鹅卵石的小巷里,在阴影下,在蝉鸣中。我们像这样走了几个小时,但是我很难确定确切的持续时间。太阳永远悬挂在地平线上方，用明亮的橙色将所有破旧的白色建筑着了色。

上帝知道这些石头、墙壁和百叶窗从何时开始就在这里了，十年，数百年？也许只是几秒钟。时间固定在现在，没有昨天，没有前天，没有明天。一切都在这里和现在。

远方，有路人从眼角看着我们。他们看起来很像我，我和我的父亲。仿佛如果我们的面孔融化了，他们的面孔便会浮出。在这些熟悉的眼神下，我们拐了个弯，他们也随之消失了。

我们到达了一条建筑物变了形的大街。太阳仍然悬挂在太平线，但是阳光越来越猛烈，使我感到厌倦。"太热了，我需要水。"随后，在中间的道路上突然从地面涌出了一口井。我冲了过去，将头伸向空洞。一股气流从下往上吹，使我摆脱了日常生活中的物体和人的束缚，并减少了我口中令人不愉快的味道。这之前，我不断恶心疲倦，好像一切都让我的身体越来越沉重，并慢慢地把我压成了令人讨厌的土豆泥。但是，在这种不适消失的那一刻，我感到一股强大的力量将我推到了井底。我摔倒了。我首先尝试抓住了井内坚硬冰冷的石头，但经过多次尝试，我发现这个举动除了烧伤我的手指以外毫无用处。所以，在我失去意识之前，我让我的身体自然下垂。

我醒来时发现自己独自站在一片结了冰的表面上。

"你没事吧?"一个滑冰的男孩喘吁吁地问道。

"我没事，谢谢。"

时间恢复了。

在"朦胧地带"旅行

每天晚上都会有一个瞬间,我会进入一种被我称为"朦胧地带"的状态。在这个时刻,我的思维和清醒会逐渐消失,我被缓慢地拖进某种梦乡。用不那么诗意的话来说,处于"朦胧地带"就是处于进入非快速眼动第一阶段睡眠的边缘。

我大部分最疯狂的想法都是在这个时候产生的。似乎每当我的脑电波变慢时,我就不再顾虑逻辑和现实了——事实上,真实和虚幻之间的界限都变得完全模糊了。这使我的大脑创造的最荒谬的故事都像日常琐事一样看似正常。

一旦我的大脑开始将文字和图像编织成魔幻的连贯叙事,我就有两个选择。第一个选择,我可以马上醒来,以失去睡眠为代价,立即写下梦乡边缘给我注入的胡思乱想。第二个选择,我可以告诉自己,当我醒来时,我会记住这个想法,并且继续入睡。根据我的经验,第二天醒来时,我很少会记得前一天大脑给我讲的离奇睡前小故事。所以,大多数时候，我会睁开眼睛，抓起手机，忙乱地写下脑海中闪过的任何东西，不管语法是否正确，不管思想是否有意义。

第二天醒来后的早晨是用来复习这些笔记的。有些时候，我写的东西会意义明确。另一些时候，我感觉我的大脑给我开了个大大的玩笑，让我乱写了一堆。但无论结果如何，我一天中最喜欢的时刻仍然是这"朦胧地带"，因为我可以逃离意识清醒的日常状态，好像到另外一个空间做了次短暂的旅行。

森林的光芒

今天,我正在安静地绘画,突然远处传来了一个巨大、奇怪的声音。

咕噜声来自一个我从未见过的生物。它看起来像牛,也有点像鹿,又有点像马,但是更加雄伟。我们从远处看着它穿过马路,消失在一条狭小的布满阳光斑点的森林土路上。

我们等了一会儿,然后跟上了它。

天气温暖而明亮,我们的头顶上覆盖着一片棉被般的白云,微风轻轻吹动着它,以至于我们时不时地可以看到闪烁的阳光。随着我们越来越深入森林,越来越远离一些徒步者的目光,阳光逐渐消失了。随即,另一种亮光出现了。原本白天普通无奇的紫色小花,像挣脱了看不见的禁忌的制约,散发出紫水晶般的光芒,繁茂的花朵闪烁着粉红色的光芒,铺成了一条道路,牵引着我们的双眼也牵引了我们的脚步。

我们发现了一片全新的土地。

在这里，月亮分裂成了成千上万的锦鲤在天堂翻转和扭动，仿佛它们在寻找回家的路，如果鱼有羽毛，那它们一定是长成这样的。锦鲤散发的光芒将周围的一切染上了温柔的紫色：草，溪流与微微吸收锦鲤光芒的鲜花，更不用说花朵散发的像银河系蜂蜜般粘在我们衣服上的甜美了……

空虚之子，便是无聊

当我脑子里有太多东西时，我什么都不能思考。

想象一下 The Doors 的 Light My Fire 的配乐以卡农的方式不断地在脑子里回荡。各种乱七八糟的想法像激动的原子一样聚集和碰撞，最终形成一团爆炸成原子蘑菇的杂音。

水火不容的想法是异质思想的云彩。无论我多么想要搅拌混合它们，它们都无动于衷。它们碰撞，弹跳，碰撞，震动，但绝对拒绝形成一团像雾一样的同质的思想。

原子蘑菇的果实是最糟糕的：空虚之子，便是无聊。

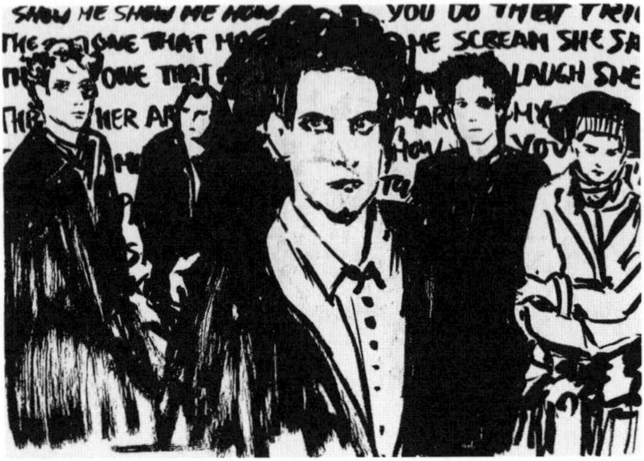
SHOW ME SHOW ME HOW
SCREAM
LAUGH

哭泣的艺术

我经常哭。看电影时我会哭，不理解时我会哭，理解的时候也会哭。我会在脑袋里哭，在脸上哭，也会因为哭了而哭，因为我不想再哭了。小时候，我曾经会无声地哭泣，只为了能够独自一人。为了不被打扰而在脸上画上笑脸，那才是王牌演技。

哭泣已成为我的艺术。但要知道，我的眼泪从来没有除去过我的面具，相反，是它们帮我乔装打扮的。多亏了它们，我笑过一千遍。

一些断章

有时我想,如果我闭上眼睛,我会在同一天的同一时间,但在另一个地方睁开它们。

每当我看到人们在十字路口过马路时,黄色潜水艇的旋律就会在我的脑海中弹跳。

永远不要认为你什么都知道。永远不要确定任何事情。当你认为自己确定时,你确定你自己确定吗?

飞机是一个胶囊,它可以让你重新启动,并为不一样的场景做好准备。不一样的生活方式。新的开始。

如果时间是永恒的

你们知道我最害怕什么吗？我害怕一切开始都没有结局，害怕时、分、秒的概念不存在，害怕时间是永恒的，像空间一样。当我思考时空的概念时，我的大脑就会冻结。时空太大了，太抽象了，我无法理解。当我无法在脑袋里模拟它时，我就会陷入困境。我会失去信号。

每一天，我都会好奇每一张脸背后的故事是什么。我认为我与他们擦肩而过不是偶然。为什么我会经过这个人？我们为什么会出现在同一条街上？

相机捕获的照片从来不是我们想要的图像。在我们按下快门的那一秒，已经太晚了。只有成为先知，预知一个神奇时刻到来，才能捕获到它。像挥动棒球棒一样，我们必须看得见球的轨迹，才能百发百中。

马龙·白兰度们

我在书店里徘徊时的状态是最平静的,我说的不是任何书店,而是二手书店。

无法解释为什么,但是每当我的指尖轻触摇摇欲坠的旧书页时,身心便会情不自禁地有一种满足感。我尤其享受泛黄的书页散发出的木头气味,当我迷失在成堆的旧书中时,这个气味便会轻轻地刺激我的嗅觉,使我的鼻孔有些发痒。破旧的书本中嵌入的麝香污垢和油腻的污渍并不会令我反感,相反,这些瑕疵使我更想触碰它们。每当我感到压力很大时,我所需要的就是拿起一本旧书,快速地用我的指尖翻阅书本,深吸那本书的味道。任何药物都无法代替这种感觉。我最喜欢的书就是由皮革包裹起来的那些书,它们散发的味道是强烈而独特的,像动物一样的气味,我称它们为"马龙·白兰度们(Marlon Brandos)"。

我喜欢幻想这些书的前任主人都是些什么人,什么样的人会因为乐趣而在让-弗朗索瓦·利奥塔（Jean-Francois Leotard）的书上记笔记？显然，有些人觉得阅读伏尔泰是一种乐趣。为什么有人会卖掉《每天一篇蒙田摘录》(*A Day Book of Montaigne*)？我猜想，在持续 N 天阅读一篇摘录以后，那人也读不下去了。有多少人在我拿到这本书之前触摸过这本书？他们的故乡是哪里？这些书又在这堆旧架子上摆了多长时间？

我永远不会找到确切的答案，我想，但我知道每本书曾经都是某个人的宝贝。说到底，不仅仅是书里的故事，书背后的故事也彻彻底底地吸引着我，那是一种叫人生的东西。

通过这些书，我的人生和许多人的人生发生了交集，深知这个，让我感到欣慰。

情绪和壁柜

我房间的整洁度反映了我处理问题的方式。

有情绪问题?把东西扔在壁橱里就行了。它仍然在那里,但是没人看得到。

所以我会把橱柜塞满,直到塞了太多东西为止,直到壁橱爆炸。

哎呀。

思乡病

我为什么会伤感?"因为我想家。我思乡。"但我为什么会想家?家里有什么我在这里找不到的东西?我的房间,太阳,我自己的空间,妈妈,爸爸,一个不会为了玩电子游戏而忽略我的人,一个不需要我开口说话就能理解我的感受的人。

我不善言辞。我的感受,我的一切思想,我不能立即轻易地出口成章在对话中表达出来。在日常交流中,我是笨拙的。我能做的只有把我朦胧的想法写下来,把它们清理干净,修剪成句子,然后不断整理。我的词句只有经过仔细排列才能准确反映我的感受。我无法在谈话中做到这一点,当我说话时,单词在我的脑子里会堵车。

我像是个轮胎,一个被放了气的轮胎。我厌倦了厌倦,也厌倦了周围的人因为我的厌倦而厌倦。思乡是一种疾病,伤感和厌倦是它的症状。

再见房间 2B-315

2019年5月,我开始整理我所有的物品,我要离开我的学生公寓了。

是时候离开这间房间了,离开早餐的沉静,门把上的钥匙与单调色彩的忧虑。在像鸽子般展翅飞走的各种时间片段中,地面从未像此刻这般光亮过。

此刻,我看着房间里的镜子,我的面孔仅仅是它所反映过的很多面孔之一。在这个空间里,在这个镜子里,曾经有过多少不同的面容,来了又离去。在这些变化无常的画面里,曾经有过什么样的悲伤与欢愉?目睹过多少恋人的呼吸与寂寞?他们的疲惫、他们的希望和他们永无止境的无聊?那些年轻的灵魂。

然而,悲伤并非是这些面容的全部。悲伤之下,暗含着青春的汹涌澎湃,像越过高高岩石的波浪,会有力地砸在沙滩上。

一切的存在,都在这里留下痕迹,存在过,并被新的痕迹取代,像盐结成晶体,浓缩了所有的青春的浓度。

在新的夏天快要结束时,这个房间将会有新的面容和声音,波浪将再次涌起,而青春将在镜面里再次结晶。

羽毛下的藏匿

一只瞳孔是玫瑰花蕾的蜥蜴

在阿尔贝·卡恩(Albert Kahn)的花园里与时代广场里滑动

一切都是空的,没有生命迹象

这就像一个在淡季空旷的体育场

紫丁香色的鸟,黄色的眼睛

拨开每根羽毛下面都藏了一张脸

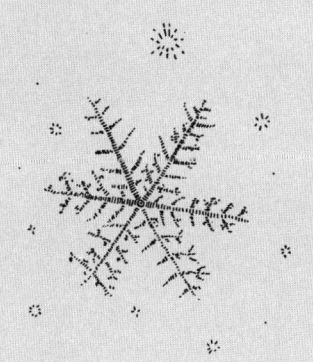

存在与消失

存在与消失

我喜欢雪花在我脸上融化的感觉,好像一片片雪花想要把我埋没在白色的风景里,慢慢地,一层又一层地。这种消失温和而微妙,就像某些人和某些记忆会逐渐从我们的大脑中消失一样,或者像新的神经连接会接管旧神经连接一样。

雪花与皮肤的每一次碰撞,都是一次小小的爆炸。看似无声而轻柔的撞击,其实是成千上万的晶体在接触到人体热量后剧烈的解体。雪花触碰皮肤的瞬间形成了一个陨石撞击地球的微观世界。

靴子踩在嘎吱作响的雪地上的声音有些孤独,留下的短暂痕迹会在一两个小时内消失。每一个脚印都暗示着我来过,也暗示着我的存在,但这是一种谨慎的存在,会因为最轻微的风吹而消失。

我想,正是这种行走与存在,却同时不断被抹去的感觉,让我如此喜欢独自在雪地里漫步。在雪中,我想到的任何东西——包括这些随意的胡言乱语和文字——都会迅速消失,不留痕迹,不留证据，除非我把它们写下来。我好像走在白板上一样，从零开始思考。漫步的过程中，我的思想有时只会蔓延一点，有时却会蔓延出许多，但一旦回到温暖的室内，一旦再次被墙壁约束，一切思想都会风吹云散，就好像什么都没发生过。

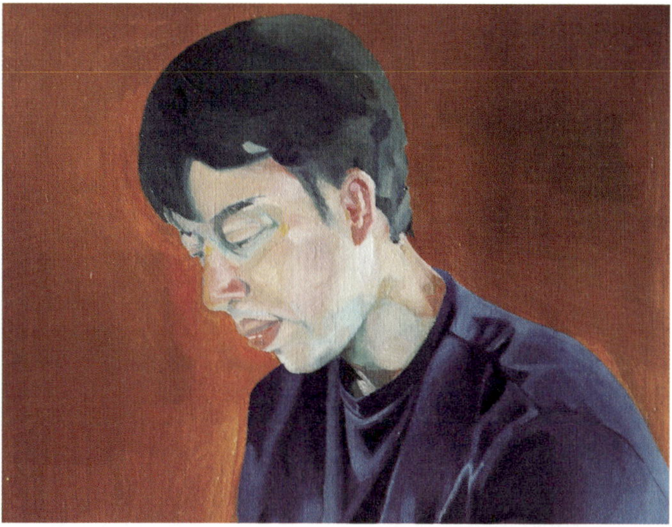

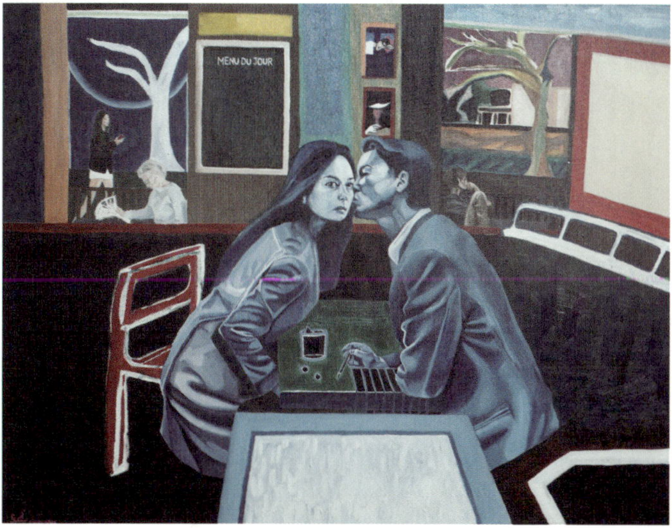
MENU DU JOUR

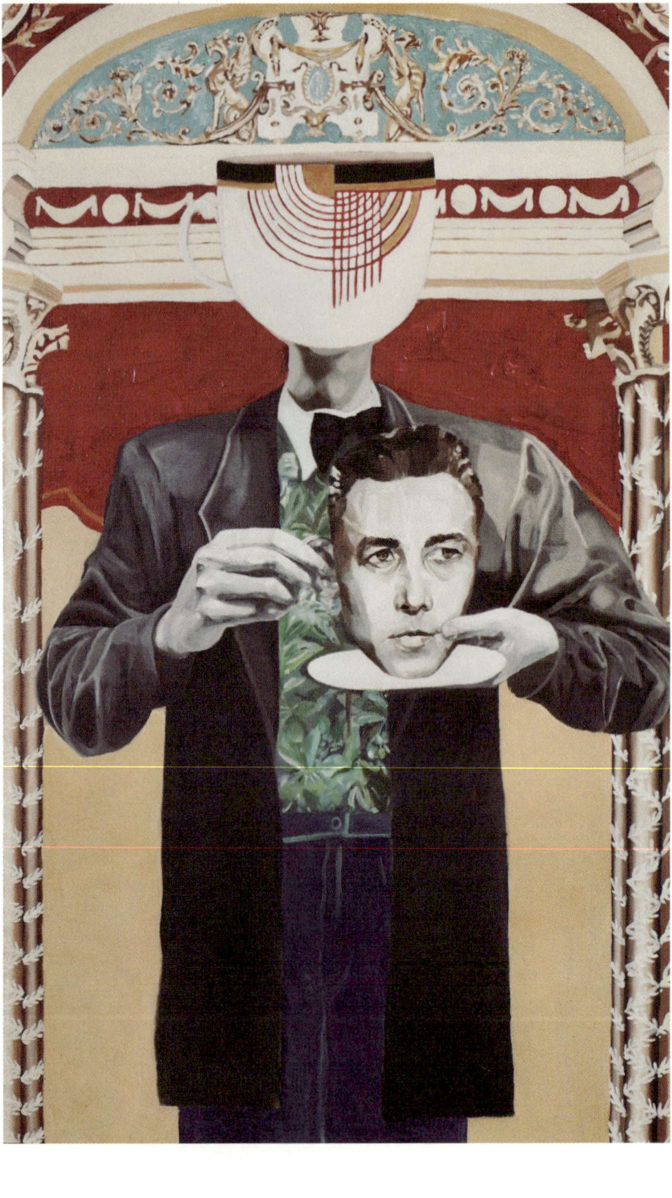

我与我若即若离的记忆

那个下午,一个拿着吹泡泡机的小孩吹着泡泡从我身边跑过,他的妈妈紧跟在他后面,他们在我身边留下了一丝香草的气味。当时是晚上五点,天开始黑了,我正从图书馆走回家。我的鼻子一下子捕捉到了那丝气息,一种甜蜜的熟悉的气息。那气息立即让我穿越到了某个夏天,我站在布拉格会跳舞的房子的楼顶上,手里拿着冰激凌,靠着栏杆,和我的哥哥背对着我的父母,静静地看着夕阳。爸爸走过来,递给了我人生中第一瓶啤酒,啤酒的味道太辛辣,我喝了不到一半便皱着脸把啤酒交给了妈妈。

记忆像闪电一样击中了我,而在我能够捕捉住它之前,它便又消失了。

回到波士顿撒满化雪盐的街道,我努力地试图重建那幅画面。我想象着不同国家的语言在我的耳后细语,舌尖上残留的麦芽味,以及被手温捂热的铁栏杆。感官记忆打开了我探索情感记忆的通道,我回想起十六岁的我，那个碰到任何事情都会兴奋，觉得自己离长大还早着呢的少女的我。我成功了，至少在那一秒钟内，我感受到了这种怀念的滋味，而且，今天的我与昨日情感的距离恰到好处。

我与我的记忆之间有一种若即若离的关系，我很珍惜这些回忆。总体上，大多数时候我完全无视它们，毕竟我的年龄还没到怀旧的时候。但是，只要它们被轻微的感觉输入触发，我便会将每段回忆拆散，再以我所选择的叙述方式将其重新拼凑在一起（"当时我很高兴""我很困惑""我全身上下都受到了启发"等）。在重新拼凑的图像里，我会为时间的线性流失而伤感，我会讨厌自己的健忘，有时候，我会混淆事物在时间中的顺序，会把现在的知识误认为是以前的智慧，事后诸葛亮一番，并自欺欺人地以为自己早就知道了许多东西。

不断记录我的生活是组成记忆这座纸牌屋的重要元素。我狂热地记录着我的现在，以便有一天我可以尽情地回到过去。我听以前喜欢的专辑、阅读旧日记、看旧视频并感叹于这些时刻离我有多么的久远。我遗憾于我的变化，但同时，我又渴望成长与改变，也会转过身来哀叹自己生活的种种版本，渴望逃脱自我。我沉迷于回忆，在等待未知的未来的同时，重温过去有一种令人难以抗拒的魅力。

今天，当我在教学楼排队等电梯时，我试图改变我脑袋里的这个记忆系统。我观察着周围的环境——隔壁教室飘来的奇特的咖喱味，走出教室路过的每一个海报——并尝试着运用这些细节形成的画面来想象在未来的我会如何回忆此时此刻，看待今天的我。我想象了将来的自己听到今天的自己最喜欢的歌曲时，也许是愉悦掺杂着悲伤的感受，我想象了未来的我会感叹今天的我太年轻太天真，但是，我失败了，因为这一切都没有发生。只有在时间的流逝中，我的生活才能以特别的方式呈现出回忆，与未来不同，回忆将是被选择的，被控制的，被确定的。

或许我的过去通过我的行为、思想、视觉与感受存在于我的体内，但我所记得的会不断变化，试图构建一种未来的回忆不过是白日做梦。我无法回到过去，只能活在当下。所以，我必须要继续前进。

关于孤独的对话

我从未如此亲近大自然。因为长时间住在城市里，我几乎忘记了除猫和狗以外，还有其他动物。而且，每当我想起猫狗，我也很难不去想他们和人类之间的关系。它们依赖我们，它们是宠物，它们在我们周围转来转去，它们生活在玛黑区35平方米的公寓里，睡在有小流苏的垫子上，那是我们在它们三岁生日时送给它们的礼物。

那么，在这里，杰克逊小镇，有很多真的动物吗？

是的，我看到了它们，比我想像的还多！

昨天我们去骑了自行车。大门向右转，如果沿着街道骑到离这里十公里的小木屋，过一会儿就会看到一片牛群，在道路的另一边，还能看到一些雄伟的公马，它们好像比我还高。我们抚摸了马，它们真的是很温和的大动物，喜欢被人轻轻地抚摸鼻子。然后，我们穿过马路去看牛，但是它们很害怕，我们一靠近它们就往后退。有趣的是，虽然每匹马都是独自待着,但是独处的它们看起来很是自在。牛却总是聚在一起,好像群居才有快乐。似乎,马儿选择了孤独,它们也满足于它们的孤独感。而牛呢——不能承受孤独的牛——它们试图在与别的牛的相伴中找到幸福感。

那你呢,你是马还是牛?

马!当然是马。一个人享受肯定比集体抑郁强……哦!你看!并不是每天都会有小鹿来你的花园里啃叶子吧!这儿是一个例外,或许在这里每天都有……

与痛苦同行的幸福

如果一年中有一个时间能让幸福普遍达到顶峰,那应该就是年末期间。这时,节日季刚刚开始,庆祝活动一个接一个。但奇怪的是,正是在这个时段,一种莫名的孤独感可能会袭来。为什么我的家人没有团聚?为什么叔叔要和爸爸吵架?为什么我要忍受这些我根本不喜欢的人的评判?为什么我感受不到幸福?幸福真的存在吗?

也许这种情绪的产生与对人们对幸福的错误定义有关。换句话说,幸福的感受,不在于我们是否找到了它,而在于我们如何对它定义。康德认为幸福是我们的欲望和由欲望延伸出的需求能得到保证和满足。但是,这样一个定义可能恰好就是我们不幸福的原因,因为我们总是需要更多来实现永远不会到来的欲望满足。真正的幸福或许就像一个与生活的婚约,不管怎样,不论好坏,都需要相信自己的誓言,努力和生活相亲相爱。

绝对的幸福如同痴人说梦,是一种不存在,生活总是有无法避免的残缺，毕竟残缺与存在是同质的。幸福在于有勇气来面对生活中所有不可避免的痛苦和不确定性。人们会死去，会哭，会受苦，但人们也可以快乐；不是在痛苦消失的短暂时刻，而是尽管痛苦，也幸福，甚至伴随着痛苦幸福。

从旧金山开往上海的地铁

白色的房间是活着的。它不是空的,它是一个充满意义的单色无限空间,它不断地自我更新并产生越来越多的含义。它是"白上白",它是一个独立的宇宙。它的画布、颜料与框架可以被无限地诠释,但它仍然保留着其本质,即白色单色的独创性。

白色的房间里有一个奇怪的精神乌托邦。我不知道自己能在黄色,紫色或红色的房间里做些什么,但是四面白色的墙壁通向的是无限的空间,一个微观世界通向一个宏观世界。我在白色立方体里面自由穿梭。我从外面的世界上撕下了彩色的衬里,然后把它编制成了线。我扭曲和操纵着线头以重新创建我的宇宙,一个平坦却丰满的宇宙,人们能沉陷进去却出不来。

逐渐地,我的思想成为自由的物体。它们从我的手掌中滑出,变成改变视线的光线,变成寻求思想激活的漫无目的的物体。

我无法完全掌握它。

它逃脱了我。

我的世界不再是我的世界。

它从未是过。

在这个白色的空间里,我希望有一列从旧金山开往上海的地铁。

风筝的高度

飞机的窗户朝着神奇的风景敞开,使我们脱离了我们太熟悉,太乏味的日常生活。

人类站在钢铁丛林下会显得渺小,而渺小会使我们谦虚,那么飞过这些丛林,摆脱束缚着我们双脚的地球,让天空像过分热情的恋人一样将我们拉向它那沸腾的心,就会给人一种无所不能的感受,让我们有一种如同成为神的幻觉。毕竟,随着海拔升高、心跳加快,追随权力的刺激也随之提升。

但是,一旦回到地上,我们就会发现自己只不过匍匐于世界的脚下。

落基山脉,横亘在我的眼前。山脉的冠冕笼罩着广阔的绿色植物丛,天空如蓝色天鹅绒被粉状的山峰雕刻。一串一串的紫色珍珠花朵形成一个反复无常的格纹,就好像哪位画家小心翼翼地以最具有装饰性的方式排列了它们。这些植物珍珠是易碎的珠宝,如果人类的手稍稍刮过它们,花朵就看不到即将到来的黎明,这脆弱的美让我们只能从远处观赏这番风景。如此，大自然这座博物馆自己建造了一个系统来保护自己，相对于被放在人类空间的容器里被人工照明展现的人工艺术品，自然的美是独立、野性和自由的。

这幅过于美丽的画布使我们感到自由自在，但无论画像丑陋或美丽，画像中的人物仍然留在画中，无法逃脱。我们这些人类不过是这个世界的风筝，线放长了，风筝飞得高了……看！它几乎到达了天堂！但是最终，线用尽了，线轴不再转动了，就这样，风筝被困住了。想想，真是没有什么可以自大的。

被再定义的假期

在日常生活中,各种习惯构成了一种生活结构,但是假期打破了那种习惯,时间是虚无的。这时候有两种选择,一个是形成新的框架,一个是面对虚无。通常,我会选择构建新的框架。

假期是"空余的时间,它没有任何预先建立的功能和用途。这段时间不属于上帝,也不属于日常、职业、社交和家庭生活。这段时间对我们每个人来说都是让人快乐的财富,但它有时也会让人痛苦和苦恼,因为人们害怕虚无",让·维亚尔(Jean Viard)写道。

假期是时间的沙漠,它是没有结构的自由时空。在这段时空中,我们要么利用暂时的自由来创造一个新的生活框架,要么选择过一段不用从一个海岸拼命游到另一个海岸的生活,一个没有开头和结尾的生活。

选择没有开头与结尾的生活有时会让人感到空虚,没有计划和工作的时间缓慢流逝,也会让人发慌。在这种虚空的时空中，固有的习惯就是稳定的力量。习惯会建立一种框架，会填空虚无的时间，让虚无充满事件、礼节、迹象、物品和仪式，这会让人安定。

因此，即使是在假期，我也选择了不断地发明与重复新的仪式和动作。这些活动将在这段荒凉的时间里充当时间的标记。它们再次构造了我的日子，使我能够避免存在的苍白。这是一个让我保持快乐与平静的生活选择，这也是我渴望创造的表现，让我来定义并延续属于我自己的宇宙，这个宇宙由我统治，它注定要抵抗其他所有的一切。

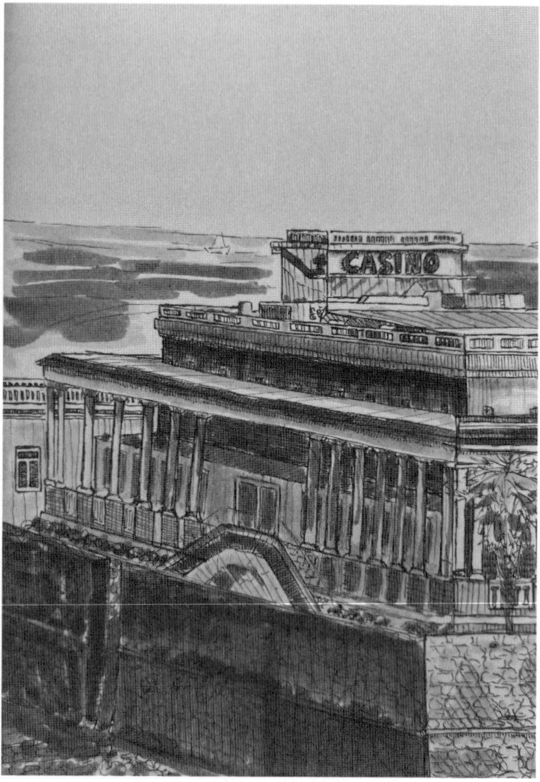
CASINO

仪式是生活的盐

在当代生活中,仪式的重要性往往会被忽略。有时候是我们不在乎,有时候是我们只看得到它过于正式和具有约束力的一面。特别是当某种仪式是被强制要求的时候,我们会容易产生反感,认为仪式感是过于生硬的东西。

但是,仪式为时间提供了基准,它们是生活的结构要素。不同的仪式标识出季节和岁月,给我们生活中的种种关键时刻一些重要的深刻记忆,不管是婚礼、葬礼、庆祝活动、生日,或是毕业典礼。它们为生活增加了一个逃离日常的维度。

我和很多人一样,有时会无视仪式的重要性,这样一来,我也就遗憾地错过了它带来的令人欣慰的情感,失去了一些期待,一些回忆。

从这种意义上来说,仪式不能简化为一种简单的社会规定和惯例。相反,仪式可以是充满情感的,可以是庄严的,可以是有自豪感的,仪式甚至也是一种给予,当我们给予别人一种仪式,其实也给予了文明和尊重。

　　仪式就像生活的里的盐,有了它,生活的滋味被强化了。

松鼠仍然在树枝间跳跃

星期六的下午,在整个冬季的大部分时间里失踪的太阳大发慈悲地露了个面。它在路上的行人脸上打上了鲜橙色的光影,并剪出人们走动的剪影。一只松鼠从一支树枝跳到了另一支树枝上,然后迅速地爬下了树,并谨慎地接近了一个拿着坚果引诱它的男人。那个男人弯下腰停在公园中间,这在像波士顿般寒冷繁忙的城市中,是一个格外罕见的场景。

愤怒的汽车的鸣叫声,推着婴儿车慢跑的父亲们,扫到路边的坚果壳……这些都是我通常不会注意到的小细节。但自从新冠病毒爆发,我的家人和朋友们都陷入了困境,不得不把自己隔离在一个密闭的空间里,自从病毒杀死了两千多人,我对自己能拥有的外出自由就有了更多的敏感。

虽然我经常会因为自己遇到的各种麻烦而感到不堪重负,但现在看来这些问题似乎都是鸡毛蒜皮,无足轻重的。至少,我可以自由地走出家门去冥想散步，下课和男朋友约会，或者在附近的杂货店买新鲜的农产品，而不必担心被病毒夺取生命。换句话说，至少我仍然可以过相对正常的生活，参加正常的日常活动，这些活动分散了我的对人类必死的命运的注意力，让我觉得生命是充实而有意义的。但是，当我们被病毒隔离，我们的活动被限制，被困在一个封闭的空间中时，我们很难分散自己对死亡的注意力，不得不被迫思考死亡的问题。当世界被病毒和疫情笼罩，无论我们在哪个网站上浏览有关 Covid-19 的新闻，死亡人数和感染统计都会成为我们最关注的消息，死亡占据了我们大部分的思维空间，突然变得离我们那么近。

我们为什么会害怕死亡？我们对它的恐惧从何而来？我们是害怕随之而来的痛苦，还是害怕不再有感知？

对我来说，可怕的不是死亡本身，可怕的是我们在活着和有感情的时候离死亡的距离有多近。正如伊壁鸠鲁所说，死亡本身对我们来说无关紧要。死亡是对所有敏感性的剥夺，因此当它真正发生，当我们真正处于"死亡"状态时，我们将不会感到痛苦，悲伤，我们将会一无所有。因此，死亡不是一件痛苦的事情，认为死亡会给自己带来疼痛也不合理。痛苦的是有感知地等待死亡，也就是我们称之为生命的等待。等待的时间越长，或者说寿命越长，我们离死亡就越近。我们离死亡越近，就越害怕自己的感知力消失。这也就是为什么我们的寿命越长，我们想要死的次数就越少。这也是为什么我们对死亡的恐惧越多，我们的生命就越少，或者说我们生活越多，我们的生命就越少。

当我意识到对死亡的恐惧来自害怕无法再感知时，我开始试图尽可能地了解自己的环境和感受，所以我会观察带着孩子慢跑的爸爸。我发现这样做对我有一些安慰的效果，因为我感觉好像我一生都在尽最大的努力去感知自己的感情与周围的环境。因此，当那个时间来临，我或许也不会后悔自己没有足够地感知过，我或许会坦然面对死亡。我同时还更加频繁地写起了日记，我认为这样做有助于记录和分析我的情感输入。也许在活动自由受到限制的情况下，通过日记记录与解剖自己的情绪——不管它是消极的还是积极的——会有助于减轻对死亡带来的无感知状态的恐惧。

最后，重要的是要意识到死亡是一种人类被迫承受的现实，生命的存在是因为死亡的存在，一方不能没有另一方。如果没有结束，生命就不会是生命。

我们会留下活过的痕迹

冰冷的风在手掌中燃烧

声音搅动了原子和它们构成的上千种物质

包括我们自己

脚在丝绸中下沉并融化

天鹅绒的深渊成为我的皮肤

拥抱着我的笑声和梦想

一个空间,隐藏着无数的隧道与另一个空间

同时也有即将来临的风暴,与四处飞溅的悲痛欲绝

尽管我们只是在这个时空中存在的短暂生命

但死亡之口,也不能吞噬生命之美

尽管生命无法留下证据

但我们会留下活过的痕迹

日常琐事

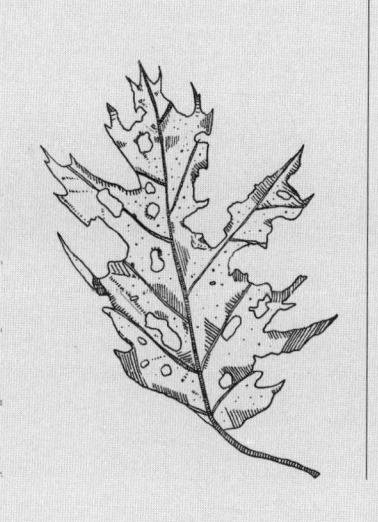

秋天的快乐

秋天是我最喜欢的季节。当葡萄开始发红，地上的梨多得让我绊倒时，我就知道秋天来了。

很奇怪，虽然我知道一年四季更替，我看到第一片落叶时总会有愉悦的惊喜。

没有什么是新的。我一年比一年大，但柔和的秋光，大自然最后一股清冷的美，以及空气中苹果酒的香味是我每年都听不腻的副歌。在这种时候，重复似乎不是一种周期性的恐惧，也不是但丁《神曲·地狱篇》中的折磨，而是一种时机成熟时反复出现的快乐。

也许在这种情况下，重复不是单调的，而是闪闪发光的，因为我知道每个季节都是有限的。而且，谁知道呢，也许有一天秋天就不再回来了。对这种消失的预期使重复性成为生命抵抗毁灭的勇敢延续。这样一看，每当秋天来临，我们庆祝的不是新的季节，而是生命在死亡面前的抵抗。

白色波士顿

12月，我回到了一个全是白色的波士顿。大雪覆盖了街道的每个角落，将城市风景变成了圣诞糖果手杖图案的田野。那天是我的生日。正好在前一天，我和哥哥、男友还有他的家人在温暖的洛杉矶一起过了个热闹的生日。但是当我回到波士顿的家，没有任何东西在等着我。

没有任何人。

确实有些朋友给我发了生日祝贺的短信，祝我一切顺利。但这一切都只不过是表面的热情，说到底我们没有那么亲近，至少不再是了。更何况，不管别人的话有多么温暖，所有的甜言蜜语都无法替代身边有亲人的陪伴。

我是否"爱"我所谓的朋友？事实上，我并没有很多朋友（大多数人也许只能算是熟人）。每当我开始与某个人接近时，我的笨拙会让我不知道如何长久地维持这种关系。

现在，我已经不羞于承认这个事实了，尽管在小的时候，我曾经被这种社交恐惧无能症严重地困扰过。

现在，对孤独这件事儿，我已经可以坦然接受了。

我把花在维持社交友谊上的精力和时间，都用在了我的创作上，因祸得福，我有了创造力和效率。换句话说，我不会感到孤独或悲伤，因为我对太多想做的事情抱有激情，没空考虑这些零零碎碎。

早上好，陌生人！

一大早，在脆皮培根的气味与煎蛋嘶嘶作响的声音的环绕下，与一群亲切的陌生人聊天是多么美好的开始一天的方式呀！

今天，我在咖啡厅等待我的贝果，一手拿着苹果，一手握着咖啡。咖啡师和顾客开了很多玩笑，老实说我没听明白他说了些什么，但不用置疑的是他很友善。一个男人戴着建筑工地的帽子走了进来，他浑身散发着喜悦和正能量。令我惊讶的是，他居然向我问了好，我也微笑着问候了他。

他问我："今天怎么样？"

"有风。"我答道。

"是的，外面很冷，但我喜欢！"他又说道。

"你是模特吗？"他突然问道。

他是怎么看出来的？

"你的站姿和外表都很可爱。"

我笑着感谢了他。

我原本想要和他多聊一些，但是我的贝果已经准备好了,我也要上课了。于是我推开门,快速地在寒冷里跑到了旁边的教学楼。像这样的早晨,无论外面有多冷,风有多大,你都会想要快点起床,迎接新的一天。

历史的一个词就是我们全部的一生

我们沿着旧金山的海湾漫步,今天是五月初。在过去的一两个星期中,温度持续上升了几度。我们在干燥的人行道上缓慢行走,情侣在跑步者之间结伴而行,这是个熟悉而宁静的场景。

如果路人没有用口罩遮住他们的下半张脸,很难看出今年的立夏和往年的立夏有何不同。小动物们似乎对人类回归到街上无动于衷,虽然在相当长的时间内,它们几乎独占了城市的街道,而充满异国情调的植物始终在甜蜜的阳光下熠熠生辉,无视人类面临的遭遇。

我们走了很久,很久。我们避开了阳光,走在树荫下,走在泡在海里游泳的人们旁边,走在可以俯视整个海湾的山丘下。挤满游客的码头通向高处的公园,公园又通向金门大桥的沿海大道,风景随着时间的流逝不断地滚动变换。

未来的某个时候,当历史学家回首现在,穿越时间,把现在的世界归纳成可描述的事件时,一切都会变得如此简单。"这个时间段或者那个时间段的特征是这个,这个日期和那个日期之间又发生了那个。"他们或许会这样说。但是从这些"这个"和"那个"蔓延出了很多其他没有记载的事情:好天气、大自然的回归、以及一个在沙滩上嬉戏的孩子。

这些我们不会在教科书中看到的幸福时刻,这些口耳相传的故事,这些我们珍惜的活生生的人性的痕迹,也许就是一个人全部的一生。

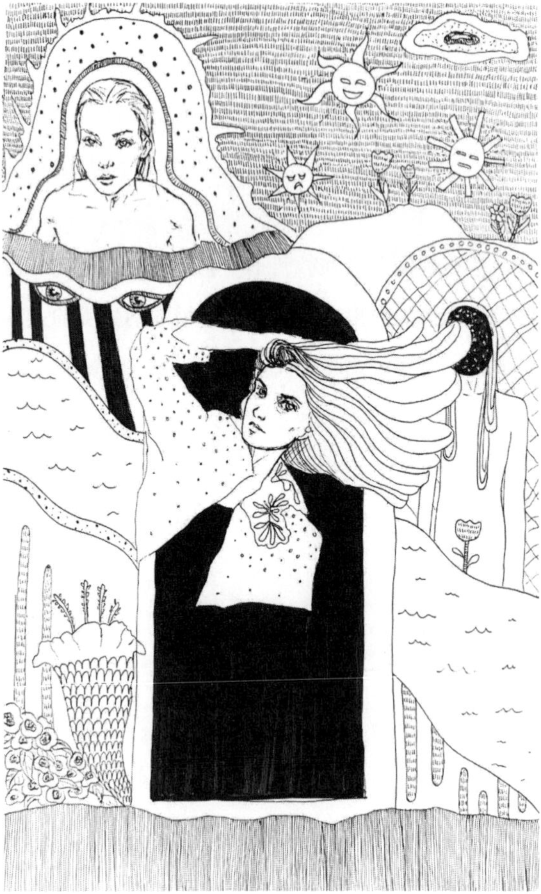

一个特殊的时期开始了

从两周前开始,我就停止了计算时间。

流行病刚开始时,我每天都要记日记,美国政府宣布隔离时间是1月27日至4月7日。我一直在倒计时,等待着官方宣布居家隔离结束的日子。但在内心深处,我很清楚这次疫情并不会那么容易结束,居家隔离无疑会延长。只要查看统计数据,看看欧洲正在发生的事情,以及其他国家曾经发生过的事情就能够知道。

尽管如此,我还是想相信黑暗中的火光比我们想像的要近,它在手指尖能触到的地方。我需要某种东西,也许是信念,那会让我忘记自己是被锁在一个封闭空间中的恐惧。这个空间没有阳光,因为阳光的路径被附近的摩天大楼遮挡住了,有时候,我会担心未来的日子不会再有改变了。

事实证明,我的焦虑是多余的。即使在隔离中,每一天仍然都与前一天有所不同。我今天读了昨天没读过的章节,这给了我一个在昨天前天大前天，以前的任何一天都没有感受到的启示。这样的发现使我能够写出以前从未写过的东西，表达出我以前无法表达的感觉。你看，这也像一种连锁反应。

但是我不知道这病毒的连锁反应对我们每个人意味着什么。我不知道谁是安全的，谁不是。我不知道该如何帮忙，也不知道流行病什么时候会结束，有很多事情我无法控制。坦白地说，我甚至无法控制自己，我的身体，我的手指，我的脑袋，我的想法！我觉得所有这些保持"社交距离"的隔离也使我远离了自己。

我不能让这种事情发生，我需要我自己，我们需要自己。我们有时间可以害怕，但我们也有时间尽最大可能尽力而为，包括尝试去帮助别人，并随时完成我们所能做的所有正确的事情。我还很年轻，我可以重塑自己，以适应新的情况，适应后来的新社会。

是的，有些东西不受控制，病毒，法律，时间，但这不包括我自己。

Chloé
Anna &
Lars

绝对没有睡着
Julien Nash
Nathalie A.
什么时候下课
Please Don't Call On Me
Alex P.

温柔的抚慰

今天大二结束了,我的老师在哭泣,她为我们所遭遇的因为流行病而面对的特殊境遇而哭泣,她为大四学生无法经历毕业典礼而哭泣,她为绝望、悲伤、孤独而哭泣,但她也为爱、敏感、真诚与温柔而哭泣。

这些天,我们非常需要真诚的温柔。

温柔是一种将他人视为敏感体的沟通方式,温柔是懂得他人的身体是有渴望的、是会受到环境的影响而感受到疼痛的。温柔可以在人群中间生长出一种良性循环,甚至可以带来治愈力,它可以安抚时代带给我们的创伤。

全球大疫情蛮横地控制了人们的身体、节奏与动作,它充满了暴力的攻击性,但是温柔使人们有可能抵抗这种侵略性所造成的人性贫困。

所以,或许,如果疫情持续下去,为了对抗疫情的冷暴力,我们应该让自己和他人沉溺在温柔中,温柔会让我们所在的空间充满一种抚慰,就像是从天上落下来的粉红色花朵。

毕竟，说到底，一个极端会治愈另外一个极端。

一个人的房间

我们以为生活可以成为一种共享的经验,街道上的许多面孔和他们背后的故事,在平常的日子里仿佛都是相同的。

我们习惯过一种被外部印证的生活,在这种生活中,我们通过自己以外的东西来确定我们的存在。歌手通过观众,儿子通过父亲,教师通过学生……但是一旦我们被隔离,我们就被迫作为个人面对自己。我们必须绝对地思考自己,我是谁,没有我存在的意义,没有印证使我们不知所措。

你不相信我?尝试将自己赤裸裸地锁在房间里,什么也不要做。你会发现,你坚持不了多久的。

所以,我们不得不尽可能地让自己和别人产生关系。歌手会为了有观众而直播唱歌,父亲会打电话给自己的儿子,教授会在网上教书,一切都是为了有他人证明我们仍然存在。

就我而言,我很幸运没有达到这个极点。我有一个人在同一个空间里陪着我，所以我没有被逼到极端。他认可我，我认可他。他让我有所反应，我让他有所反应。即使彼此被剥夺了身体在空间里的自由，我们也会彼此提醒，我们还有精神上的自由。

自由是在埃莱娜·费兰特的笔迹中畅游，自由是在虚拟世界与朋友继续奔跑、跳动、交流，自由是在完成一项任务之后又完成一项任务，以抗拒强加于我们的、我们不能控制的外部条件。

自由也是在一切都变了之后仍然相信自由的存在。

此时的孤岛

人际关系是对我们自身存在的肯定。看到和被看到，听到和被听到，激发共鸣和得到共鸣，作为人类，我们彼此依存。我们寻求被照顾，被关爱，并且将这些感情传下去。但是，当我们突然发现自己与世隔绝时，我们该怎么办？

隔离中的旧金山，每个人都是一座孤岛。

我的眼神与对面大楼里的一个男人的眼神相遇了。他站在那儿，看着关在屋子里的我贴在玻璃上的脸庞。我想知道，他能够理解我的感受吗？他是否像我一样渴望呼吸一口新鲜空气？

经历了那些无声的、虚拟的互动之后，我渴望穿过彩色玻璃层与更多的真实的人产生关联。

我想了解一个被隔离回家的大学生在家里到处闲逛的生活，想知道他不知所措的状态。

我想为那个盯着电脑屏幕看了几个小时的男人解惑，想走出去对他说声嗨。

然而现实世界不是童话，非常时期，人们保持距离，互相远离，人们不与陌生人交流。

　　幸好，我还有一些彼此关爱的亲人，虽然我无法透过眼前污迹斑斑的玻璃看见他们，虽然他们在千山万水之外的，但这时候，很稀有的，电脑屏幕不是人与人之间的屏障，而是让我靠近和触及到他人温暖的通道。

十四天，回家等待中的日记

第一天

我仍然听得到前往酒店的巴士上的自己的耳鸣。凌晨三点，巴士在深圳的黑夜前行，耳鸣时而像是我梦境中微弱的背景杂音，时而又是将我拉回现实的警钟，让我面对在暗淡蓝灯照射下疲惫的同车旅客。从洛杉矶飞到深圳机场，在等待了六个小时，完成了所有的防疫安全流程后，我终于到达了酒店。

早上，在酒店的床上醒来，被微弱的空调吹凉的床单安托着我长途跋涉后敏感又无力的肌肉，我从来没有像现在这样，觉得能睡在中国某一个酒店的床上简直让人感动。

开始了十四天的入境隔离。酒店的窗户很大，即使是下雨天阳光也充足。我感觉今后这两个星期，我的大部分时间都会在窗户前度过，试着摄取足够的维他命 D。

现在该如何？接下来又该如何？这段时间我是

要过得有点意义,还是该趁此机会好好休息?这些细节我之后再理,现在的重点是把时差倒过来,我需要从这半梦半醒的状态跳出来。

第二天

隔离的第二天。我得知了隔离期间我可以租一台酒店健身用的单车。这让我高兴坏了,立马就下了单。可惜的是,单车嘎吱作响,可能年久未修了,我的身高骑车也蛮尴尬的,骑上去不太顺畅。可是,总之,有这个比什么都没有要好。我很开心可以告诉大家我的装备有所升级。

收到了妈妈的朋友寄来的问候包裹,里面有水果、巧克力和最重要的咖啡。咖啡对倒时差和打败下午的睡意太重要了。问候包裹里还包括了一束向日葵。这束花让我意识到没有花的房间是多么的毫无生气,从现在起一直到两个星期隔离结束,这束花就是我与大自然唯一的联系了。

最大的问题是食物。困扰我的不是食物的味道,而是饭量。因为在房间里关着消耗不了多少能量,我自然也不会饿。因此,我打电话给前台,请求他们一天只给我送一顿午餐,不用送早餐和晚餐。前台的小姐姐听到我的要求之后感叹道:"太少了，饭还是要吃的！"我尝试再次说服她，告诉她我不可能一天吃三顿饭，每顿饭还是两碗米、一碗汤、一素两荤。我强调说我不想浪费食物。说了半天，她最后终于答应告诉厨师少给我盛点饭，然而，实际上，我餐盒里的食物一点都没少。我还是吃不完。

说点好的，我的精神状况一直不错。我不会无聊，我有很多事情要做，比如写文章和画画。在隔离中，我有两种娱乐方式，一个是通过现代科技通信设备与家人和朋友视频聊天，另一个就是通过读书与文学大师有精神上的交流。这次我选的是荣格与哈贝马斯的陪伴。老实说，他俩不是最好玩儿的人，但是阅读他们的作品可以保证我的大脑不短路。

第三天

尽管前天我一觉睡到天亮，昨晚也吃了褪黑素，但今天还是在凌晨四点半就醒了，原本以为我已经摆脱了时差的困扰，现在却又回到了起点。

我昨晚没吃的晚餐还放在外面递餐用的桌子上。每天晚上七点到九点都会有人来收垃圾，但他们一定是认为我只是睡着了没有取食物，却不知道我其实是不想吃。我今天要断食一天，我能感觉到我的脸在我走进这个房间后明显变得更圆了。

当你被困在一个房间里，无处可去时，你对每一个微小的变化都变得非常敏感：空气湿度的气味，房间亮度的改变，空调的出风声和温度的变化。躺在床上，我注意到有一盏灯在我的头顶上不断地照耀着，它不像一颗星星，而是像一个黑色的太阳，比它周围的黑暗更亮。

天啊，我出现幻觉了，这不就是月亮吗？

第四天
我决定举办一个一人派对。

我天天都上网看我的朋友在世界各地各种玩耍、跳舞，然后就想到，我也可以。于是，我通过外卖叫了几个灯串、一包气球，还有派对帽。我想，酒店的工作人员看到送来的外卖肯定一脸诧异，但是他们还是很友好地立即给我送到了房间。我现在不得不关在隔离酒店的房间里，多亏了外面协助的工作人员，他们是我和外面世界的摆渡船。

不打扮的派对就不能算是派对。对我来说，派对最好玩的部分之一并不是派对本身，而是派对前的准备过程，选择一套衣服、化好妆、打理好头发等等。今天如果没有人赞美我的外表也没有关系，我可以做我自己的欣赏对象。我可以做我自己的陪伴。

在国外，我经常听到有人说他们时不时会来一次与自己的约会，一个人出去吃饭，一个人逛街，一个人去音乐会。我一直很好奇，想找哪天尝试尝试，却从来没有真正的做过。可不，今天这机会就来了。

第五天

隔离让我对时间变得更加敏感，为了让时间过得快一些，我试图将自己的每一天都排得满满的。

我一起床就会喝咖啡、打电话给妈妈、写作、写日记、画画儿、工作，甚至是花些时间来学我一直在学却没有认真学的编程。

我也和多年没有联系的朋友重新建立了联系。因为分别而变得有些陌生同学，刚开始对话时虽然有些慢热，但很快，我们就进入了有意义的深入谈话。我们聊对世界的不同观点，或交流某些我们共同的信念。我想即使是内向的人，与人交谈也会有助于理清思路。今天我和朋友聊天时就发现，大多数时候人们需要新事物带来的兴奋感，却往往又不想下功夫去真正了解正在发生改变的新世界。因此，人们会通过不需要付出太多努力的方式寻找这种兴奋感。美国文化中流行的同时与好多人约会就是这么一种方式。在工作上取得突破也能带来一种兴奋感，但是它需要长期投入时间与精力，没有约会、打游戏什么的那么方便。

即时的满足是方便的，但随之而来的满足持续时间也会比较短暂。你越努力工作，就越珍惜回报。例如，我现在确信，比起一下飞机就能见到父母，在酒店待上两周后我会更珍惜待在家里的时间。

第六天

我以前特别爱哭。刚高中毕业，开始上大学的时候，我每周至少会哭两次，不管是为大事、小事还是根本就没啥事。我只要坐在那里，呼气，泪水就能轻易地从我的眼睛里涌出。但是最近，我发现我已经很久没有哭了。当然，我有过一两次泪目的情况，但我不记得我上一次红着脸、满脸鼻涕、肿着眼睛哭是什么时候了。

这是好事吗？我变得不那么敏感了吗？还是说我对痛苦有更强的忍耐力了？或者，我只是把一切都藏在了心里，忽略自己的感受，用繁杂的日常任务分散自己的注意力？或者，我真的长大了，学会了用不同的视角看待事物，一种更基于解决问题和理性的视角。这种改变给我带来了什么？它又带走了什么？

我觉得我学会了在感性思维和理性思维之间转换，但我不再能像以前那样大声哭出来了。或许，我只是努力地去看我生活中美好的事情，然后告诉自己真的没有什么好哭的。我妈妈总是对我说一句话，除了生死，一切都是擦伤。尽管如此，有时候，我还是会怀念那个能放声大哭的自己。

第七天

隔离对我最大的限制就是我不能运动了。通常，我习惯了每天早上都出去跑步，一周去几次健身房，如果坐得太久，就会出去散步。而这几天，我感觉我的身体越来越僵硬了。

被封闭隔离在房间之前，我从未意识到定期锻炼对我的情绪和健康有多么大的影响，这不仅仅在于内啡肽的释放。当我在徒步登山时，我会感到亲近自然，心情自然舒畅。当我走进一个挤满了很多努力让自己变得更好的人的健身房时，我会感受到积极的动力。

最近,我一直在用高强度的间歇训练来补偿我的日常跑步,但是我很想念在经历第一英里跑步的不适以后出现的兴奋感。

第八天

隔离中的我重温了汤姆·汉克斯的经典电影《荒岛余生》,在这部电影中,被困在荒岛的主人公查克用排球幻想出了他唯一的朋友——威尔逊。

虽然与主人公相比,我所在的情况要好得太多了,但我的房间里大量的气球让我想起了威尔逊。也许,没有多少人可以说他们有比查克更多的朋友。

严肃点儿说,谢天谢地,现代科技让我没有完全与社会隔绝,迫使我结交想象中的朋友。事实上,现代科技的发展远远超越了社交便利。这次回国,从登机到下飞机,从过海关到定期的核酸检测,每一个流程都因为科技发达而变得非常高效。微信从这方面来说也就不仅仅是一个社交应用,它完全是一个超级应用。

我记得是在 12 岁的时候,朋友推荐我下载微信的,那时这款软件才刚刚出现。当时,它能提供的顶多不过是即时通讯。今天，付费，坐地铁，甚至是抗疫都有它的份儿，世界变化真大，拥有一个虚拟的真朋友，也许很快就会是现实了。

第九天

倒计时感觉现在才正式开始。隔离已过一半，这是最后阶段了。

隔离第二天收到的向日葵已经谢了。台风来了，台风把天空染出了橙色光影，偶尔还会有闪电鞭子一样地抽过。

不得不说，这样的天气有点令人沮丧，非常昏暗的天空促使我读了更多的书。外面下大雨的时候，我总喜欢靠窗读书。不知何故，一下雨，所有的电子屏幕都失去了魔力。雨滴轻轻敲打着玻璃，还有有节奏的翻页声，就像一支精致的管弦乐队，为我提供了一些急需的安慰。

我进入了一种疲倦和走神的状态，我在迎合这种倦怠感。在过去的几天里，我努力保持住积极和高效的工作状态，但现在，我需要懒散和下沉一会儿，这对于我的精神和身体的恢复是必不可少的。

第十天

达到了一个临界点。我想不出任何更多的创新活动来给我的隔离生活增添点乐趣。这就像在两个人的关系中到达了一个点：你们完成了所有令人兴奋的约会，最终不得不进入一种常规状态。每天重复一样的活动，感觉激情逐渐下降。

不过，人不必一定要永远是积极的。我知道有些人整天就靠睡觉来打发时间，这也是一种生活方式。对于我来说，我会画画，我会玩水彩，我的创造力会偶尔爆炸，这意味着一旦我开始画画，就会停不下来。作为艺术家，会在被灵感和激情驱动时开始创作。然而这些天，我不得不像人工降雨一样迫使自己去挖掘创作的情绪，因为创作是唯一让时间飞逝的方法。糟透了的是，天快黑的时候我就不得不停下来，毕竟没了自然光，色彩变得非常不可信任。

酒店房间的顶光太差，能有一盏台灯就好了。

第十一天

我习惯于分析和解读事物。每当我的感官被输入或接收到信息时，我的大脑就会编织出一个网络，将我刚刚接收到的新信息与我过去收获的知识与经验联系起来，这就触发了我各种奇怪理论的发展。我会把我已经处理过的信息放在放大镜下，从一个新的角度来审视它们。

今天，雨开始下得更大了，所以我走近窗户观察每一滴雨水的重量是如何影响它的飞溅的。我还听了一个关于时空和爱因斯坦相对论的播客，把它和我的隔离状态联系在了一起，开始思考时间的度量是如何影响人的精神稳定的。最后，我尝试了在拖鞋的鞋底上画画，为什么不呢？再说，我的画纸也快用完了。

第十二天

我意识到，尽管有 iPad 和 Kindle，我还是会被纸质画和纸质书吸引，我很好奇这是为什么。从逻辑上来讲，数码画板和电子书都是更方便的选择。30 本电子书的重量比一本纸质书还轻，携带一支苹果铅笔也比携带 5 支画笔和 3 支铅笔要省事得多。

也许是因为有形的、触摸得到的、经典的纸质物品带有一种浪漫的内涵，也许是因为指尖翻动书页、手掌摩擦纸张的感觉给我带来了一种屏幕上无法再现的平静的快乐，也许，我选择实体是出于一种优越感:"我不像其他人,我不满足于便利。"但说实话,这种优越感是毫无意义的。当然,也有可能是因为觉得自己像1960年的法国知识分子,带着小小的"口袋书"。但科技带来的便利应该得到庆祝,因为它让阅读和艺术变得更亲民、更大众化。

艺术和文化只属于精英的观点已经太过时了。

第十三天

我已经有两周没出过门了,我很想回家。但奇怪的是,我对这个房间产生了依恋,我好像得了斯德哥尔摩综合征。隔离一周后,我就感觉自己完全忘记了时间和日期。我几乎投降了,接受了这个房间就是我的命运,我准备好在这里度过我的余生,就好像我从未见过太阳、从未呼吸过新鲜空气,好像我的一生都在冬眠。

我意识到明天将是这么久以来我第一次和有血有肉的人在同一个空间。虽然通过每天与朋友和家人的视频会议,我保持了沟通能力,但我想知道,我的空间意识和对其他身体的感知是否会在一出门就发生变化。我还会记得如何在别人面前表现吗?事实上,作为一个社交尴尬的人,我想我从来都不擅长和人打交道。

第十四天

隔离解放的这一天,深圳迎来了自我隔离以来第一个阳光明媚的日子。我们一大早就离开了酒店。我在机场等了 5 个小时,迫不及待地想见到我的父母。能够再次处于人群中的感觉真好,所幸的是,我发现我并没有忘记如何与他人打交道,也许是因为在十四天的禁闭之后,我太渴望与人交流了,我反而觉得在社交沟通这件事儿上我变得更在行了些。

我的父母来机场接我了。我拥抱爸爸的那一刻,就好像我身体里的某个开关关闭了,让我披上的成人外壳立刻融化了,露出了那个三年前独自出国留学的、过度羞涩与紧张的 17 岁女孩。

一切都和我记忆中的一样。自从我上次回家以来,我熟悉的环境发生了一些变化,熟悉的商店关门了,新建筑拔地而起,我们的房子也翻修了,邻居也不再是以前的邻居了。不变的是我的妈妈仍然在用百合花装饰家里,我的爸爸仍然给我手制最可爱的欢迎礼物,我也仍然对院子里的街道烂熟于心。街道似乎更窄了,可能是因为我长大了。

我感到如释重负。

一切都是未知的

  每当两条道路合二为一时
  看着汽车越来越近,我的心就会跳动
  然后,我会想象每种可能的事故情况
  翻转的汽车弹跳起来,汽车干脆地撞到墙上……

  会是哪一个呢?

女性 & 爱情

两个人

我爱上了你的陪伴

在这几个转瞬即逝但同时无限的小时中

海洋和星星交融成冲流

穿过我们之间的狭小空间

你是一个矛盾的存在

你的栗色卷发滴落着温柔

你的手指轻轻地在我的皮肤上游荡,就像水彩一样

自由地染在我的腿、我的背、我的脖子的空白画布上

溪流对你来说不够,或者说

你觉得它对我来说不够?

你有力的手指,你紧缩的手掌

我的身体是一片越来越汹涌的大海

你在我胸口的湍流中航行

你的手像暴风雨中的锚一样紧紧抓住我的胸膛

深夜无声的痛

在星云的面纱下揭露

天空晴朗,地平线突出

大海的深蓝色与黎明的紫色分开

留下一条微弱的金丝出现

一道亮光

它摸索风暴的起源

探索狂风留下的残骸碎片

我白色的皮肤上可以看到绿色的痕迹:

它们是回忆、惩罚和漫长的告别

两个人的日常

每天早晨都是一样的,我们在第一缕阳光的照耀下跳下床。你会坐在办公桌那儿工作,我会在沙发上用一杯咖啡的时间看书。然后,我会开始晨练,在地板上锻炼 30 分钟,在自行车上一个小时。而你,你还会在办公桌那儿。

然后,即使我无处可去,我也会洗个澡、换身衣服。我注意到这简单的行为能够让我在这种情况下更有动力,好像一切正常。而你,你始终在办公桌那儿,但这次,你会在打游戏。

然后,我会去厨房准备午餐。工作日的午餐基本上都一样,抓两把球芽甘蓝,再加两片培根和两块鸡胸肉烤 23 分钟,烤箱温度 425 华氏度,多一分钟少一分钟都会有很大的影响。当计时器响起时,我会把你从办公桌拉开,让你坐在厨房柜台,否则你会留在办公桌,在电脑前吃饭。我不喜欢两个人各吃各的。

我所有的小活动似乎都改变了你的"自然栖

息地"。我在这里放一个笔记本，在那里搁一个硬盘，我巧妙地将色彩塞入了你原本全是深色的衣柜中。在我的逗留期间，你的卫生间桌面也少了很多空间。至于你的金属书架，你现在可以在《极限控制》和大学毕业证之间找到艺术品和音乐了。不是说我的存在使你的存在更加赏心悦目，相反，我非常喜欢你淡淡的墙壁颜色和你的极简主义生活。但是，我很高兴能够在这里和那里留下一些我存在的痕迹。你不清除它们让我很宽慰。

最终都会成霜

我在你与另外一个也是你的人之间行走,你在我的面前带领我,而我走在你的影子里。

微风吹进了这间因为某些缺失而让空虚发出震耳欲聋的巨响声的房间里,那木头的气味仍然残留,仍在呼吸。

显然,那不见的东西仍然存在。

就像经典小说提供了现代书中很难找到的浪漫主义一样,在这个狭小房间的密度里,仍然可以创造广阔的思想空间。思想带来了自由,是伤口滋养的天鹅,让我能够飞翔。

沉默、风沙与尘埃,最终都会成霜。

金属蛇

胸罩是一条金属蛇

它慢慢地勒着你

将鳞片嵌入你的肉中

并在皮肤上滑动留下痕迹

慢慢地 悄悄地　　你无法呼吸

粉嫩

　　　　苍白

　　　　　　　淡蓝

成为一个女人

我看到自己的脸变得更圆,臀部变得更宽,胸部一天一天轻微地隆起,不动声色却肉眼可见地变化着。

这些变化是我无法控制的,好像我的身体被某种在我体内的黑暗所操控,它使我难过并让我始终感到焦虑。但与此同时,我感觉我离女性,离我在广告牌和杂志上看到的女演员和模特,以及所有男孩子都在谈论的女生更近了一些。

尽管我内心的某一部分有点喜欢这突如其来的变化带来的新鲜感,但是在大多数时候,我会为自己不断变化的身体感到尴尬和困惑。我穿大号 T 恤来隐藏自己的曲线,隐藏即使在宽松衣服下仍会露出的不合适的内衣痕迹。我觉得找既不是最美丽的也不是最优雅的,我或许是死板无趣的一个人。

要过好几年,我才开始接受我的新形象,接受我正在成为一个女人。

美是有差异的

几天前,早上醒后,我在社交媒体照片下面看到了这样的一句评论:"讲真的,最近胖了……"

当我的目光从一个单词跳到另一个并最终抵达句尾的省略号时,我的脑海中浮现出了一连串思绪:这是一种侮辱吗?如果不是,为什么我会感到侮辱?为什么这句话听起来如此负面?是因为他说我胖吗?但是胖有什么不对?我胖吗?胖影响了我的颜值吗?我为什么会这么想?这是否意味着我需要减肥?当我瘦到肋骨露出、手臂细得像筷子似时,当我余生都在谴责食物中度过,那样的我才会美吗?我感到非常困惑。

从美国回来后,我意识到我在美国的短短三周内胖了五公斤。那段时间,我一日三餐中的两餐都是在外面吃的,每顿饭还要吃三道菜,一天两个甜品都不是事儿。我的每一天都沉溺在各种牛排、糖浆和含糖量爆表的巧克力蛋糕的味道中。我承认,那些日子过得稍微有点极端。

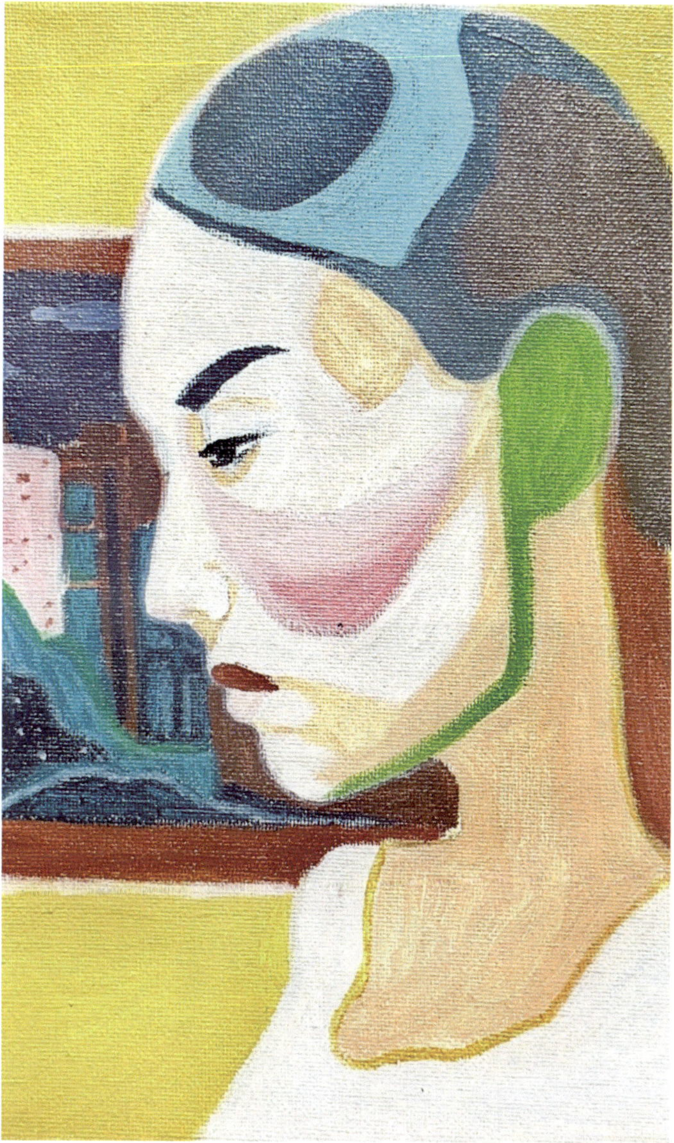

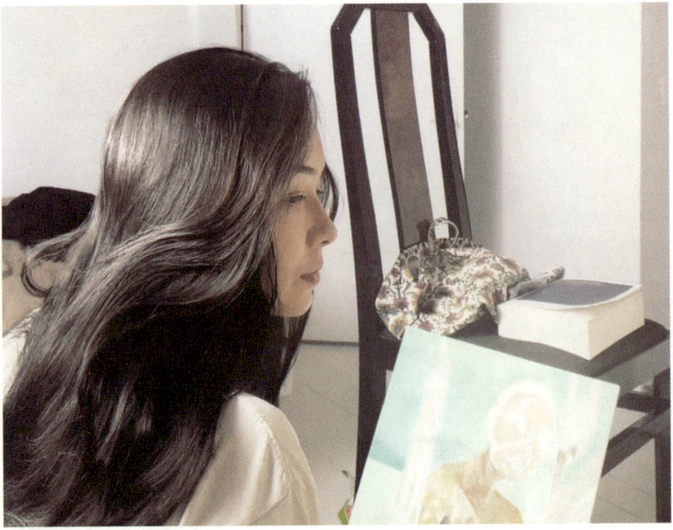

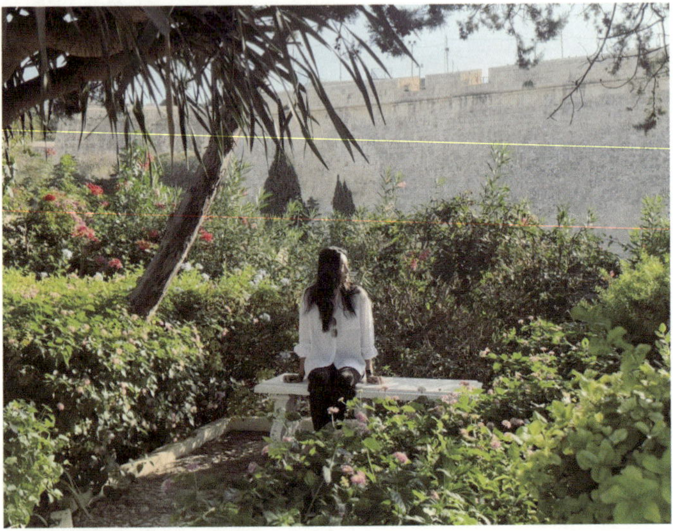

那时我大一刚刚结束，迎来了期待已久的暑假。我很高兴与我的男朋友重聚，更高兴我的父母终于从太平洋的另一边飞过来看我了。所以，我脑子里唯一想做的就是尽我所能地庆祝这突如其来的快乐。因为从小在我们家，庆祝的形式就包含了一家人共进晚餐与品葡萄酒，而且从小星巴克的巧克力麦芬就成为了我缓解忧郁的良药，用美食来表达我的喜悦是自然而然的。我想让我父母尝遍我在旧金山最喜欢的餐馆，我想和这些我爱的人们共享美食，让我们的味蕾同时绽放，并且把一起度过的甜蜜瞬间锁定在食物的口味，质地和味道中。这样一来，以后，无论我的家人离我有多远，只要我再次尝到这些食物，我就能解锁和释放这些被捕获的记忆。例如，只要我吃一口香草巧克力冰淇淋蛋糕，我就可以重温哥哥毕业典礼时我们共度的时光，每当我给自己做炒鸡蛋三明治，我就能够感受到家的舒适，只要我吃一颗薄荷糖，我就能穿越到在旧金山和我的男朋友行走在山丘的时候。我要在如此短暂的时间内锁定许多记忆的奢望，让我迅速地胖了。

像每个女生一样，我当然会关心自己的外表。在美国，体重涨了几磅并不是什么大不了的事，因为那里的文化相对来说更加接受多元化的美，没有人会对我的体重评头论足。因此，即使我的腰围涨了几英尺，我仍然很自信。在一个移民国家的文化中，美没有特定的定义，无论高矮，无论肤色黑白，无论身材胖瘦，美丽的价值是让你与众不同，充满个性，是自信心让人变得美丽。甚至，在美国流行的政治正确标准下，一些极端的，原本被传统审美视为是缺陷的特征也可能是具有价值的。例如尽管患有白癜风，超模温妮·哈洛（Winnie Harlow）始终被认为是美丽的，她用自信和勇气，创造了自己的逆袭之路，从而凸显了她的美。至于超大号模特阿什利·格雷厄姆（Ashley Graham），她的曲线并没有阻止她成为超模，成为美丽的化身。我不想陈词滥调，但在美国，"你的缺点让你完美"的氛围真的特别强烈。因此，美国人并不纠结于他们的腹肌是否像希腊雕塑一样轮廓分明，他们更不会去在乎自己的锁骨上能放多少个硬币，因为，对他们来说，美没有一个通用的定义。美有传统的美，但与众不同，并对自己的差异充满信心，也会让你变美丽。

不同的是，在一些亚洲国家，对美的定义并没有那么包容。虽然人们对待差异的态度越来越开放，并开始接受美丽可以多样化的观念，但大多数人仍然认为这世上存在着某种既定的美容标准：高鼻梁，苍白的皮肤，V形脸，大眼睛和苗条的轮廓……这个名单长着呢。许多人认为，如果你的皮肤太黑或你的大腿太粗，如果你的下巴太短或你的鼻翼太宽，你就被排斥在美之外了。于是，无数人竭力去迎合这种美的标准，并为此节食、依赖于整形手术，或者不知疲倦地将自己的照片P到亲娘都不认的程度。在这种对美的追逐中，个性和差异性都失去了。

我很好奇，这些人有没有问过自己为什么某些特征象征着美丽，某些又不是？是什么让长腿比短腿更好看、双眼皮比单眼皮更漂亮？是谁这么定的？我经常听到人们用"这就是约定俗成"来回答这些疑问。可是，为什么要遵循这些标准并且盲目跟随？这些标准给我们作为一个人带来了何种价值？

对我来说，美应该是健康的，有思考的，无论是什么容颜，一个自信的，充满活力的人都会有属于她的独一无二的美丽。

女性的两难

今天,偶然地,我从爸爸的书架上抽出了法国"无国界作家"阿梅丽·诺冬所著的《诚惶诚恐》。

我自己正处于一个被坚强的中国女性所包围的环境中,我周围的女性每天都在追求职业的成功,还要保持生活的精致,同时承担家庭的重担。阅读这本描写在日本职场的女人为了过上一种有自我的生活而付出一切代价的书,是一种很奇怪的感觉。我看到了生活的真相,有点残酷。

如果我们把一切都放在事业上,我们就会放弃家庭。如果我们成为家庭主妇,我们将放弃梦想和野心。在家庭与职业之间找到平衡,我不知道我的母亲是如何做到的。

一个黑人妈妈

如果判断一个酒店的位置好坏标准是看当地人是否会在周围逗留,那么我的酒店的位置可算是非常糟糕。在纽约没有什么地方比时代广场更加游客化了,也没有什么地方像时代广场一样让当地人如"避开瘟疫"般地尽量远离。这次来纽约,我住在时代广场附近,在这里,除了因为在附近的大楼工作而偶尔穿过时代广场的"金融小哥"之外,其余的人群主要是穿着短裤、放着暑假的年轻人,和穿着西装、很有可能是从德克萨斯州来这里出差的外地商人,当然,还有像我一样想探索纽约生活的游客。虽然我住的地方是真正的纽约客不屑的外地人区域,但我还是觉得这里的剧院区晚上亮着的广告牌可真是活泼好看啊。

在纽约最初的几天,我一大早就急急忙忙地出门,在下午之前都不会回来。每次我回到房间,就发现我离开时乱糟糟的床、满满的垃圾桶和湿透了的毛巾像变了魔法一样,被整理得干干净净的。我对收拾我的房间的人心存感激，但我们从来没碰过面，她像一个田螺姑娘，无形地存在着。

5月9日是个星期日，我像每天一样从外面溜达回来，惊讶地发现我的床还没整理好，毛巾湿漉漉的，垃圾也没有倒空。这突如其来的改变虽说让我有点不适应，但是由于我原本就不介意打扫卫生、收拾房间，我关上门顺手就整理了床铺，并按照记忆中酒店折叠毛巾的方式收拾了毛巾。在酒店我没有办法倒垃圾，但东折折西叠叠毛巾被子什么的，我还是能做的。

一个小时后，我突然听到了敲门声。我半开了门，发现自己和一个身穿制服的黑人妇女面对面。她身材丰满，容光焕发，头发短到头皮，蓝色眼影和她的蓝色制服相呼应。看到我打开门，她害羞地露出了一个微笑，目光转移到我身着的雪纺连衣裙上，然后大声说："我好喜欢你的裙子！"

原来，她就是我一直没有碰到面的"田螺姑娘"。

她对我解释说："因为今天是母亲节，我们今天不打扫房间，但是我想确认下你是不是洗护用品都齐全。你需要更多洗发水吗？或者更多的乳液？咖啡？"

"嗯，让我看看……"我回道，然后转向浴室的洗手池，数了数小瓶淋浴产品。在转身的同时，我随手把房门开得更大了。我正想告诉她都齐了，我不需要更多东西，却突然听到她难以置信的声音："谁帮你铺的床？"

我愣了一会儿，原来打开了门，她可以看到整个房间。

"哦，我自己铺的，我喜欢保持整洁。"我回答说，对她的惊讶有点困惑。

"看看你的房间，你肯定是一个很爱干净的人，"她指着我靠在墙边的鞋，和我整齐靠在台灯旁边的书继续说到，"我的女儿和你一模一样。她每次出门也一定会叠好被子、收拾衣服，确保一切都干净整洁，她就是那样的人。她对人们说'我妈妈打扫房间为生，我怎么可能不自己收拾好自己的空间'。"

说起女儿，她的眼睛闪闪发光，她不再掩饰她那被酒店职业性规定所限制的亲情和友善。也许，是我们的短暂交流使她放下了戒心，她感受到我愿意给她一些聊天的时间——毕竟我与住在隔壁房间的商务人士不同，也许是因为我和她女儿的年龄差不多，生活习惯也有些相似，从而激起了她对女儿的想念与爱。

"这样吧,让我留一些干净的毛巾,这样你需要的时候有的用。"她说道。

她小心地走进浴室,在毛巾架上挂上了新毛巾。"你有没有不用的脏毛巾?"

"我把它们放在水槽下了,"我指着洗手池说道,"因为房间的淋浴有点漏水,我每次洗完澡都得拿毛巾把地砖擦干。"

"看到你有多干净吗?"她笑着说,"好了,如果你还需要其他任何东西,你就告诉我。"然后,她走了。

在接下来的几天里,尽管她从来没有回到过我的房间——至少我没撞见过她——但是我时不时地会在我的楼层的走廊里遇到她。我们不会过多地讲话,她总是会以最温暖的笑容向我打招呼,并称我为"宝贝"和"甜心"。她不知道我的名字,我也不知道她的名字,但是每次见到她时,她散发的母爱总会使我的一天变得更好。

这个母亲节,我不在妈妈身边,她的女儿也不在身旁。或许我在她身上感受到了我妈妈的能量,而她也在我身上看到了她女儿的影子。

精神才是不凋谢的花朵

雪有一种安抚人心的作用,它能冻结片刻时间,冻结一片风景,让一秒感觉像永恒。有时我觉得它停止了所有生物的生长,包括我自己的身体,我的指甲,头发,细胞,皱纹。确实,我最近注意到我脖子上多了一些小小的折痕。

我 21 岁,开始考虑变老的问题,或者说,这一生应该怎样活。岁月不再是一个抽象的词,我在母亲身上,看到自己。

看着母亲刘海下羞涩地藏着的一缕缕银发时,我好像看到了我的棕色头发的色素也会逐渐消失。不知道我的头发在什么时候会变成那样美丽的颜色?我会像她一样将发丝染黑吗?看着她在客厅灯光下按摩自己的肩膀时,我感受到了多年来支撑着她美丽身体的关节的僵硬与疼痛,这个身体在生理和精神上养育了两个美丽的孩子。

每当晚上我听到她的脚步声时,我都会看见自己的身影徘徊在走廊上。母亲不再有年轻时那种明亮的美，但她的思想仍然在发光。一个人跨越时间的，除了美好的身体，更重要的是她的内心力量，学习新的知识，保持对世界的好奇心和思考，给与亲人关爱。我看到她越来越多，也看到自己越来越多。容颜的美重要，但我更希望自己有一种超越外部容颜的美。内在的美，可开出不凋谢的精神的花朵。

我不是一个热爱社交的人，我放弃很多同龄人的社交和娱乐，把大量的时间用在独处的阅读和创作上，对外的封闭激发了我的想象力，我内心的张力。我最具有创造力与思维能力的时候，是我安静独处的时候，在一个人的环境中，我沉浸在自己的创作工作中，那是一个属于我的无边界的世界，在那里，我很自由。年轻，不仅仅是外在的，更是精神的。

衣服的社会标签

大约两个月前,我带着一个塞满了五件T恤、两条裤子、一件裙子的小行李箱从波士顿跑到了旧金山。原本我连那条裙子都不想带的,我只打算去旧金山和我的男友过一周的春假,但我有先见之明的男友觉得新冠的疫情发展可能会带来隔离,校园说不定也要关闭。摩羯座,你们懂的,一切都喜欢安排好。他非要我收拾一个月的行李。事实证明,他对了,我这一整个学期都被困在了旧金山。刚开始我觉得只有几件衣服让我怎么过啊,整周只穿同一件衣服,也无法玩搭配,每天早上出公寓和我打招呼的柜台小姐姐会觉得我无趣到没有衣服换,想想就很难接受。结果日子过下来,我发现担心完全多余。世界处于隔离状态时,外面就没啥人,偶尔遇到点人,人家也毫不关心我穿什么,事实上我都不在乎我到底穿了什么。

大家都在开玩笑地讲述各种参加网上会议只关心上半身不在乎下半身的笑话。实际上,这事我也干过。我每周三都会在 4:30 醒来,戴上隐形眼镜,换上一件得体的套头衫准备上东海岸八点的早课。我的同学们在视频上看到我着装讲究得体,但他们不知道的是,我没有穿长裤,我连家居短裤都不穿,我只是穿着内裤盖着毯子坐在沙发上听老师讲课。这种上下分离着装的行为让我产生了好奇心,我忍不住去想,为什么我要努力整洁给我的教授和同学看呢?而当没人能看见我时,我却会随便穿一件超大的老头风的套头衫,从更广泛的角度来看,为什么居家隔离前我们要天天打扮,居家隔离后我们又不怎么注意穿着呢?

　　罗兰·巴特的《流行体系》给了我一个非常全面的答案。巴特说,每件衣服都有意义。它们之所以有意义,是因为与它们相关联的词,我们穿这件衣服是因为我们希望与这些词所具有的价值相关联。也就是说,如果一件衬衫的标准定义是"上半身的服装,由棉或类似织物制成,有领子、袖子和纽扣",可在阿依莲衬衫和巴黎世家衬衫之间做选择时,为什么我们大多数人都想要巴黎世家而不是阿依莲呢?因为巴黎世家被形容为奢侈品,与它有关联的词汇大多数都是"高级时装""昂贵""高级"等。换句话说,它的生产者制造了一种与产品相关的标签,即物体本身的模拟物。所以说,我们真正想要的不是衣服本身,而是衣服的名牌,以及与之相关的词语和符号。因此,自然而然,我们更愿意在公共场合穿巴黎世家的衬衫,因为它比起阿依莲衬衫更像是一种社交声明。

同样,我上网课时换上了一件漂亮的 Moussy 套头衫,因为套头衫比睡衣要得体(除非我穿的是 Olivia von Halle 或 Atelier Intimo 的睡衣)。传统意义上来说,与睡衣有关的词汇是"床上的""懒散的"和"私人的"。套头衫反而散发着"学生"和"放松但不过于休闲"的气息。但是在上网课之外,在我无法发送社交信号的私人领域中,我不会在乎自己穿的衣服。我不在乎我父亲的里茨查尔兹(Charles of the Ritz)运动 T 恤的含义,也没人可以下意识推断出我缩了水的羊绒裤代表着什么。隔离时,我没必要对他人证明什么。可见,穿和不穿,穿和穿啥,说到底是个社会标签问题。套头衫除了使用性,也成为了人设的一部分。

我的身体是一颗行星

一只手掌是一个王国
另一只手掌是另一个王国
我的静脉形成河流
我的头发
是拥有一千零一个答案的垂柳
两个王国处于紧张状态
我的身体是一颗行星

世界&城市

共享并保持个人边界

地铁站是一个奇怪的地方，它既是公共的又是私人的。它的公共性在于它把成百上千的人聚集在同一节车箱里，每个人都在被他人审视的状况下。但在某种意义上，它也是私人的，因为通常每个人都只关心自己的事情，并尊重彼此的私人空间。也就是说，在地铁上，你可以瞥见别人的生活和精神空间，但又同时保持相对的距离。

这是一个让我觉得很安全的地方，我有一种归属感，觉得自己是某个社区的一部分。但我又不会过多地打扰他人，同样，我私人空间的界限也会受到尊重。我可以观察别人的生活，看到他人的故事。地铁上擦肩相遇的人，我可能永远不会在其他地方和他们重逢了，我们不会再有任何的关联。但在此时此刻，在同一个空间里，我们短暂地共享了一些东西——一个眼神，一个扶手，一个座位。

也许这就是人类典型的生活模式，共享的同时也保持着个人边界。

巴黎街头

坐在巴黎街头的咖啡馆看人来人往的街道就像是在博物馆欣赏一幅画,只不过这幅画里的人物会不断变换,风声、雨滴与树枝被踩断的声音更是都能够被听见。这种场景很适合当世界的旁观者,给现在与思考一点时间。

在这种时候刷手机真是有点可惜。

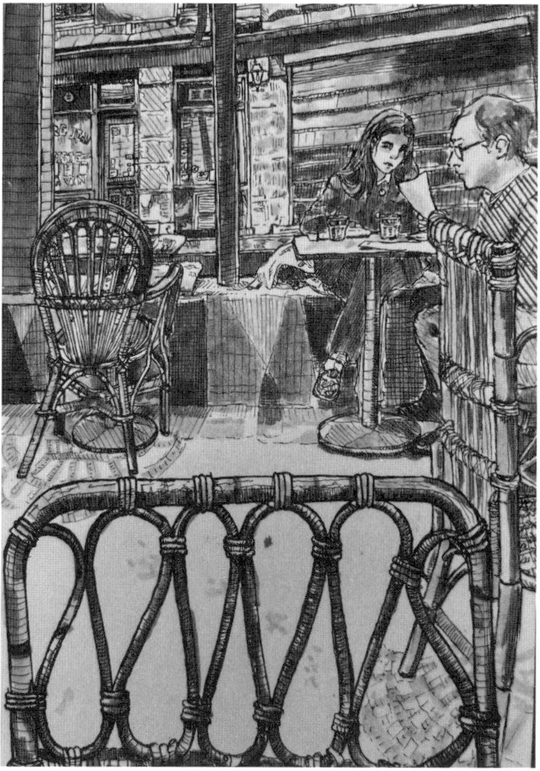

纽约的一次聊天

我在纽约认识了两个"奥利",奥利弗与奥利维尔。

奥利弗是半个德国人、半个美国人,26岁。他从小在法兰克福长大,上德国学校,高中毕业以后才回到美国,到达特茅斯上了学。这之后,他一直在纽约住着,在金融科技领域工作。奥利维尔是法国人,32岁。他从小在巴黎长大,中学上的是声望很高的亨利四世中学,大学读的是国立巴黎高等矿业学校,毕业之后又来到了美国,在哈佛商学院读了工商管理硕士,目前在 Facebook 工作。

有趣的是,奥利弗与奥利维尔除了名字相似以外长相也很相似,只是浅褐色头发、蓝色眼睛的奥利弗散发着一种严肃的日耳曼光环,而深棕色头发、褐色眼睛的奥利维尔整体要放松自在很多,性格也比较开放,就像典型的法国浪子。尽管两位奥利近十年来都融入了一个新的国家、一种新的文化,但两者都保留了各自文化背景的特征,这些特征塑造了他们的生活方式，但同时他们的举止谈吐也还是被美国习惯影响了。

奥利弗与奥利维尔都是礼貌友好的模范青年，但奥利弗在表达自己或分享观点时表现得要有约束得多。他不是一个喜欢主导谈话的人，更倾向于提出问题然后耐心地听对方说话。这是一个很体贴的行为，但考虑到我是一个安静且有时害羞的观察者，这却让我有点不自在，有点尴尬。倒是无所畏惧和健谈的奥利维尔，在某个晚上的八点钟，在一个隐藏在纽约钢铁丛林的日式地下酒吧，与我进行了一次令人难忘的、具有启发性的谈话。

奥利维尔身材高大、肌肉发达，他看上去完全就是美国人叫做"stud"的那种男人，一个迷人的、酷毙了的、极其自信的男性。他说着一口流利的美式英语，口音非常正宗干净。虽然我和他都是法国教育的背景，但随着我不断地因为忘记法语词汇而混着法语和英语而跟他聊天，我们的对话渐渐地完全被英语主宰，导致旁人很轻易地把我们误会为美国人。

奥利维尔的父母都在耶鲁教书，他也在耶鲁上了一个学期的大学。但是，在他22岁时，因为被一位法国女孩迷得神魂颠倒，他决定回到法国完成学业——哈，这是小青年常犯的错误，所幸的是这小小的弯路并没有影响到他的前程。几年后，他在大学毕业之后又回到了美洲大陆寻求发展，现在，他已经在纽约生活八年了。

奥利维尔的话题，主要围绕着两个方面：女生和著名的西海岸东海岸辩论。关于女生，他的主要重点是证明"女生比男生成熟"是一种错误的想法。"当然，你们女孩在某些方面更成熟。大多数时候你们不制造麻烦，你们通常早年学习也更加认真，"他说，"但你们也有表现非常幼稚的情况。比如说，你们很难应对被别人拒绝。"

"我有女性朋友经常会跟我说'啊，我喜欢这个男生'。但每次我问她们'你为什么不约他出去呢？'她们都说'他没有迈出第一步'或者'这该由他来问我'。但为什么呢？如果你那么喜欢一个人，为什么不迈出第一步呢？那是因为你害怕被拒绝，"他说，"我们男生早就习惯了被拒绝。"

他继续说道："从小我们就不断地迈出第一步，不断地被拒绝，所以现在长大了我们也不在乎了。有了经验，你就会知道被拒绝是正常的，它是常态，你不能因为被拒绝了一次就被打垮。你们女孩比较复杂。你们没有这种经验，所以你们现在就很害怕被拒绝。"

我们对这个话题进行了更多讨论。我提出了一个想法:"也许女生不迈出第一步是因为她们习惯了男生这样做。我不知道这种习惯和传统来自于哪里,我也不知道它是什么时候发起的,但它在社会中是持续存在的,尤其是在更传统的文化中。有些人甚至会称之为绅士与英勇的表现。"奥利维尔表示同意,但补充说:"保持这种习惯没有任何价值,因为它会让女生变得被动,甚至态度消极。"因为正如奥利维尔所说,"迈出第一步的女性会散发出自信"。我们同意这种现象是需要改变的,鉴于文化改变不可能在一夜之间神奇地发生,我们一致认为,改变始于个人层面的行动,即女性自己意识到自己的主观能动性,理解被拒绝和失败并不是世界末日,而是生活中正常的一部分。奥利维尔总结说:"不投篮就是投失。"

之后,我们转到了下一个主题:西海岸和东海岸之间的文化差异,特别是各个海岸的"科技兄弟"(tech bro)文化。自从我来到这里,我注意到纽约的每个科技兄弟之所以来到这里是因为他们不喜欢湾区的科技文化、旧金山的政治。奥利维尔证实了我的观察,他说他之所以定居在东海岸而不是硅谷，是因为纽约能够提供更加多元化的人群。"因为我的工作，我在这里每天打交道的大多数人仍然都是技术兄弟或金融兄弟，但与湾区的不同之处在于，如果我愿意，我总是可以在这里结识其他人：艺术家、创意人员、作家……旧金山真的只有一个人群，各个行业的人没有机会混在一起。"他补充说，旧金山是一个"可爱的小镇"，但它缺乏纽约无处不在的喧嚣和繁华的大都市氛围。

然而，这并不意味着东海岸就完美无瑕了。自称为纽约狂热粉的奥利维尔也承认纽约周边缺乏户外活动。"确实纽约有公园，你可以四处走走，骑自行车，如果你负担得起，你也可以去航海，但它不像在旧金山，你可以去海滩冲浪，甚至去不远的太浩湖徒步和滑雪。"奥利维尔还批评了纽约随处可见的工作狂心态。"人们在这里比在旧金山更受工作驱动？"我问道。"哦，是的，这里的工作节奏要快得多，人们的工作时间要长得多，尤其是如果你从事金融工作。这里没有人有自己的时间，而且很多人甚至会因为忙碌和没有时间而感到自豪。"但这并没有阻止奥利维尔在纽约玩得、住得、吃得开心，他甚至决心在这里建立一个家庭并将他的孩子送到纽约法国学校。问他如何处理缺乏阳光和海滩的问题？旁边就是迈阿密，他说。

我们的聊天就这样结束了，因为第二天早上我要赶回西海岸，而他也正好准备前往迈阿密。当我在路边等我的 Uber 时，一辆汽车疾驰而过。司机狂按喇叭，播放着响亮的嘻哈音乐，有人突然在苍白的夜色中、在人群中欢呼雀跃，大声喊道："这就是纽约，宝贝！"

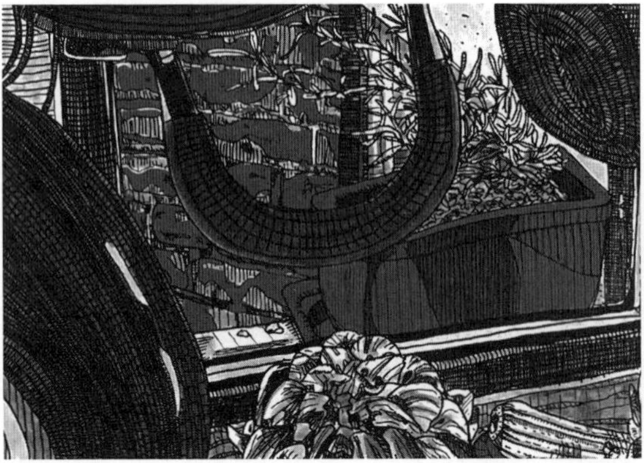

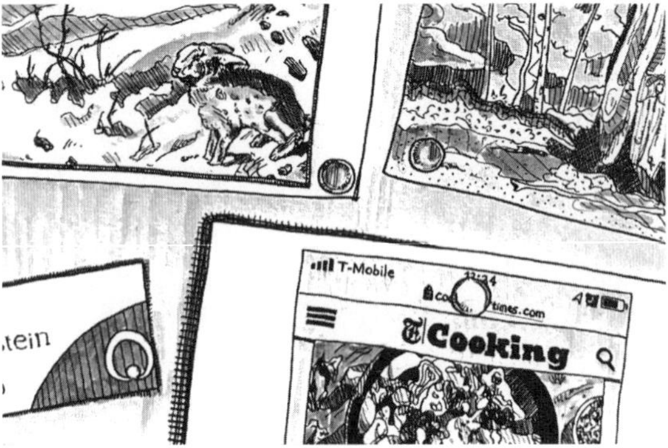
T-Mobile
Cooking

笔直的纽约和更高的上海

切尔西是发现纽约艺术场景的最佳地点。在纽约的短暂周末之旅中,我遇到了一些有趣的伙伴,在策展人西蒙·沃森的带领下,我们参观了这个地区的许多画廊。之后,我们在一家美式小餐馆——The Orchard Townhouse——吃了午饭,并且思考了纽约的过去、现在和未来。

西蒙说的一些话让我印象深刻。他把纽约的今天比作古罗马辉煌的最后时期,那个时候的罗马仍然富有魅力和活力,但不再是创新和新鲜事物的前沿。

纽约是一个站得笔直的城市,但其他城市比它要站得更高,比如上海。西蒙称赞上海过去 10 年的发展超越了今天的纽约。"上海的每个年轻人都容光焕发、精力充沛、兴奋不已。"他说,纽约人明显缺乏敏感度。

我同意西蒙的看法。当被要求向美国人描述上海时,我经常说,上海是洛杉矶和纽约的结合;它既有洛杉矶的空间,也有纽约的都市气息和活力。

尽管纽约可能正在衰落,但我们都认为,这座曾经是世界上最伟大的城市,在几乎不可避免的衰落中,有着一种忧郁的甜蜜,而我们能够见证它的衰落是一种特权。

无论如何,我喜欢纽约,我想知道十年后它会是什么样子。

心灵天文馆

我又回到了波士顿，回到了我的学校生活中，这是疫情开始以后我第一次回到这座城市。我忘了我多么怀念走在褐石建筑当中被意想不到的大风裹着的感觉，我忘了踩在被雪水浸湿的落叶上是多么的让人愉悦，我也忘了我多么喜欢跟随着严肃的路人急促的脚步行走。

无论我走到哪里，我都有喜欢观察和吸收当地人生活细节的习惯，他们的生活就像是一块块细小的碎瓷片，我看他们在说什么，在做什么，他们对一切的态度都被我像马赛克拼图一样拼在一起，融入我自己，成为我的一部分。在硅谷，我接纳了"科技兄弟"对生产力的痴迷，在上海，我吸取了这座城市强烈的规律性，在法国，我找到了积极生活的向往，我是在不同的文化和生活中，在不断学习和交融中成长起来的。

我们都有一个心灵天文馆，里面的星星会根据外界接收到的信息而发光或变暗。这些星星是你的特点——你的经历、技能与环境——它们拼凑成的一片不断变化的繁复星空。

印象派的暴风雪

波士顿的冬天常常有暴雪,那种时候人们都会躲在温暖的室内。而我,却会系上一条围巾冲到暴风雪中去。雪中走起路来有点困难,整个城市变成了一片白茫茫。雪光给城市披上了一个安静的外衣,但风不停地呼啸着,从树上飘落下来的雪块砸在地上发出低沉的声音,这些声音交织在一起制造出无人的喧嚣。

我有一种强烈的冲动,我希望能有"我是这个世界上唯一的人"的感受,希望我可以大声尖叫但没有人会听到我,希望我走过的所有道路都是我的,并且没有人能从我面前走过。暴风雪为满足我的这种想象提供了完美的条件,街道上人迹稀少。

零下11度的时候,在户外皮肤很快就会被冻得潮红,好像身体试图紧紧抓住这寒冷世界里最后一丝温暖和生命的气息。在这样的空间里,还存在秩序吗?当你眼前什么都看不见、白噪音持续嗡嗡响、大脑也因为温度不能正常工作,逻辑就似乎脱离了这个世界。

被大雪覆盖的建筑和雪雾后面隐约的灯光，雪中的树枝和窗户，看上去都像印象主义大师的点彩画，为朦胧和含混不清的街道增添了一种神秘的元素。这一刻，我脑海中浮现出德彪西的音乐，虚幻缥缈，和眼前的城市交融在一起，恍若梦幻，非常不真实。

严寒开始慢慢地吞噬我，就像冰水里的青蛙，僵冷从脚一点点地往上走，最后，心脏被冻得缩成一团。我挑战自然的勇气也在消失，我无法想象，如果我的头上没有屋顶，没有暖气，没有食物来帮助我度过暴风雪，我会怎么样。如果没有技术发展带给我们的便利生活条件，人类在面对大自然的恢弘中会处于什么位置？当寒冷慢慢地侵蚀了我的身体，我开始感觉不到我的手指存在时，我不得不结束雪中沉思，让自己从这油画般的白色风景中拔出身来，躲回了自己舒适温暖的房间，像这座城市的其他60万人一样。

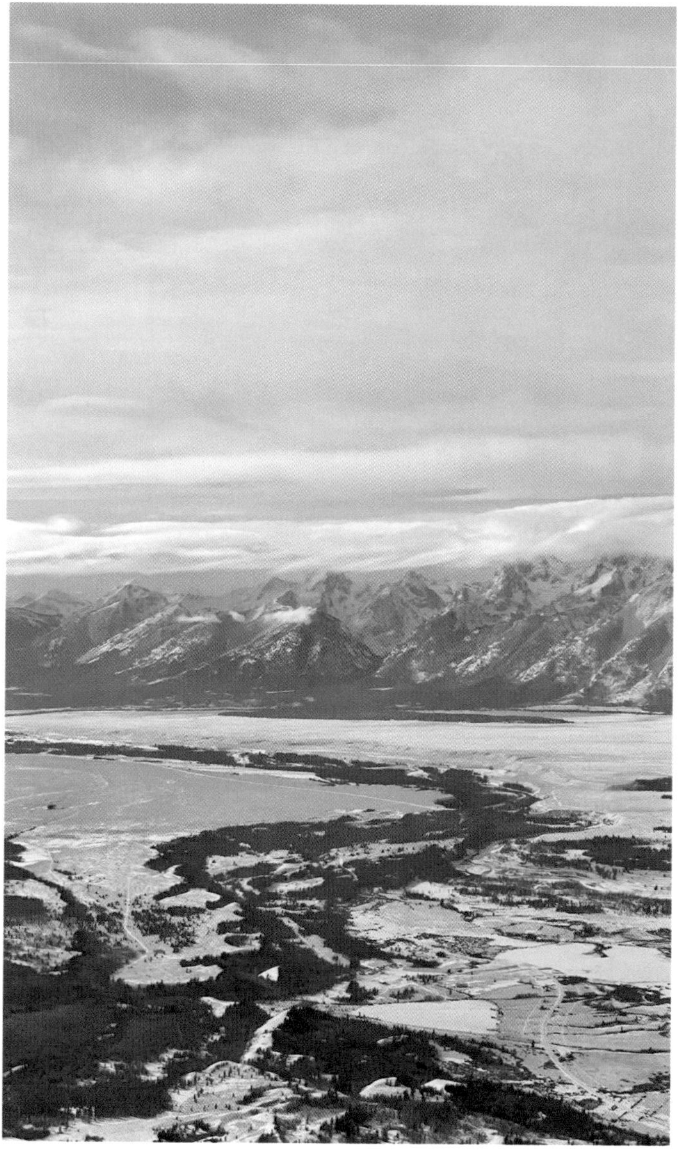

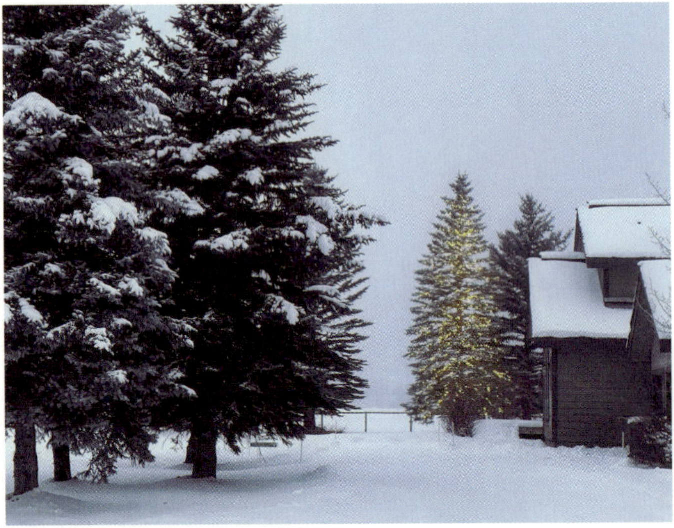

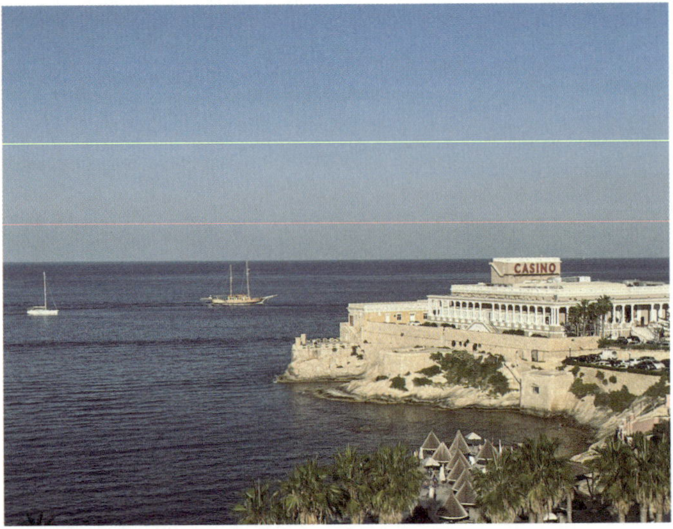
CASINO

在海滩上

阴沉沉的海滩让人想起夏天的雪、夜里的阳光,和无忧无虑的母亲,总之,都是常识混乱的、矛盾的修辞。但一旦看到它,便会完全更新我固有的对海滩的印象,重新建立我对世界新的感受和体验。

习惯了威尼斯海滩那种人比沙粒多的海滩,半月湾是我遇到的第一个游客不多的海滨小镇,一个典型的北加海滨小镇。虽然半月湾主街店铺的布局、招牌上的泡沫字体和游客多的海滨小镇一样,但少了太阳和游客,小镇看上去有些奇怪。没有人群的喧闹,你几乎能偷听到小镇书店和市政厅之间通过风传递的密语,发现它们真是八卦的一对。

找到通往海滩的路有点像一个 Leap of faith(信仰之跃[1]):你只能沿着悬崖上的一条土路走,你不

---

[1] 信仰之跃,出自克尔凯郭尔的《恐惧与战栗》,指人的认识能力有限,无法证明自己信仰的合理性,选择自己的信仰是一次惊险的飞跃。

知道它通向哪里，只能祈祷在岩石之间能够找到一个狭窄的开口，可以让你把脚趾伸进沙子里。

事实上的飞跃是由一只急躁的狗完成的。它收到了远处海浪的呼唤，却不能用它的吠叫回复。于是，正当它的主人忙着交谈时，它从悬崖上跳了下来，摔进了沙子里。听到远处传来的狗的呜咽声，它的主人吓坏了，而这只狗却觉得自己赢了。

唯一能找到路的是那些一对一对穿着卫衣和宽松运动裤的少女们，海滩是她们常去的地方。她们见面并不是为了做任何具体的事情或谈论任何具体的事情，她们只是习惯聚集在一起，看着大海冲走时间，并且互相讲述她们已经讲过一百遍的故事。每次讲故事的时候，她们还不忘稍微改变一下用词和语调，让对方更加积极地融入故事，虽然，实际上同样的叙述她们已经听过十几遍了。

当然，也有可能，她们真的忘了这些故事有多么熟悉了。在这里，生命的点点滴滴都埋藏在沙粒中，随风飘散。

被唐人街安慰

我出去散了一个没有目的地的步。我的向导是城市外墙上的涂鸦,每一个涂鸦,我都会走近瞧瞧,我跟着一个接一个的涂鸦走着。

当涂鸦变得越来越大,并且包围着我的商铺招牌大部分有了东方氛围的时候,我意识到自己在唐人街迷了路。旧金山的这一部分让我想起了我回不去的家乡,我被熟悉的面孔围绕着,我发现周围的汉字我都读得懂。这里的面包房出售的都是中式甜品,豆沙就是我童年的味道,可惜我的男朋友吃不惯。只是,与上海丰富多元的城市景观不同的是,这里的建筑风貌似乎统统都被困在了上个世纪。

唐人街保留了中国文化中最传统的元素:兵马俑,"中国皇后",北京集市,五颜六色的中国龙和舞狮。在这里,中国不同地区的文化都经过了混合和重新组合,最大程度地体现了中国特色。所有这些元素似乎对于建立海外华人的庇护所至关重要,它们似乎也表示着海外华人拒绝同化于美国社会的态度。

这里的集市很丰富，人们聚集在拐角处的生鲜市场挑选新鲜蔬菜。因为超市购物的流行，这种场景已经很少见了，很怀旧。我在路口拐了个弯，很惊讶地发现自己站在了我的另一个故乡巴黎的门口。一座被青铜包裹的、底部是咖啡馆的、像是文艺复兴时期的建筑就这么立在摩天大楼中间。

就这样，在这短暂的48分钟，我仿佛回了趟故乡。

喜欢美国的一个原因，就是它的多元化文化。这意味着每个人都可以在这里找到自己文化的影子，找到与自己产生共鸣的因素。而我对中国的想念，被唐人街安慰了。

不被看到的城市阴影

春天的时候,疫情发生了,而此刻,我在旧金山。

乍看之下,旧金山是一个普通的城市,无非就是"科技专家"的聚集地,它是世界上最昂贵的城市。这里的豪华公寓容纳着有钱人,这里的街道是流浪汉的庇护所。

这座城市的舒适程度因地区而异。Marina 和 Mission 区布满了色彩,充满着灵魂,而一般情况下,我们需要花些时间才能看清是什么使旧金山的金融区与其他金融区不一样。举个例子,我们该如何想象一个没有鸽子、没有树木、没有花园的社区?一个没有鸟儿翅膀颤动或树叶沙沙作响的地方?一个无性格的地方?在这里,季节的变化只能从天空看出,春天只能通过空气的质量或卖家从郊区带回来的鲜花篮来感受,这是一种在市场上售卖的春天。

了解一座城市的便捷方法是观察那里的人们如

何工作、如何爱、如何死去。在我们的大城市里，或许是因为气候的影响，死亡、爱与工作都是虚空而疯狂的。这个城市的居住者是高科技巨头之乡摩天大楼中的工蚁，他们总是渴望致富，他们基本只对商业感兴趣。用他们的用词来说，他们最看重做生意了。当然，他们也喜欢简单的快乐，比如喜欢女人、美食和海水浴。

大多数人的娱乐，是在星期六晚上和星期日。一周的其他几天他们都在试着赚大钱。傍晚，当他们离开办公室时，如果不去健身房，年轻人们会在固定的时间在酒吧和酒馆见面。有时候，他们也会在同一条林荫大道上漫步，手里握着一杯热乎乎的无咖啡因咖啡。

在这个城市中，最惊心的是人们死去的难。用"难"一词形容其实并不完全恰当，"不适"反而更加准确。生病从来不是一件好事，但是有许多国家和城市会让一个人在患病的时候仍然感受到被呵护。病人需要温暖，病人希望有所依靠，这对患病的人来说相当重要。但是在旧金山，每个人只看到手中业务的重要性，而周围的环境与他无关。黄昏的美丽很短暂，生活和娱乐的品质很重要，人必须是健康的。在这里，疾病是丑陋不堪的，令人生厌的。病人会非常的孤独。想想一个即将死去的人，他将死在被忽略的空虚中。也许就在同一时刻，一群人正在咖啡馆里打着电话谈论股票、提货单和折扣。如此干涩的城市，死亡——特别是现代社会的死亡——让人非常难受。

在富裕和生机勃勃的旧金山，老去和生病是不被看到的阴影。

对于没有任何征兆的疫情以及随之而来的一系列事件，我们现在只能记录事实。一个纪实作家的任务只有在事情发生时表示"此事发生了"，并且在引起人们的关注时，知道成千上万的人和他一起成为了事件的证人。这成千上万的人群能够自己在心里留下正在发生着的事件的笔记，其真实性只有他们自己心知肚明。

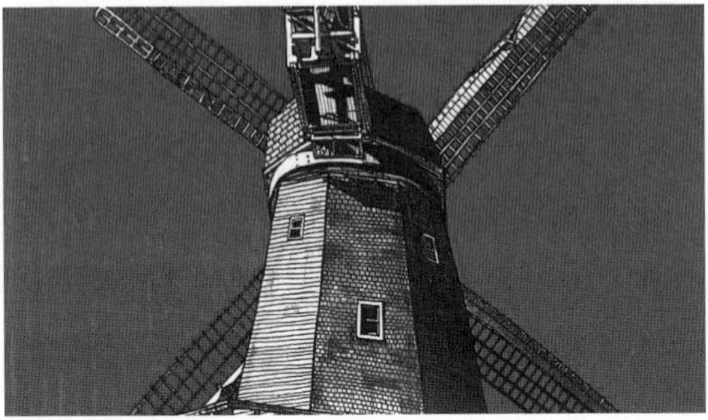

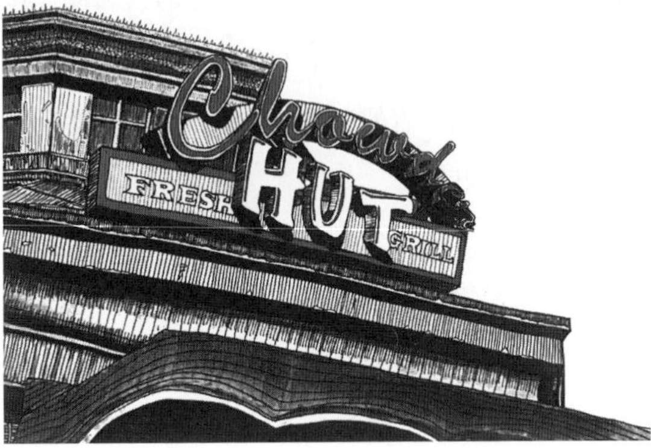
Chowder
HUT
FRESH
GRILL

如果风景是有感知的

旧金山有一些当地人会尽量避免的地方，我说的是渔人码头、吉拉德利广场、伦巴底街，那些在纪念品商店的明信片上看到的色彩饱和度超高的地方，这些景点属于每年来这座城市旅游的 2580 万旅客。

在疫情的这一个月里，这些地标被遗弃了。这座城市曾经被霓虹灯照亮的皮囊失去了光泽。它的毛孔曾经被街头艺人的音乐滋养着，呼吸着西班牙油条的肉桂香。但如今的它，干燥、掉屑、暗淡。

我们关注自己的孤独感，但是因为我们的存在而变得生动迷人的风景和街道现在又怎么样呢？如果风景和街道是有感知的，它们能听到的那唯一听得见的音乐，是寂静和沉默。我试图猜想离开人的世界会有怎样的感受，它们会像我们一样在这种脆弱的情况下感到迷茫、失去意义吗？我不知道。

只是，世界有大自然的陪伴，也许一点也不想念我们。土狼会拜访它们，通常被人类无情除根的野花也会在它们的耳边轻声细语,天空因为没有污染而更蓝,被囚禁的人类,给了世界喘息和修复的机会。

也许没有我们,地球呼吸得会更好。

一切都是时间问题

我很想和你走出家门,去看看人类,去观察被改变的世界。但是作为一个公民,我们不得不服从政府在这特殊时期公布的要求:居家隔离。

于是,我们只好做中场休息,将目光从外部世界转移到我们的厨房里来,好在烹调食物的气味总是会让人平静,我要制作一个千禧世代最爱的香蕉蛋糕。

将烤箱预热至 350 华氏度,将香蕉切成薄片,然后捣碎。想象香蕉是过去几天你所经历的所有烦恼,你死劲压碎它们释放你所感受到的那些压力,然后,在里面加入三个鸡蛋,代糖和杏仁酱,再将榛子粉与一茶匙发酵粉和小苏打混合。

人类可以发明香蕉蛋糕,人类可以发明无糖的糖。但是人类不能发明更多的时间,更多可以对病毒做出反应的时间,更多可以准备对抗病毒的时间,更多可以让我们享受我们曾经认为平凡的世界的时间。

我们曾经认为微不足道的生活细节现在是我们最想念的，是我们的希望和期望，像蛋黄和蛋清在搅拌碗中的旋转一样，融合在一起。本能地，我们想加快蛋糕材料的混合，但是太快了材料就溢出碗来。放慢速度真让人不得力和沮丧，可我不得不去适应它。

在添加巧克力豆之前，将所有粉类添加到混合物中。巧克力豆在蛋糕的糊状中编制图案。那图案像人们在混乱中寻找的格式一样，一种我们将赋予其意义并创造新的惯例的格式。一种可以让你适应新的现实的格式。

这个新的现实包括一个新的节奏，我们甚至可能相对于过去的节奏更喜欢这种新节奏。你只需要带上雾化外界的遮光罩即可度过每一天，以一种愉悦的精神坐下来写作、工作、画画、保持忙碌。

这样，我们不会忘记过去的节奏，但同时也可以想象未来的节奏。可能，这就是活在当下。

然后，将蛋糕转移到烤箱中 50 分钟，随后冷却。请记住，现状也会降温。一切都只是时间问题。

我和我的花园

六个月的冬天换来了一个春日

我对天气感到满意,我很怀念阳光

但是我不喜欢别人把我的公园,我的公共花园偷走

可怜的花园,天冷时没人在你身边,每个人都离弃你,放弃你

但是我,我爱你

我拜访你,我欣赏你,我与你分享我的音乐,我的播客

我在你身上行走,帮你放松骨头

我,是你真正的崇拜者,其他人都是假的仰慕者,我会一直回来见你

天气糟糕时,你会独自一人,我也会孤独

我们最终还会见面的,你和我。

说到底,聚会结束时,你只有我,我只有你

咱们会重聚的

艺术与美

美是一种思想

我清楚地记得在高中时写过一篇哲学论文。主题是"艺术是否应该是美丽的?"我们班分成两个阵营,一些人认为艺术应该是装饰性的,也就是说是美丽的;还有一些人认为艺术作品需要表达一种思想,艺术才能是艺术。

昊美术馆让我想起了这个辩论。那里有几个展览在展出,一楼是空山基和 MR. 的作品,二楼是博伊斯的作品。空山基的性感机器人和 MR. 五彩缤纷的作品是视觉盛宴,而博伊斯的作品却是模糊字迹的褪色海报和又长又慢的影像。一楼观展的人们通常忙着和空山基和 MR. 的作品拍照,但我没有看到什么人会给博伊斯的作品拍照。仅从被拍摄的频率,就可以清楚地看出哪个艺术家更具有观赏性,哪个更具有哲理性。

我想不起来在课堂上我们讨论出了什么结论,但我认为艺术重在表达思想。在某种程度上,即使是最具装饰性的绘画和雕塑也在表达一种想法,毕竟，美本身也是一种概念。考虑到满足这一标准是多么容易，难怪正如博伊斯所说，"每个人都是艺术家"。

爱上法国新浪潮电影

明亮但柔和的色彩、胶片的颗粒感、慵懒的角色、摄像机不多不少轻触现实皮肤的能力，这一切都是法国二十世纪六十年代影片吸引我的特质。我喜欢新浪潮片用低廉预算创造出来的美，即以最少的成本但充分的才能与想法制作出好电影，在法国六十年代的片子中，特效和好莱坞明星都是无关紧要的。

侯麦、特吕弗和戈达尔的电影魔力在于简单却意义深切的对话，以及轻松随意的事件过渡，在这些电影中，我们离开了黑色电影的险恶世界，我们拥抱了噪音、速度、节奏、街道、青年，尽管总会有一点忧郁……总之，重要的是环境叛逆但经典的《三十光辉岁月》(*Trente Glorieuses*)导演的想法场景，这些电影中的青春和怀旧是各个时代的年轻人都在寻找的东西。十几岁的时候，我们每个人都疯狂地渴望远走高飞、四处冒险、通过探索外界来探索自己。新浪潮电影中的成年儿童完全满足了年轻人的妄想。哪个男孩不想在意大利像《怒海沉尸》的阿兰·德龙那样过上好日子？哪个女孩不想像《祖与占》中的让娜·莫罗一样成为一段三角恋的女主人公？乔治·德勒吕的作曲更是让观众在感情的旋风中越走越远。

青春、休闲、怀旧以及对电影和文学之父的尊敬的这种不可思议的融合，是这几个月来带我踏上旅途的翅膀。新浪潮为我打开了一扇过于美好的可以看到外部风景的窗户。

这些对当代人来说节奏缓慢的电影使我逃避了当前的时空框架，在那个电影世界里没有疫情，没有寒冷，没有冰雹——即使电影人物处于冰天雪地里，他们处于的寒地也是《瑟堡的雨伞》当中色彩缤纷，充满活力的世界。通过电影，我重新获得了疫情使我失去的身体的活动能力。我跟着《狂人皮埃罗》在法国南部经历令人振奋的冒险，通过《面包店的女孩》在巴黎街头拐角追逐一名金发的神秘女子，伴随着《克莱尔的膝盖》里面的人物享受安纳西阳光明媚的夏日。我像《午夜巴黎》中的玛丽昂·歌迪亚与欧文·威尔逊一样，期待在更美好的时光中找到更美好的一个世界。

当然，虽然我沉迷于所谓更美好的法国六十年代电影世界，我也不得不提醒自己，电影像当今社交媒体一样，仅仅是精心构成的虚假世界而已。它们展现的是人们最向往的感情、经历与生活。我敢肯定，在六十年代法国生活的人们肯定也有许多不满与问题。或许，像《午夜巴黎》中玛丽昂·歌迪亚所扮演的角色一般，他们向往的世界也是过去的某一年代；那可能是十九世纪的美好年代、十六世纪的文艺复兴，或者是十五世纪的中世纪。

我想，如果我们可以像看待过去时光一样怀旧地看待我们今天所生活的年代，也许我们会重新发现对现在的热情与渴望。看看我们今天的生活，我们有远程办公的可能性，更灵活的时间表，初为人父的男人有时间看着新生儿一点一点长大……也许我们会意识到我们与侯麦或夏布洛尔的角色生活在同一个世界中。我们的眼睛就是我们的相机，温柔的滤镜由我们来安装。

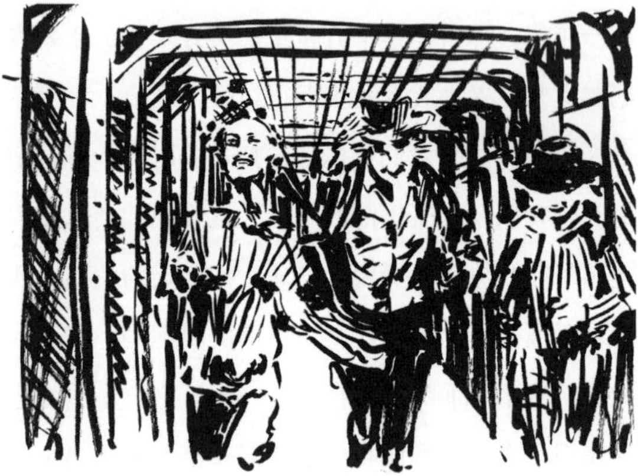

与世界共享一支笔

每一天都是一篇独立形成的故事。

每天,我们都会把发生的事件串在一起,形成一段叙事,如同写一篇文章。我们选择喜欢的事件,选择将这些事件组织在一起,并且表达我们对这些事件的理解。"今天我们去公园,明天我们再去喷泉那边。"我们可以仔细地计划所有事情,但并非一切都会顺利执行。世界总会给我们准备一个我们无法设想的惊喜,它是我们每一天文章的合著者。

与世界共享一支笔可以确保未来不是一本可以随便翻阅和预料的书。当然,有一种逻辑指引着某些事情比其他事情更可能发生,但是你绝对无法阅读将在未来发生的确切对话,无法看到未来的人物、情况与台词,这些不确定性将由世界来告诉你。

因此,每天,你都会发觉写作的乐趣,同时,你也会发现各种你无法掌握的转变。你是作者,也是读者。你是指挥家,也是观众。在我看来,这是与世界万物共存的最佳方式。你拥有强大的力量,但不会过多,以免变成无所不知的叙述者。而成为无所不知的叙述者,也许会因为知道的太多了,不再具有解不开的谜题,反而丧失了好奇心。

伟大的正午

"正午思想"是一个由尼采创造,加缪采用并发展的哲学术语,它指的是地中海正午最灿烂的阳光所锻造出的最炫目的那一刻,超越的那一刻。这阳光的强烈可以照亮荒谬的最深处,它是在德拉克洛瓦的画中,自由女神高举的那支长矛,一支如此锋利的矛,引导着人们反抗生命中的阴影,追求光辉的呈现。

尽管加缪的作品很荒谬,但他从未放弃表现地中海沿岸的一切美好。他把绿松石色的潮汐看成一首充满激情、再现人类生活起落的华尔兹,他还在沙沙作响的橄榄树声中听到了对生命的颂歌,而橄榄树是被天空和大海养育出来的温柔生命,反过来又滋养着我们。

"地中海只有一种文化,"加缪写道,"它不是一种装腔作势的抽象文化,也不是一种谴责文化。它是一个存在于树木、山丘与人类之中的文化。"荒谬是加缪的出发点,乐观勇敢地抗争并寻找人生的希望,才是他的终点。

科学并不是绝对客观的

"你想学习文学？可是学这个好像没啥用啊！"

"数学和物理更为重要。"

尽管我很讨厌听到这些话，但自从我选择读文科的那天起，这些话便一直无情地在我的耳边徘徊。

我的大多数高中同学像他们的父母一样，都确信文科学生是"垃圾"，他们认为只有理科生才能在现实生活中取得成功，而一个人的价值，是由能否成功来决定的。这也是为什么我上高中那会儿，一百个学生里只有十二个文科生。从那时起，我就已经习惯了人们说科学是一个更具有社会权威的学科，这种权威建立在科学是客观的观念上。据称，科学的主张，方法和结果不受任何偏见的影响，例如特定的观点或价值承诺。因为这种所谓的客观性，科学被认为具有帮助我们公正理解世界的力量，而这种力量确立了它的优越性。但是，我认为科学从根本上说并不是客观的，而这恰好使它没有那么优越。科学是建立在信仰和范式之上的，因此，它所谓的客观性是主观信念的结果，而这也剥夺了它的客观性。没有客观性，人们便不能宣称科学赋予了我们对世界完全和公正的理解，这就是为什么科学不是一个至高无上的研究领域。

科学主义树立了"科学是了解我们的世界的唯一关键"的想法。对大多数人来说，科学似乎不带有偏见并且客观，如果这个想法是真的话，科学主义的观念是有道理的。然而，人们忽略了一点，科学首先是人类创造的信念。就像弗里德里希·尼采在他所著的《快乐的科学》一书中说的那样，科学源于人类想要了解更多的渴望。人类创造科学是因为相信通过科学的进步，我们可以拥有一种无私的知识，使自己更好地理解基督教上帝的智慧和善良。也就是说，根据尼采的观点，科学是建立在一种信念，一种信仰——对真理的渴望——的基础之上的，而这种渴望又是主观的，因为它承载着个人价值承诺。因此，建立在信仰基础上的科学并不是客观的。如果科学是因为其客观性强而拥有优越性，那么通过证明科学从根本上是建立在信仰和个人利益的基础上，尼采的理论便打破了科学的优越性。没有客观性，

科学再也无法提供对世界的公正理解，而没有这种力量，科学就失去了作为至高无上的研究领域的地位

此外，科学是主观的，不仅因为它建立在信仰的基础上，也因为它建立在美国物理学家托马斯·库恩称为范式的一系列假设之上。范式是普遍公认的科学成就，它们一度提供模型问题和解决方案，以便科学家可以在其基础上进步并取得进展。正如库恩的著作《科学革命的结构》所讨论的那样，科学是建立在许多不断变化的不同范式上的，这意味着科学无法在一个特定的范式上安顿下来。举个例子，从亚里士多德和柏拉图的"两球宇宙"到托勒密范式或哥白尼，再到开普勒和牛顿的理论，多年来范式不断地被创造并取代。范式的替代被称为范式转换，它使科学不仅仅基于一个绝对真理，而是基于真理的各种观念。也就是说，因为有许多不同的范式和竞争意见，科学是主观的，并且永远不会完全客观。因此，科学基于那些随着时间推移而不断变化的观点，并且是一种通过集体方式来研究和理解世界的方式。因此，库恩的理论表明，科学是一系列总是在变革中的范式，因此科学是主观的。由于科学是主

观的，它失去了客观性所保证的对世界的绝对理解的能力，因此，科学作为一个研究领域就失去了它的最高地位。

在马德里邂逅毕加索

我在马德里的大部分时间都待在酒店房间里。由于航班延误和难以忍受的时差反应,我只在城里闲逛了一个小时左右,纽约的月亮就越过大西洋,把我拉入了梦乡。

我甚至没有像往常一样在新城市参观博物馆。我的大脑几乎没有足够的能量来处理当前的时间和日期,更不用说在一个庙宇一样的建筑里处理整个城市被浓缩的文化和历史了。

我在阳台上喝着咖啡,试图消除压在我身上的困意。虽然我无法在普拉多欣赏西班牙大师的杰作,我却注意到我用来放置双脚的椅子看起来非常熟悉。是的,椅子的藤编,我在毕加索的画里看到过。

《有藤椅的静物》和布拉克的几幅画是我中学美术老师教我们立体主义的入门画,无论我的老师如何解释这些图像,我总是很难在扭曲的渲染图中区分具体的物体和面孔。但我记得,藤椅给毕加索原本具有象征意义的作品带来的一丝现实主义,这给我留下了深刻的印象。虽然毕加索融入藤椅是对技术和艺术之间关系的质疑,但我却认为它缩小了抽象艺术和现实之间的差距,提醒观众即使是最抽象的艺术作品也来源于日常生活。

因此,我,一个无名的小人物,在一个世纪以后,碰巧在毕加索的祖国重现了画中的场景,是再自然不过的。我拿了画中的柠檬片给苏打水调味,用画中的刀切了我的炸丸子,又用毕加索的扇形餐巾擦了擦嘴。

我们都吃饭、睡觉、做梦、玩耍,我们的行为都是类似的。但不同之处在于我们对日常的认知与理解。有些人会把一顿饭变成抽象艺术,而另一些人会把它冲进厕所。

人是艺术的核心

佛罗伦萨是文艺复兴的摇篮,在这里兴起的人文主义、新伦理、新知识改变了欧洲之前被黑暗时代的阴影笼罩的艺术界。文艺复兴时期的绘画和雕塑对观众的影响超越时代,那个时期留下来的雕塑,至今仍像散落的珍珠一样在全世界被人膜拜。无论是文艺复兴时期的艺术还是现代艺术,对人的关注应该是艺术的核心。那时的雕塑家们用人体来表达揭示人类情感、激情和心灵的深度,虽然现在已经进入了人工智能时代,我们站在这些艺术品面前仍然能产生共鸣。

对于文艺复兴时代的人来说,今天的我们或许看起来像是被科技主宰、说着奇特白话的奇怪生物,就如我们在现代的科幻电影中看到的未来人一样。但无论在哪个时期,人类最深刻的兴趣都不会改变:了解自己和自己的物种。因此,一块大理石雕像能穿过岁月永恒地影响观众这件事,也就不足为奇了。

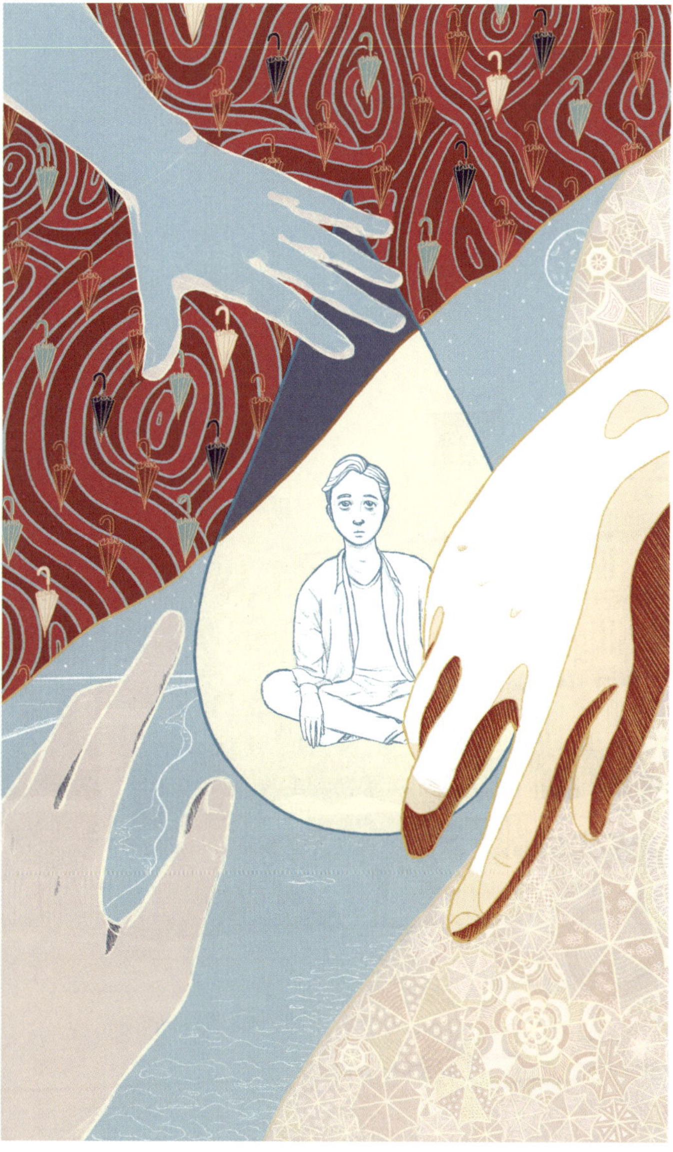

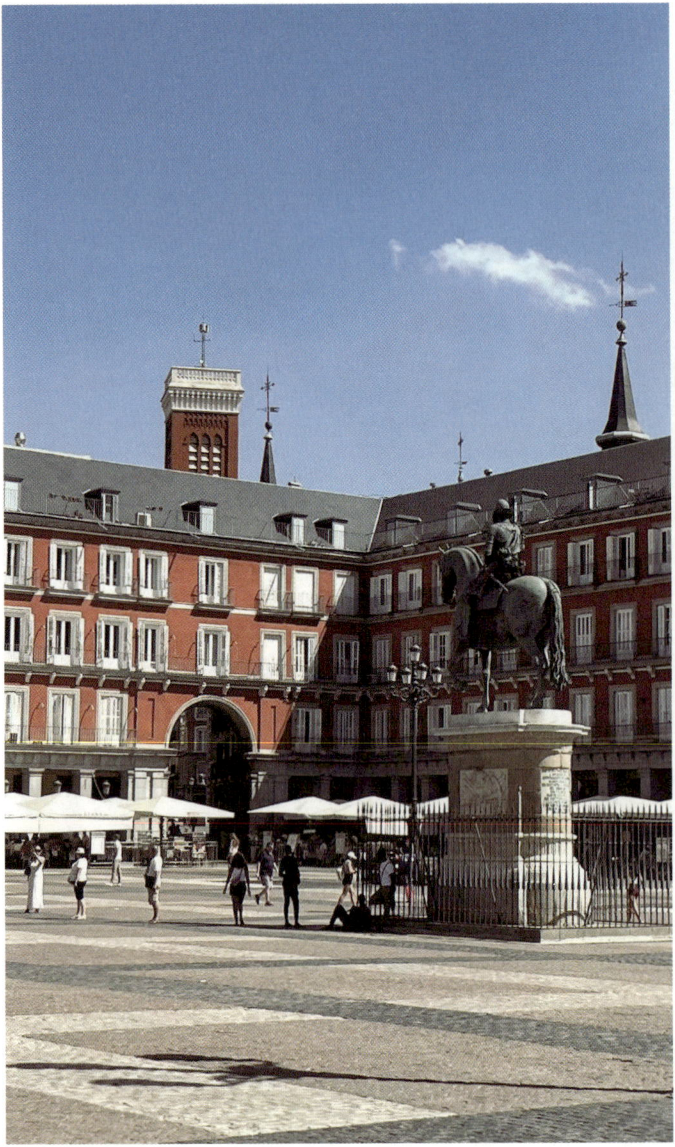

活在数百年前的大理石雕塑人,与今天凝视他的生物人并无太大区别。在一个强调个体意识的社会中,我们都觉得自己是一个独立于历史和过去的小世界,而事实上,我们是生活在过去的人编织的带着金色光芒的文化和历史延伸时间中的,就像我们的后代也将生活在由我们的画笔描出的时代壁画中一样。

作品后面的思想者

每一件艺术品都是艺术家的经历和观点的超凡投射。你会发现，当一群艺术家聚集在一起描摹同一个模特时，没有一件作品会看起来像另一件。思想与艺术是同一回事，毕竟艺术作品来源于思想。

如果将每个人的思想都呈现在画布上，我们将发现非常独特的作品。尽管一幅画的笔触强度有时会与另一幅画的笔触强度相似，但笔触与颜色和形状的磨合会创造出每幅画的独特的精神。有些人会尝试模仿其他人，但要注意，模仿永远不会超越原作，因为每件艺术只有一位领导者，那就是在笔墨色彩之后的那个思想者。

两种工匠

有些工匠保存过去,有些工匠编制未来。

一流时装屋的工匠保留了艺术和手工传统。这种文化遗产象征着我们所向往的某种微妙的声望,但它遥不可及,是一种我们只敢用眼睛爱抚的放纵。工匠用一针一线在白纸上绣制画面和诗歌。他们讲故事,他们用每个设计和每个系列创造一个神话般的宇宙。他们让你梦想成真。

也有不保留过去的工匠,相反,他们编织通往未来的道路。他们不会使用柔软的彩色织物,而是使用绣有铜线和玻璃纤维的金属板。他们也在变魔术,带我们进入一场冒险。没有比科学发现更伟大、更奇妙的冒险了。他们创造了自己的世界,一个可以让任何地方的任何人敞开视野的盒子。这个盒子不是毛茸茸的,用料也不是丝绸,它通常是棱角分明的,寒冷而坚硬的。

但是,尽管寒冷,这些美丽闪亮的零件还是有种莫名的温暖。这种温暖来自人们的低声细语,他们曾经梦想着成为无尽的自然的主人与拥有者,但有一天,这个梦想的遗骸将只剩些金属拼图。

主观的景象

有一只猫一直在我们的花园里走来走去。我不知道它来自哪里,也不知道它要去哪里,它经常躺在这里晒太阳或单纯躲躲雨。

我有试过接近它,但那样我就会把它吓跑,所以,我唯一能做的就是像这样隔着玻璃和它说话。

我发现自己经常会透过玻璃窗往外看,看到事情发生,但却不参与其中,如同从画框外面,望着画框里面的画面。我很喜欢成为观察者,而不是被观察的对象,但话说回来,通过描绘和写出我所看到的东西,我不可避免地也把自己放在了作品中。我会通过无法摆脱的个人视角来扭曲我看到的一切,并通过受我精神状态影响的内心的眼睛来赋予其新的生命和颜色。

我画布上的女人并不是她自己,而是我眼中的她。我画出的手的张力,眼睛里的闪光,只是印象和推理,很可能她的实际感受和我所看到的完全不一样。而用我的方式看到的她很可能与你眼中的她

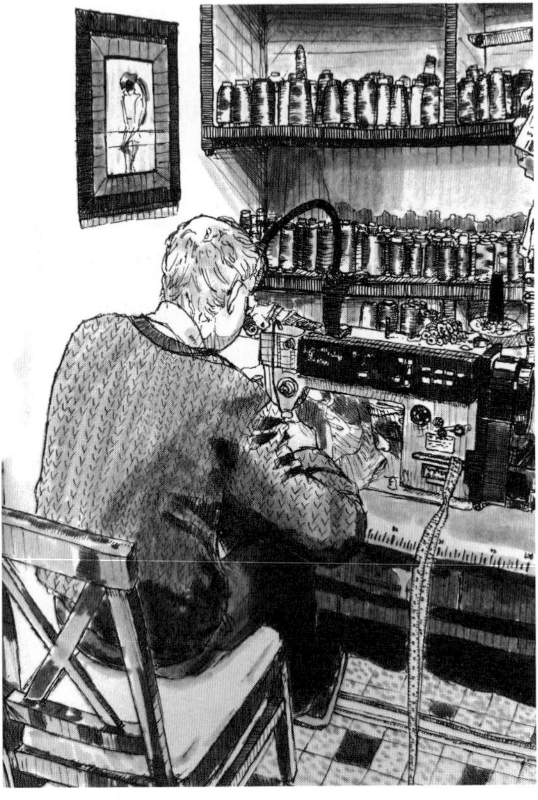

并不相同,你也许会看到另一个完全不同的女人。

说到底,艺术家的角色是成为他人。我们有的是镜子,不是脸。我们的作用是让最个人的感受成为最集体的感受。我们会把具体和细小的事例和情绪放大与扭曲成每个人都能感受到的景象,那是一种主观的景象。

消费主义的僵尸

看了僵尸片先驱乔治·罗梅罗导演的 1978 年上映的《活死人黎明》，这部电影真实地表现了盲目消费的可怕，不管是在当代生活中还是在美国的上世纪七十年代。

电影中，僵尸世界的末日席卷了美国，幸存者们选择在一个大型购物中心避难。在那里，他们享受着"享乐主义的生活方式"，但是一帮骑自行车的人很快闯入并抢劫了这个地方，顺便将成千上万的僵尸送入了商场废墟。在电影的最后时刻，僵尸挤满了购物中心的自动扶梯，密密麻麻地拥挤着，和我们熟悉的典型的假日或周末购物人群没有什么区别。

电影里的僵尸暗示了美国 1970 年代后期对资本主义和无意识消费的恐惧。在这里，僵尸是消费者，他们漫无目的地在商店中漫游，"这是他们生活中的重要场所"，一名幸存者对僵尸在商场中的存在做了描述：

罗杰：恩，我们在（商场），但是我们怎么会回来呢？

彼得：谁在乎呢？我们去买东西吧！

罗杰：手表！手表！

彼得：让我们得到我们需要的东西。我要电视和收音机。

罗杰：哦，哦，打火机油！还有巧克力！巧克力！

彼得：（沿着衣服走道走）嘿，貂皮大衣怎么样？

幸存者从本质上被资本主义意识形态洗脑了，除了占有和消费之外，他们看不到周围破碎的世界，而这种盲目足以使他们无法意识到他们的生命已经陷入了危险。

少就是多

我带着一本维特根斯坦的书去了纽约,所以我花了很多时间思考语言,以及语言是如何影响我们对世界的体验的。语言是如此强大的工具,思想是由单词组成的,所以在某种程度上,你知道的单词越多,你能形成的想法就越多,你的精神世界也就会因此而更丰富。然而,我觉得真正的力量不在于把大量复杂的词汇记在脑子里,而在于巧妙地用最直接的语言表达最强烈的情感和最清晰的逻辑思维。

换句话说,少即是多。

当然,顶级的语言大师肯定知道最繁复的单词,但他们不会仅仅为了显摆而使用它们。相反,就像立体派画家精通具象绘画,但却把自己的表达分解成儿童般的绘画一样,语言大师的每一笔——每一个词——都是精确的。

我发现我仍然会因为喜欢一些单词在我舌头上的发音,和喜欢不同单词在一起读时的巧妙节奏而使用它们。但我正在学习将实质凌驾于形式之上,并在简单中找到抒情性。

因为缺乏被教育而自由

语言的表达是有限的,这就是为什么我们经常会使用视觉和音乐来传达语言不可描述的东西,也是为什么我认为动画、歌剧和电影可能是目前存在的最丰富的艺术媒介,因为音乐、动态的人物和文字都在发挥作用,来渲染情感、意义和想法的丰富性。

尽管我使用文字和画笔的时间足够长,可以画出我思想的轮廓,但由于我缺乏音乐背景,我的表达能力仍然很差。我多么想拿着小提琴尖叫和微笑,或是拿着短笛给鸟儿插上翅膀。

被局限于使用视觉艺术和文字,对一个创作的人来说,就像外语能力能应付日常的生活,但却不能完整地表达深刻的意义和独特的思想。对音乐语言的不通在我的大脑中造成了交通堵塞,而疏通它的唯一方法就是回到我已经熟悉的媒介,我已经拥有的技能。

但这种无知的好处是,当我拿起一种乐器时,我不会有正确演奏方法的限制。没有基础意味着我可以跳出框框思考——实际上，对我来说，根本不会有任何框框。

这是"小白"艺术家的福与祸。你永远无法与传统的大师相比，但你可以创造出自己的游戏规则，因为缺乏被教育反而获得了一种自由。

音乐是种过滤器

音乐是生活最强大的过滤器。当你走在大街上时，你耳朵里播放的一切都会影响你的情绪，你的能量，甚至会改变你看待周围环境的方式。判断那个从商店出来的女孩是在等待一个可爱的邂逅呢，还是情绪低落，这取决于我是在听"碎南瓜乐队"还是 Patrick Watson 的音乐。身边溜过的滑板少年，他们滑板是在释放焦虑，还是只是在享受运动的快感，这取决于我耳机里 Mac DeMarco 的音乐是否在播放。客观发生的情境，被我耳机里的音乐过滤，决定了我的主观情绪。

我收集了很多小众歌曲，正是因为如此我每时每刻都戴着耳机。但最近，我意识到这个习惯的形成可能源于我试图逃离头脑中的沉默——一种会迫使我面对一些让我想避免的情绪的沉默。当我的思绪过于激动时，音乐能让它们安静下来。我越焦虑，听的音乐就越嘈杂、越复杂。快节奏和复杂的作曲有一种控制力量，穿透我思想和情绪的屏障，到达我的大脑，让我躲在音乐中逃避自己的麻烦。

但我已经意识到，躲避实际上无助于缓解任何悲伤，反而，负面情绪只会积聚更多。面对问题，真正有帮助的是找到问题的根源并处理它，而且只有在让自己的大脑安静和有空间的时候，才能进行思考。

所以，现在我每天散步的时候，会试着少听点音乐，让交通灯的滴答声和偶尔的汽车喇叭声成为我生活这部电影唯一的背景音乐。我通过接受自己的思想，也接受了外在的世界。当我不再伴随着 Talking Heads 紧锣密鼓的节拍急急促促地走路时，我和身边世界的连接就建立了。

沉浸在音乐制造的屏障里可能会让人觉得自己是唯一的主角，但我所有真正能主导自己状态的时刻，却都是在没有音乐的情况下发生的。

一个仰慕者

仰慕的感觉来源于我,却投射在别人身上
仰慕,是一种无法单独存在的感觉
没有仰慕者,就没有被仰慕之人
我,更喜欢当仰慕者而不是被人仰慕

我仰慕大自然
仰慕被沙粒碰撞时发抖的野草
它散发的那新鲜的绿色气味使空气分裂
它瑟瑟发抖时发出的细语 有时会被吹倒触地

我仰慕大海
仰慕那让我在湿硬的沙子上留下脚印的泡沫
我在波浪的语言抹去我的生命之前
留下了短暂的痕迹

我仰慕美丽
那种头脑美丽 因此外表也美丽的那种美丽

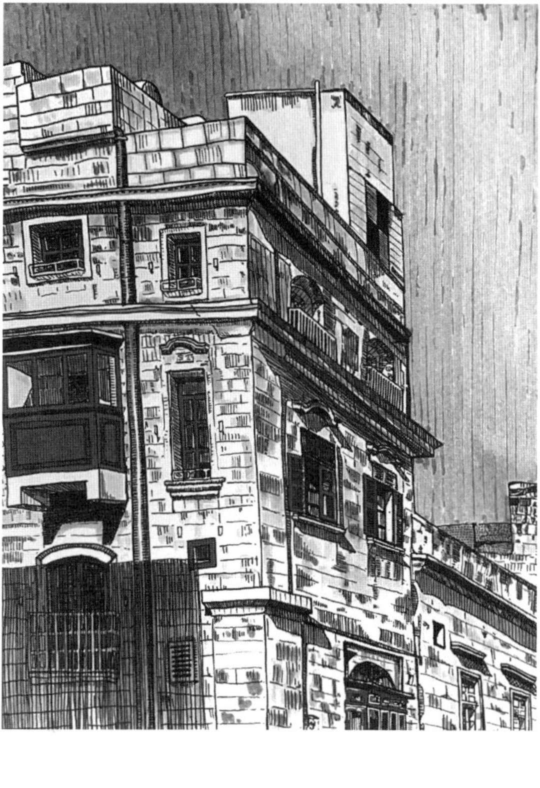

而不是完全肉体上的美丽

在时间的流逝里

肉体的美丽会渐渐空洞

就好像它根本从没存在过

我在寻找一个男人 我要仰慕他

在他身上发现那些可以超越我的东西

下一个路口

星期天的早上，巴黎仍然深陷在沉睡之中，天空失去了夏日的明亮，厚重的云在灰色的锌屋顶上翻滚，模糊了天与地的界限。

我沿着拉丁区的鹅卵石，向索邦大学紧闭的大门走去。平时通常充满玻璃杯碰撞声和喧哗交谈声的咖啡馆此刻非常安静。前一天晚上热闹遗留的唯一痕迹是漂浮在浑浊的雨水坑里的烟头，它们看起来像是在池塘里航行的小船，那些孩子们在卢森堡公园里推来推去的纸船。

秋天已来临。破裂的树干散发出苔藓般的湿气，滴落在落叶上。我的靴子重重地落在昏昏欲睡的树叶上，没有发出一点声音。湿气压低了它们清脆的破裂声，软化了它们噼里啪啦的崩溃。这段时间以来，我第一次感到如此平静。

我上一次来巴黎的时候，完全是另外一个人。事实上，我甚至不确定我当时是否有资格被称为一个完整的人。那时的我没有真正的身份，只存在于与他人的关系中：我的教授，我的同学，还有一个从同学中延伸出来的松散的朋友圈。也许，还能算上校园咖啡厅柜台后面的克里奥尔女士；每天早上，当我在上课前等咖啡的时候，我都会和她简短地聊几句。

我从未追求过这些关系中的任何亲近，他们都是主动地来接触被动的我，他们总是以我无法避免的眼神接触开始，用一个我无法忽视的"你好"，或者，在最不得已的情况下，一封我无法拒绝的小组作业邮件，打破我沉默的围墙。当对方简单的问候变成问题，通常我不会马上回答，而会巧妙地把问题转回到提问者身上，让他们对自己的悲伤和喜好进行单方面的倾诉。我会用反光碎片把自己掩饰起来，好像我是个无定形的物质，可以融化成任何符合容器形状的东西，以适应这些不同的交谈者。我的身份如此流动，如此易变，以至于我可以滑入任何东西的模子里。如同某个叫"罗曼娜"（"Romane"）的人，是"罗马-安娜"（"Rome-Anne"）的结合体。其实，连我的名字也不是我自己，而是我父母相遇的城市和我祖母名字的组合体。我不能独自存在，我总是被别人定义，被身边的人或者环境定义着。

*

沿着 Soufflot 街，朝着卢森堡公园走去，香烟船让我有了探望真正的小帆船的欲望。一个女人站在 Saint-Jacques 街的一家面包店旁，黄油的甜香味偶尔从吹着微风的通风口吹出，预示着面包店即将开张。"开放时间：周一至周六，7:00-19:00。周日，8:00-13:30"，门牌暗示着。6 点 40 分，伴随着从门缝传出来的雷鬼音乐的微弱节拍，面包师把一只只烤好的美味点心挪到橱窗。在黎明的黑暗中，酥脆的黄油糕点在温暖的灯光下闪闪发光，就像丢失已久的水下箱子里的宝藏。今天，做面包的男人只会当几个小时的面包师，他还有一整个下午的时间要去做一个父亲，去看望他的孩子们。当然，如果有热情的美丽女人来买面包，也许他还有空档带她出去喝杯咖啡。

自从我到了这座城市，我常常会忍不住想走进一家这样的面包店。但每次，在我研究完橱窗里一个个泡芙上的冰糖图案，还有覆盆子馅饼上的糖浆后，在我打算推门的时候，我的勇气会突然消失在那扇有着装饰艺术风格的门前。我害怕自己会像往常一样再次陷入身份混乱的漩涡，我害怕一个"你好"会发展成"你今天过得怎么样",这简单的问候会迫使我不得不进行陌生人之间的寒暄,并且根据对方的回答来展现另一个我。不,那已经是过去的那个时期,另一个阶段的行为了,现在,我想把它们抛在脑后。我来到巴黎,正是为了观察一个与我的世界不同的世界,还有寻找我在这个世界里——或之外——的位置。我希望把自己描绘成一幅有我自己风格的画,无论取景和角度如何,我都保持不变,我需要一个稳定的自我认知,而为了找到它,我必须避免任何可能打乱画面的交流。

我最接近找到自己的一次经历是在大三的时候,在校园的电梯里,十月的一个早晨——一个比巴黎秋天的黎明更温暖、更明亮的早晨——因为教授有事,我早上九点的课提前结束了。像往常一样,我的书包在下课前 5 分钟就收拾好了,这样我可以绕开同学们在离开教室告别时的闲聊,避免漫长的寒暄和不得不露出的尴尬与僵硬的微笑。一个人坐电梯回家,大而快速的步伐往往意味着我精心设计的保护个人空间的努力是成功的。当然也有失败的情况,比如说,我看到有人在电梯门快关闭的时候跑来,我会为他们按着开门钮等待,并开始思考和他们共同分享电梯的这几分钟,我要沉默着看看哪面墙，每次听到电梯铃"叮"的一声，我就感到那种奇怪的沉默即将到来。

那个十月的早晨，像往常一样，我冲出教室，直奔电梯。我选择的路径是离电梯所在的墙最近的路径，就像赛道一样，靠墙越近的路径总是最短最快的。我的快速离开是值得的，我成为唯一一个等电梯的人。我按下电梯按钮，开始为一天中出现的崭新的一小时空闲时间而感到高兴。我并没有什么特殊的安排或任务要做，但一想到因为得到更多的时间而获得了更多的自由，可以去做任何让我高兴的事，不管行动或不行动，都让我很愉快。但正当我的思绪飘忽，想着要用线上象棋或无脑的网络媒体来消耗我新获得的自由时，走廊突然传来了越来越大声的人声，我听到了越来越接近的脚步声。然后，一个高大的女性身影很快出现在视线中，径直朝我的"私人电梯"走来。电梯门开始关上，但她似乎没有加速，她继续缓慢而响亮地用鞋跟踩着地砖，好像她确信电梯门会为她敞开着似的。电梯门确实为她敞开了，是我替她按住了开门的按钮。她不知道我是谁，但我不会因此而无礼。

她从帽檐下抬起头来，露出了被一缕金色刘海遮住的半只眼睛，她张开了狭窄的嘴唇，展示了带谢意的淡淡微笑，然后转身面对了门。电梯发出嗡嗡声，开始缓慢下降。我站在角落里，凝视着电梯按钮，但也注视着按钮后面铜色的墙板上反射出的她模糊的身影。她穿着发旧的牛仔裤，白色背心紧紧地裹着她结实的身材。她的手臂在肩膀下有一个轻微的凹痕，投下了只有大理石雕像才有的鲜明阴影。虽然她微微斜戴的帽子遮住了她的上半脸，但她细小的眼睛仍然在帽檐下闪闪发光，衬托着她那突出的、有个小坡的鼻子，她的方下颌在头顶灯光的照耀下显得很紧致。不知道为什么，她打动了我。我一直觉得中性的外表特别耀眼，但她身上还有别的东西。她不只是漂亮，她的美有一种不可思议的、略显不安的感觉。

当电梯落地，她的身影最后消失在地面上的人群中时，我才意识到这种不可思议的亲切感源于我们是相似的同类。我们在人体学上是一样的，同样的身高，同样的身材，同样的棱角，但她像太阳一样灿烂，我像月光一样清冷。或许是她的金发和灰蓝色的眼睛造成了这种差异，我的头发和眼睛都是深棕色的。又或者，是她的自信和冷静与我的动荡和回避形成了鲜明的对比，如果我站直了，她也许是我？我心里有了一个延伸成感叹号的问号。

后来我发现,在电梯里时,她也在一直研究我。因为在那次相遇的几天后,她就在社交媒体上向我发送了关注请求。在当今社会,发送关注请求就相当于发出"你引起了我的注意"的直白信号。不久后,在我生日那天,她最好的朋友(我大一时的小组项目伙伴)发布了她的照片来庆祝她的生日。和她有同一天的生日让我更加相信我们是同一枚硬币不同的两面。

尽管我再也没有和她说过话,也没有遇到过她,但我仍然经常想起她,并且相信她也会想起我。毕竟,尽管在不同的轨道上运行,太阳和月球仍然在引力的作用下保持着基本的联系。偶尔,当时机成熟时,它们的路径会有交集,在校园电梯里呼应出神奇的日食。

*

我走到了卢森堡公园门口。平日里在天亮前,这里会有数十个晨跑者进进出出。但在周日早上,只有几个老人在街对面的长椅上坐着休息。数十亿的雨滴和任性的狂风划破了长椅的墨绿色油漆,露出浅棕色的木板,就像时间在老人们的手上留下的棕色斑点。再晚一些，当这座城市从宿醉中醒来时，长椅上便会坐满读书的学生、闲聊的朋友、以及看着孩子们在碎石地上尖叫和踢来踢去的父母。但此时，寒冷的黎明只属于孤独的老人，属于他们缓慢的步伐，还有轻抚他们头发的风的低语。一天中只有在这个时候，他们才能看到自己曾经熟悉的那个巴黎，一个人行道被皮鞋擦亮而不是运动鞋擦亮的巴黎。在老人们记忆中的巴黎，圣母院的尖塔仍然矗立在那里，就像在1968年学生抗议运动中他们年轻的身躯一样。当城市空无一人的时候，他们让思绪穿越到过去的时光并不太难。

巴黎的各种店面商铺可能已经改变了——曾经的鞋店可能被改造成设计师精品店，书店也被改造成建筑工作室——但城市最外层的外壳，也就是奥斯曼式的建筑，几十年都没有变。建筑上不变的石灰石守卫着老人回忆的立体模型，记忆一动不动地反映在他们的眼睛里，就像凝固在卢森堡公园里的舞动的半人羊雕像一样。

我轻轻地从静坐的老人身边走过，向大门走去，用眼角的余光谨慎地瞟了他们几眼。他们谁也没有抬起头来看我。对他们来说，我就像一个幽灵，是他们回忆中的未来的投影，此刻，他们正努力地想要回避思绪中的未来，但未来的影子却缓慢地在他们的手上、手臂上、脖子上前行，一直爬到他们的眼睛上。最终，这个影子会渗透到他们的内心，濡湿他们的灵魂，突然引发出他们对死亡渐近的痛苦的提醒。他们会意识到，停留在过去虽然甜蜜，却是不现实的。我们这代人的存在对他们来说是一个太阳黑子，让他们关于美好时代的回忆有了阴影，就像老去的身体有了尘埃斑点一样。我们代表了未来，而他们已经是过去。但在此刻，在巴黎周日的黎明时分，空阔的街上，我们还没出现，世界是属于他们的。

我摇了摇公园的侧门，但除了发出刺耳的声音以外，大门一动不动。一个牌子上标着："十月份开放时间：7:45-18:45"，我来得太早了。或许我该转头回到蒙帕纳斯去，我想，但我走得有点喘不过气来，同时，我也被长凳上静坐的老人近乎沉思的状态迷住了。他们的脸上几乎没有表情，除了眉宇间有一丝丝忧伤，他们几乎是安详的。我不知道是否我，一个生活经验如此之少的年轻人，能够让自己多动的身心屈服于这样沉稳的状态。如果我坐在长凳上，回忆我所看到的一切事物和我所到过的地方，我是否也能进入如此宁静的状态？如果，相反,我不去考虑过去,而去考虑未来,那又会怎样呢?于是,我穿过马路,沿着一排绿色的长椅走去,找到了一张空着的长椅坐下。

当我坐下时,我隔壁坐着的一位身穿羊毛大衣、戴着皮革手套的老人转过身来,瞥了我一眼。我感觉糟透了,就好像我刮坏了一幅我不该碰,甚至是不该看的画。我回头看了他一眼,挤出了一个微笑表示歉意。他回报了一个淡淡的微笑。随后,我们俩都扭头重新面向了公园,静静地坐着。

公园铁栅栏尖上的天空逐渐亮了起来,开始变成了钢蓝色。除了几只鸟的啁啾声和我的邻座先生偶尔的清嗓声,周围一片寂静。好像过了很久很久,一个安静、深沉、又沙哑的声音打破了这种单调:"我经常在那里喝咖啡,员工们都很友好。"这声音把我从某种冥想中拉了出来,我转过头去寻找声音的来源,我的长凳邻居正指着凳子后面的商店,看着我说。我回头看了看后面那个简陋的露台,说:"哦,是的,这地方看起来真不错。"说完,他又转身面向了公园,我也一样。

沉默再次降落,占据了空气。我看着成堆的落叶,看着风痛苦地把它们拉扯在地,叶子爬过的地上留下了淡淡的潮湿的水印。它们缓慢而艰难地移动着，水汽渗进混凝土的细小裂缝中，留下了树叶形状的影子。远处，一个身穿黄色背心的男人推着一辆手推车走过来，手指间攥着一把扫帚，他一边走一边扫着树叶，把它们堆成沿街散落的小山丘。每扫一下，他的扫帚都在模糊叶子留下的潮湿图案，一个个原本分明的叶子痕迹在瞬间就被连接了起来，融合成了一个黑色的、没有形状的斑点。男人用几个简单的手势就掩盖了树叶以鲜血痛苦画出的自我信息。我知道，再过几个小时，当太阳出来时，连那团剩下的毫无意义的水迹，也会被晒干消失。

不忍心看这落叶舞蹈悲伤的结果，于是我回头去看我的邻座，用聊天来终止了这场风和树叶的表演。

"您经常来这儿吗？"我说，并微微地把脸颊转向了他。

他也转过头，注视了我一会儿，说："我住的地方离这里只有几条小巷，所以我经常来这里呼吸一些早上清新的空气。"

"这样啊，这地方看起来真不错。"我答道，意识到我又重复了遍刚才说过的话。

"你这么早出来干什么？"他开始掌控了提问

权,"我猜想你大概整晚都没睡。"

"不,我只是个早起的人,过了6点就睡不着觉了。"我用简洁的回答让自己缩了回去。

"你太年轻了,不应该那么过得那么老成。在你这个年纪,我从来没有在8点半之前醒来过。等醒来以后,我还会花一整个小时和我的朋友们喝咖啡。当时我们都住得很近——实际上,就在附近——有事没事就会在咖啡厅聊天消磨时间。"他停顿了一下,看了看扫地的男人,"夜晚做的美梦都太迷人了,不应该在早上6点就被打破。趁你还能做梦的时候,好好享受它吧。"

"您不怎么做梦了吗?"我问道。

"还会做梦,只是我不再像以前那样记得它们了。"他回道。

"既然可以生活在现实中,为什么要把时间花在虚幻的梦中呢?"我继续追问道。

"虚幻?"他重复了一边,带着一丝惊讶。我突然意识到,我的问题有点没心没肺地破坏了他的梦境。但他笑了笑,继续说,"梦想和现实一样真实。你做梦时体验的所有感觉和你清醒时体验的感觉是一样的。你仍然可以看到、闻到、听到和摸到,只是这些感觉都更加活跃了。做梦基于现实增

摄影 Roy Pan

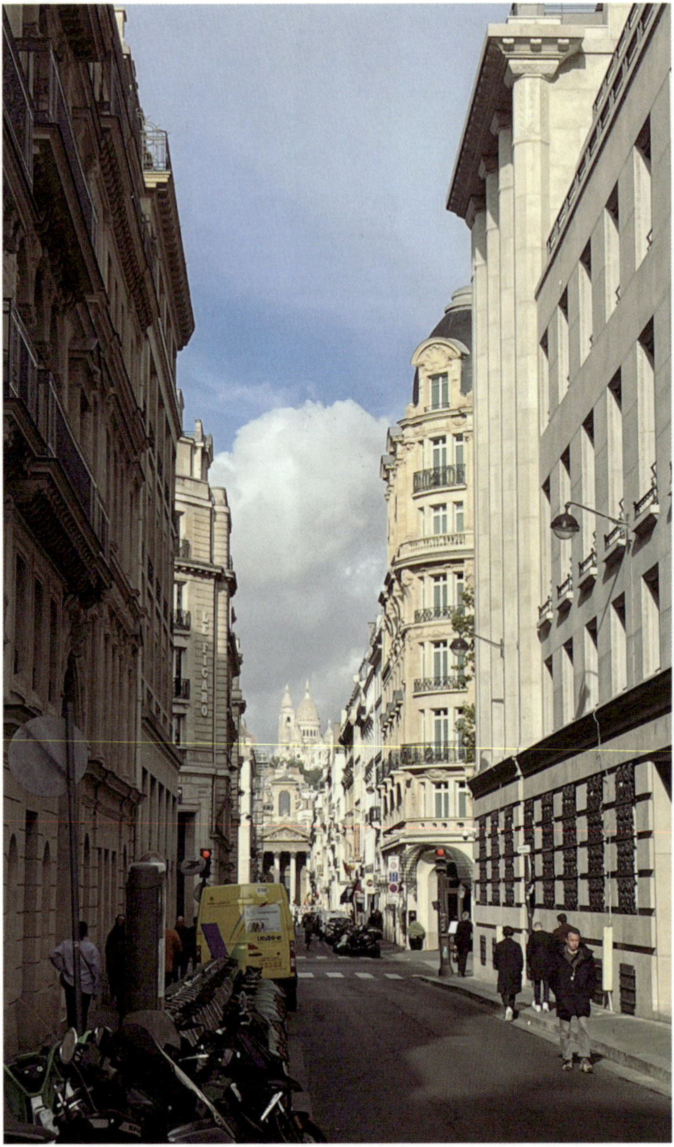

强了你的感受。"

他举起手,轻轻划动着食指,开始画出他面前树木的轮廓。"在梦里,你能够看到清醒时永远看不到的动作,遇到一些没有名字的颜色,你甚至可以闻到颜色的气味,或者看到香味。"

"但是这些梦境不会孤独吗?"我说,"梦境完全是属于你自己的世界,它无法成为一种共同的体验。你不能邀请别人进入你的梦境,即使有人出现,他们也会在一瞬间就消失了。梦境的世界可能是美丽的,但它的美丽只有你自己才能体验到,那是一种不能分享的美。"

"确实,但是在这点上它和你我相遇的这个世界并没有什么不同。现实世界也是一个孤独的世界,所有的面孔也会模糊和消失。只是在这个世界,它们需要几年才能消失,"他回答道,"我三四十年前认识的面孔,已经开始像我梦里的面孔一样模糊了。我发现自己在努力回忆自己母亲的脸。我只能模糊地记得她微笑的弧度,还有她右睫毛上方的痣,我想。"他敲了敲长凳的木头接着说:"这些长凳也让我想起了她直竖的肩膀。见鬼,她是个厉害的女人。但我想不起关于她的其他事情了,她的脸在回忆中非常模糊。"

他脱下手套，双手插进口袋。

"我觉得在睡梦中面容模糊得更快，是因为梦里的世界里有一个加速的时间轴。你在一夜之间就经历了一整个人生。你经历的每件事情都更激烈、快速、纯粹——有点像你们年轻人玩的手机——它们也消失得更激烈、快速、纯粹，"他歪着头，直勾勾地盯着我的眼睛说，"你应该好好看看我，看看十年后你能不能画出我的肖像！"

我迅速转移视线，把目光移开，然后小心翼翼地把视线落到他的脸上，勾勒出他的下巴、脸颊、前额、嘴巴、鼻子——除了眼睛以外的所有特征。即使不直视他的眼睛，我也能感觉到它们散发出一种吞噬的气息。它们从左到右，从里到外仔细观察着我的每一寸灵魂，就像一个没有光束的手电筒毫不掩饰地扫射着我。

看到我没有说话，他继续说道："你知道，在物理学中，大部分未知都是通过黑暗来描述的。暗物质，黑暗流，黑洞。任何我们无法照亮的东西都是黑暗的，但我不想在本应黑暗的地方强求光明。我花了一生的时间试图理解为什么世界是它所是的样子，我们从哪里来，到哪里去？我们生活的这个星球到底是个什么球？为什么我们被困在地上，而鸟儿却可以在天空中飞翔？整个宇宙有多广阔？我一直在寻求合理的解释来了解这个世界。但是，只要我用理性来断言一种解释，理性就会自我否定。我们推翻旧的范式来建立新的范式，只是为了用更新的范式来推翻新范式。我做了所有这些努力和所谓的'发现'，却最终，发现自己又回到了起点。只是这一次，我的双手布满了皱纹，也被关节疼痛折磨着。"

他从口袋里掏出了双手，用右手轻轻搓了搓左手指关节，又戴上了手套。"因此，在把我的一生都奉献给回答各种为什么和怎么会之后，我得出的结论是，我们投射在真理上的任何光芒都是扭曲的，而接近真理的唯一途径就是陷入黑暗。这种黑暗就是我们在睡梦中看到的黑暗。这个无意义的、短暂的、不断变化的空间比任何物理定律或细胞图都蕴含着更多的真理。最后，科学图表、Hilma af Klint 的绘画，或者说巫师的魔法书没有什么不同。它们都只是有时合乎逻辑，有时纯属神话的符号。"

说到这里，他艰难地扣上了大衣的扣子，转过身去，把身体的重量放在了已经磨损的长凳靠背上，然后费力地站了起来。

"好了，我今天已经够让你困惑了。你一定

要保证充足的睡眠,然后记住我的脸。"他竖起两个手指指着自己的脸,幽默地说,然后,他就离开了。

我看着他枯干的身影在街上慢慢地走着,就像被风吹动的落叶一样。他从街道清扫工的身边走过,向他点了点头。那时,清扫工已经把所有的落叶扫成了一堆,开始把它们收集到了一个容器里。一半的街道已经干净得没有一片叶子,光秃秃的水泥地看着就像一张未被触及过的纸,恢复了一种毫无情绪的表情。

最后,我的新朋友向右拐了个弯,从我的视线中消失了。

他的眼睛是什么颜色来着?我想不起来了。

*

老人走后,我在长凳上又坐了一会儿,想着他所说的话。在他的身影消失很久之后,他的话仍然回荡在早晨的寂静中。一个个词汇漂浮在空中,缠绕在树枝上,在树洞里滑进滑出。他似乎坚持认为,世界上不仅仅存在着一个真相,而是有许多不同的真相,万有引力定律是我们认知的一种真相,而每一个人的故事也是另一种不同的真相。或许，他把真相和可能性，假设，混为一谈了？再或许，他把真相和事物的表象、事物的显现搞混了。因为真理的前提是只能有一个：它是普遍的和不变的。真理不是通过我们的感官和知觉传递的，表象可以是多样的，但真理是隐藏在这一切表象之下的东西，是我们的感官接收器无法破解的东西，也就是说，是我们的智力无法处理的东西。它是幻象之下事物的存在的真正状态，如同在某一处的树，即使我们听不见、看不见，它也仍然会倒下。

然后，一个可怕的想法击中了我。如果我是对的，世上只有一个真理，一个超越我们感官所投下的虚幻阴影而无法触及的真理，那就意味着，即使我确实有一个真实的、不可改变的自我，我也永远无法触及它。我的眼睛，我的耳朵，我的触觉——我所有的感官都触及不到构成真实的我的清晰的数据。无论我的大脑有多么聪明，就像一个匹配了错误输入的有效数学公式，它永远不会产生正确的输出。

当然，我可以从我之外的第二方或第三方那里收集关于我的数据，但其他人的数据收集过程也会和我一样发生误差。因为他们也用他们的耳朵、眼睛、触感与世界互动，于是我，这个存在他们世界里的生物和他们的互动，所提供给他们的数据也会是有误差的，也会模糊的——他们因此也无法真正地知晓我是谁，我是什么。培根和委拉斯开兹都画过教皇英诺森十世，但真正的英诺森十世是哪一幅呢？哪个都不是。事实上，这两幅画像都描绘了教皇英诺森十世，但教皇斗篷下的那个人，乔瓦尼·巴蒂斯塔·潘菲利（Giovanni Battista Pamphilj）的真相到底是什么，仍然是一个谜。

*

天空现在已经足够明亮，大门上方的尖刺清晰地划破了天空的蓝色。两个公园管理员懒洋洋地下了车，解开了公园门上缠着的铁链。他们的汽车发出的轰鸣声和他们交错的聊天声正式标志了清晨那一段旧巴黎时光旅行的结束。老人们开始一个个从长凳上站起来，不慌不忙地穿过街道，走向公园。两个管理员中年轻的那一位靠在了大门旁，他的同事走回了发动机轰轰作响的汽车。他身材单薄修长，脸上留着和卷曲的头发相呼应的胡渣，看着越来越多的人走进公园，年轻人用亲切而半公式化的

"你好"问候了每一个经过的人。有时，他会在路人走到他的面前时说，另外一些时候，他会在目标离他还有几步远的时候就向他们抛出一个事先准备好的问候，在极少数情况下，他会在路人已经从他面前走过时再扔过一个"你好"去追逐他们，迫使他们转过身来和他打招呼。

我研究了他几分钟，然后推断出了他并没有根据公园游客的位置来安排打招呼的时间，而是按照一个固定的时间间隔，大概是每8秒说一次"bonjour"。为什么呢？我不知道，我只能假设他做这个工作已经很久，每天要对人说太多的问候，已经有了习惯和本能。我猜想在他上班的第一天，每一声问候都是有温度和意义的，而现在，日复一日年复一年之后，这些词汇基本上只剩下一种声音，一个外壳，并不包含更多的意义。我静静地观察着他，越来越确认自己的推断。为了证明我的正确性，我穿过街道，向公园大门走去。加入了稀稀落落的进公园的游客的队伍。在我快接近这个年轻的迎宾员时，我有意放慢了速度，计算着自己的每一个脚步，希望正好在一个8秒的时间点出现在他面前，听他说一个新的"你好"。

  1——2——3——我在心里数着，小心地调整着步子的大小和节奏，4——5——6——我刻意的步态看上去一定有点滑稽，这个年轻人几乎不看其他的任何人，只是直视着我，好像我带着一种挑衅。7——8——完美！当我心里的数字数完时，我的脚刚好落在了他的旁边。"你好。"我们同时说道，他的男高音与我的女低音对应着。"你好。"他又压低嗓音说了一遍，仿佛不想给我机会让我再说一句话。

我没有回头，直接从他身边走了过去。"第二个问候打乱了他的惯性，"我暗自高兴地想，"现在，他得重新开始找回节奏了。"

没过多久，管理员就以同样的节奏和语调开始向新来的人打起招呼。我破坏了他的游戏，哪怕只是一分钟，也让我体会到一种恶作剧的快乐。

是扰乱别人的模式让我开心吗？我真的喜欢纯属没事儿找事儿地搞破坏吗？并不是。我只是很享受那种发现表面行为下的隐藏模式，并且打破它们的感觉。生活中，如果你意识不到这些模式，它们就会很容易主宰你的时间与精力，在你毫无意识的情况下像潮水一样吞噬你。但，一旦你抬起头来，注意到运行世界的逻辑和规则，你就能够破解密码并控制局面，就像我控制了这个迎宾员的小游戏一样。我和迎宾员之间的游戏只是一个无害的例子，但同样的逻辑可以适用于其他更多的生活场景。

*

我终于走到了目的地帆船池塘，在我心中这地方是公园皇冠上的宝石。之前那个小小的游戏带给我的快乐已经迅速地消失了，我的眼中因此而产生的喜悦火花，很快就被早晨寒冷和昏暗的景象熄灭。我发现自己又回到了从黎明开始就伴随着我的麻木中，就像一个让人感觉强烈的被撕裂的伤口很快就愈合了，被激活的感官再一次沉寂下去。

这个时间，装着小帆船的手推车还没有被拉出来，池塘的水面还很平静。地平线上唯一可见的船是一艘桅杆破碎的船，躺在公园里随处可见的绿色金属椅子脚下。我一直认为这些小椅子比沉重的长凳要好得多，它们既好看又轻便，还有灵活的配置，大型聚会时可以随意地把它们摆成一圈，大家都可以坐下，每个人都可以互相看着对方交流。喜欢独处的人也可以带一个小椅子放到树荫下去，这样他就既可以保持自己独处的舒适感，又能观察到别人的活动。

我在想，在公园里工作了这么长时间，那个迎宾员是否注意到了这些椅子的巧妙之处？或者，他还注意到了一些被我忽略的其他细节？

我捡起了一只断了桅杆的船，把它的帆缠在还挂在甲板上的桅杆头上。帆的布料是黑色的，它应该是一艘海盗船。其他都是挂着不同国旗的船，只有这条船不同寻常，别具一格。孩子们要么喜欢它的独特性，要么因为它的不合群而讨厌它。也许只有少数孩子属于前者？就是那些长大后会支持漫威电影中反派的孩子吧。不过，是谁把船弄坏了？是一个过分热爱海盗船的熊孩子？还是一个还未长大的超级英雄？

我检查了一下船身，没有发现任何裂缝或重大损坏，只要船只的重量均匀分布，它应该仍然能够漂浮。但是还挂在船上的桅杆严重地向右倾斜了，于是我跪在地上，捡起了一把砾石，撒在了甲板的左侧。我用一只手把船放到水里，另一只手把砾石一颗一颗地放下去，小心翼翼地不让它超载。碎石似乎起了作用，当我松开手时，小船可以自己立起来了。但任何多余的移动都可能让它倾倒，我不敢用力推它。我虽然帮它重新站了起来，却不能完全恢复它的功能。也许，它累了，只想静静地躺下，我却非要逼它去做超过它极限的事，这对它是不公平的。作为一艘帆船，它的旅程已经结束了，它说不定接受了永远被陈列在架子上的命运，或者，它可以成为回收木材，被做成一只铅笔，获得第二次新的生命。

然而，我还是强迫它浮在水面上，静止地漂浮在一个黑暗的水塘之上。如果遇到强风撕开它的帆，它就会再次沉落在这池塘里，成为塘底的垃圾，从而失去了获得重生的机会。我想，我是在用我的意志要求它，生活就是如此，不管你有多受伤，只要你还有一口气，你都得振作起来，继续鼓起勇气来面对这个世界。

这是吉米告诉我的。

*

吉米是我同一所高中的同学。每次回家的校车人满时，他都会坐在我旁边，但我们从来没说过话。直到有一次他摔伤了脚，再也不能在午休时间和伙伴们一起踢足球了。受了伤的吉米，开始坐在我们学校门口的台阶上，和我一起吃午饭，一起嚼着食堂买的难吃的三明治。

吉米是个停不下来的人,他对我滔滔不绝地讲述他的生活,好像他要用嘴的活动来弥补受伤的脚不能活动的遗憾。他似乎想告诉我一切,从他姐姐的准男友,到他家的仓鼠从楼梯上摔下来的悲剧,他父母对基督教装饰的痴迷,以及他对曼联的热爱。他甚至对我泄露了他最好的朋友最黑暗的秘密,尽管他对朋友发过誓要守口如瓶。我不太担心他会到处扩散我的生活,因为他什么都没问过我。我们的关系完全就是他说,我听。

一天晚上,在我们坐校车回家的路上,他一边盯着自己的手指,一边喋喋不休地说个不停。那有点不像他,因为平时他说话时总是会非常自信地直视着他的对话者,"这样才能让人们认真对待你",他曾经这样说过。但那天晚上,他看上去并没有那么自信。"每天,"他说,"我醒来的时候,我都要把我的皮肤和骨头钉在一起,否则我的活力就会流失。但即使这样,能量泄漏从未停止过。每次我修补好一块皮肤,另一块就会被撕开一英寸。我的生活就是不断地修补再修补,无休止的努力,我正在等待泄漏停止的那一天。也许,一旦我的皮肤被一层又一层厚厚的补丁完全覆盖,我的能量就终于可以不再流失了。但是,那样的我还会是我自己吗?

我想，等我老了我就会知道了。"

只是，吉米永远都不会知道结果了。毕业 2 年后，在一次 18 英里的跑步比赛中，他的心脏停止了工作。

我没有去参加吉米的葬礼，因为觉得我不合适。虽然通过他的讲述我几乎认识了他生活中所有的人，但我却从未觉得自己是他生活的一部分，而且，上大学后我搬到了另一个国家，也真是去不了现场。我只是在吉米最好的朋友联系我以后，在心里遥远地和他道了个别。在事情发生后没过多久，吉米最好的朋友，唯一注意到我曾在吉米的生活中充当过树洞角色的人，给我发了条信息，让我从我所在的地方送一些土来埋葬吉米。他说，吉米在世界各地的朋友都参与了这次行动。于是，我从家里的花盆里抓了一把土，匿名寄给了他们。我知道吉米不需要我的名字就能认出这是我寄送的土，因为土壤里的每一个矿物颗粒都包含着他给我讲过的故事。那份土不同于巴黎公园里的薄薄的白色泥土，被吉米的故事浸润过的土壤是乌黑、沉重的，它散发着浓郁的苔藓气味，让我想起那些没有被人类的手触及过的森林的黑暗之心。那花盆里面生长的橄榄枝也非常结实，虽然它还只是一棵小树，但它的枝叶都很粗壮。有一件事是肯定的，这颗小树的活力永远都不会流失——至少，在我把它从有保护的花盆里转移出来之前不会。等小树长得再大一些，它会被移植到一片新的陌生的土壤里，那时候，它就不得不与更强壮、更粗壮的树木争夺矿物质了。

*

一个微型的自由女神像复制品守卫着卢森堡公园靠近 Guynemer 街的东北入口，它隐藏在茂密的橡树之间，坐落在一个由精心修剪的树篱组成的方形底座上。与自由女神在美国的姐妹所拥有的那个巨大的、可攀爬的宝座相比，这个基座是如此的小以至于显得有些可笑。这姐妹俩，一个是通往天堂的阶梯，让人们兴奋和振作起来，每年有数百万张面孔从她的顶部皇冠俯瞰城市，她是高高在上的女神；而另一个却只是和公园里其他铜像混在一起的小铜像，一个普通的披着斗篷的青铜女人，背后的建筑让她显得格外渺小，尤其是，巴黎的建筑甚至都不怎么高，为了保护城市的标志性景观，市政府规定建筑物的高度不允许超过 5 层。如果公园的自由女神小姐从她的基座上下来，我们大概会是同样的高度。没有了高耸入云的身体，自由女神小姐看上去像一个下课后拿着课堂笔记和香烟在公园里闲逛的学生。夸张而巨大的体积，重量和皇冠可以完全改变同一个形象的意义，这是多么让人惊讶的事啊。

*

阳光下，我的影子与公园周围建筑物的阴影融为了一体，就像我整个人沉浸在冰川湖里。一排排笔直对称的建筑环绕着我，我走在一条延伸到很远的狭窄上坡鹅卵石路上。熟食店，Monoprix 连锁店，书店……各种各样的文字装饰着这些建筑一层的店面，衬线字体、无衬线字体、全大写字母、不大写字母、白色轮廓的黑色单词、黑色轮廓的白色单词、没有轮廓的斜体金色单词……这些大大小小的字体是唯一区分这一排排相似建筑的元素。尽管表面装饰不同，店面上的字都在暗示同样的事情："顺着这条巷子走，你就可以在这街上随心所欲地漫步。"这种暗示，给人一种虚假的拥有自由意志的错觉，就像我在上学期间服从的那些老师给我们的错觉一样。每一个年级，老师会以不同版本的带着同一种权威的声音重复同一句话："你想写什么就写什么，只要它是在题目的范围内的。"他们每个人都试图阻止我的想法逃出他们画的那个框，他们不喜欢我的想法像食肉植物一样蔓延，最后吞噬了他们给与的那个中心。常常，又大又红的"牵强附会"和"跑题"的批示成了我的论文上的常规标记，但这丝毫也不能改变我，我自豪地佩戴着这些红字，从未妥协过。与父亲对我说过的话相比，老师们的批示对我毫无意义。我父亲年轻时也非常擅长写作，他的文章总会在每周一被老师在全班同学面前大声朗读，他应该是我的老师们喜欢的那种学生，并希望我也能像他一样。但是，现在的父亲却始终支持我的特立独行，他鼓励我不受制约地思考，他告诉我："如果你行事谨慎，你将一事无成。与其融入一贯的平庸，不如以你自己的独创脱颖而出。你是对的，你要留下你自己的轨迹。"

父亲的话我铭记于心，我试图在所有的学习中，拒绝墨守成规，同时在生活的各个方面寻找属于我自己的道路。当然，每一个方向和每一种努力都是在我仔细考虑后才做出的选择，我不会盲目地去冒险。在我身边的一些人不假思索就跳下享乐主义的深谷的时候，我会仔细计算得失比，然后再决定是跟着他们一起跳，还是自己掉头从深谷里爬上来。并且，我很快就得了结论，大多数的深谷都是不值得跳的，因为我没有兴趣成为尸体堆中减缓下一个人的下落的另一具尸体。这种理性而谨慎的思考结果，就是每天我都在一个人努力地往上攀爬悬崖。当没有更多的悬崖可攀登时，我就在悬崖顶上修建了一座塔，一座属于我自己的精神之塔。我每天像一个工匠一样地工作，砌砖，抹水泥，疲倦时，我就会从我留在塔墙上的孔眼往外看，观察那个热闹的享乐主义的世界。当我的塔还只是一个简陋的地基时，我还能看到那些人一个接一个跳下深谷的场景，他们会在着陆时形成的肉质床垫上愉快地交流，直到下一批人落下来砸在他们的脸上，埋没他们。我的塔正在一点点地增高，享乐主义深谷里的人的微笑渐渐模糊，那些人脸上的五官好像消融在皮肤里，难以分辨。现在，当我往下看的时候，我已经分不清每一个人的轮廓了，很多的身体叠在一起，分不清谁是谁，如同春天的一片野花，个体消失了。

在云层之上，天空永远是一种中性的蓝色。

没有风雨，没有阳光，没有起伏。

高度过滤了从下面传来的嘈杂的声波,周围一片静默。

我很好奇地面上的热闹是否还存在着。

*

Assas 街的尽头是 Alphonse Deville 广场,那是一个三角形的混凝土小岛,周围有几丛灌木和一个厕所。在岛的中央隐藏着一个小的棱角分明的空地,那里摆着三张长椅,面对着一个竖立在灌木丛中的干瘪男人的雕像。雕像的后面立着两块和它一样高的铜板,凹凸不平的表面上刻着一段文字。我好奇地在这雕像前停了下来,这个人估计是个作家,我想,他的背后刻着的是他一生的作品。

雕像男人的眉毛像笔刷一样浓密,与他的光头形成了鲜明的对比。他的表情很严肃,嘴唇紧闭,一个长而突出的鼻子主宰着他的脸,如果让我想象果戈理的短文中,拟人化的鼻子是什么样的,那就应该是这样的。在他狭窄的肩膀下面,他的一只手插在口袋里,另一只手微微弯曲,手指绷紧,好像在试图抓住什么东西。一张毫无表情却警觉的脸,一副紧张的身体上,他的整个肢体语言都显示出某种不安。他让我想起了大学派对上那些站在角落里，不跟别人说话的笨拙的孩子，也是所有的肢体语言都在尖叫着说他们并不适合热闹的派对，他让我想起了我自己。

事实是，我的社交恐惧症并不是因为我不热爱人类，我并非是一个厌世者，我的不适，来自于我不知道如何在一个与他人共享的小空间中生存的绝望。它根植于这样一种感觉：我的身体、我的存在都是多余的，在别人轻松流畅的谈话中，我是一个不合时宜的重物，那些四处流淌的语言的溪水漂浮在我之上。在一个闲聊、笑声、音乐和碰杯声融合在一起的房间里，我只能把自己躲在身体里，筑起一层保护壳，以免被热烈而汹涌的话语淹没。

我藏在壳里，能听见人们的对话，看到他们的表情，注意到他们的语调，并将他们华丽的语言包装剥离出来，试图找到话语真正的意思。悲哀的是，我无法用一种与我的谈话者的语气相匹配的方式来包装自己的回应。我的这种残疾，使得任何从我嘴里说出来的东西要么非常生硬，要么让人难以置信。我对自己的语言变得非常敏感，参与闲聊好像逼我在没有舌头和声带的情况下说话一样艰难，我会大口喘气，试图从我的肺和喉咙深处发出声音，但无论我怎么用力，发出来的声音都是一团没有形状的东西，一声没有结构的咕哝，如同一声鹅叫。

此刻，我眼前的这位雕像先生脖子前倾，拳头紧绷，目光严肃，和我每次考虑是在聚会上尝试接近一群人还是干脆离开时的困扰状态一模一样，而每一次，我最后都选择了离开。每一次，我都觉得那不是一个值得跳下去的悬崖，于是我就会转过头继续独自建造我的塔。

*

我走进了另一个公园，Boucicaut 公园，这是个我十分熟悉的公园，我以前经常来这里，曾经有一次，我还在这里的 Le Bon Marché 买了很贵的蜂蜜和鲻鱼子酱。

那一次在这个公园发生的事，我至今都还印象深刻。通常购物后，我会直接前往 Sèvres-Babylon 站，融入地下的人群，十分钟后回到我在塞纳河另一边的临时家里。但那天，当我走出商店时，突然一阵寂静攫住了我，然后是一种极度的眩晕感。我周围的人群开始绕着圈走，正午的阳光不再是温暖的阳光,而是变成了冰冷的标枪向我射来。引导顾客进入商店的斑马线膨胀成了巨大的动物,张开它的大嘴巴,好像要把我整个吞下去。我开始颤抖,摇摇晃晃的,松开了我的鲻鱼子酱和蜂蜜罐,抓住了街上的一根栏杆。过路的几个人以巴黎人擅长的那种冷漠而不受困扰的"看透一切"的方式瞥了我一眼,然后,一个有一双闪闪发光的棕色大眼睛的姑娘,弯下腰捡起了我的东西,和蔼可亲地递给了我。"你没事吧?"棕色的大眼睛噘起嘴唇说道。"我很好,谢谢。"我回答道。环顾四周,眨了眨眼睛,以便重新适应刺眼的阳光。我恢复了平衡,放开了杆子。冰标枪不见了。动物们爬回了地里。人们又开始径直走过去。那个有棕色的大眼睛留着棕色卷发的圆润女孩对我笑了笑,说了一声"那就好",然后她走进了商店。

我害怕眩晕再次袭来,于是我走向了公园,坐在公园深处靠近围栏的长凳上,那里人很少。我担心如果再次晕倒,会吸引来很多好奇的目光。幸运的是,我的体温恢复了正常,血液循环也很流畅,幻觉中的动物们也消失了。我又回到了我一成不变,平淡无奇的现实世界,我的世界只有我,我的鲻鱼子酱,还有我那瓶昂贵的蜂蜜罐。"感谢上帝,这蜂蜜的罐子足够结实，否则24欧元就付之东流了。"我一边想，一边检查着我的包里没被摔坏的幸存者，觉得这罐蜂蜜以一种特别的方式证明了它的价格是合理的。

正当我把罐子放回包里准备起身的时候，我看到对面的长凳上坐着一个又高又瘦的年轻人，正以优雅的姿势翻看他的手机，他微眯着眼睛目不转睛地看得很认真，虽然凌乱的棕色头发让人觉得他好像刚从床上爬起来，但他精心分层搭配的服装——敞开的蓝色衬衣里露出的白色T恤和米色休闲裤——又表明着他其实很在意他的外表。"他明显想要呈现出一种看似不经意的风格，法国男生的风格，"我想道，"或者，他本身就是一个不经意的法国男生，很难说是究竟是哪一种。"然后一阵风吹开了他的衬衫，在他的T恤的左上角，也就是心脏所在的地方，露出了"MoMa"的字样。"一个穿着时髦看似低调的法国男生，而且喜欢美国的现代艺术，听上去像是个完美的人。"我想。

那一次之后，我又去那个公园溜达过好多次，我告诉自己，那是为了再次感受受大自然的陪伴，那个穿着蓝色衬衫和米色裤子的男生对我来说是一种让人愉悦的大自然。我确实也偶然碰到过几次那个"大自然"坐在那里,通常是在工作日的下午三四点左右。直到有一天,他照例坐在他常坐的长椅上,一位娇嫩、甜美的女孩走了过来,问他是否知道哪里可以买到香烟。他指了指街道,但女孩没懂,于是,他站了起来,陪着她走了过去。

从那以后,我就再也没见过这个穿蓝衬衫和米色裤子的男生。

此刻,再次来到这个公园,我突然有一种想要重温上一次感觉的冲动。于是我转过身,向公园深处走去,找到了那张熟悉的长凳。我在长凳上坐了几分钟,然后觉得这真是一个愚蠢的、浪费时间的举动,因为这不过是公园的一张普通的长凳,什么都没发生。

远处,教堂的钟声开始响起,我一遍遍地数着那响亮的钟声,数到十,钟声停止了,被巨大的声波振动的空气微微地抖动着,像天使的羽翼掠过。

时间在我无意识中飞快地流过,我以为坐在板凳上的几分钟,原来是几个小时。

*

久坐让我的牛仔裤变得又冷又硬,像一块硬

湿的帆布一样紧紧地裹着我的腿,我站起来,感受到腿部血液的再一次流动。早晨的太阳已经高悬在天空中,像一个破裂的溏心的蛋黄,汁液把灰色的屋顶染成了明亮的橙色,让这座城市意外地看起来像个热带天堂。但是我仍然保持着警觉,国家气象局今天发布了早晨霜冻警报,预告了日出时的低温,这是冬天给我们的错觉,太阳和寒冷联手玩了一个游戏,太阳会用它漂亮的孔雀尾巴引诱人们出门,然后寒冷就能咬到第一对敢从门里探出头来的脸颊。

我走出广场,发现 Sèvres 街上聚集了一群移动缓慢人群,拐进 Bac 街,一些头发蓬乱的中老年妇女成双成对地占据了街道。她们穿着朴素的长外套,戴着羊毛手套,提着皮革手提包,阳光下的剪影看上去一模一样。"多冷的早晨啊!"其中一位妇女她叹息道,耸了耸肩,肩头几乎碰着了她的耳朵,好像要保护脖子不受寒的样子。"是的,而且这只是开始。"她的矮个子女伴接过话头,带着无可奈何的笑容。一个婴儿在她们身后哭了起来,他的妈妈,一个有棕色皮肤和木炭色眉毛的年轻丰满的女人,用她的羽绒服把孩子抱得更紧了,她发出了一长串嘘声,试图安抚他。矮个子的女人转过身看了一眼哭泣的婴儿，然后又看了一眼他的母亲，其他的女人们也跟随着她的目光一起看着那母亲。我觉得那矮个子女人一定是这群妇女的某种领袖，指挥着整个群体的行动，并且总是说最后一句总结的话。

这时，街道上响起了年轻活泼的声音，女人们被这声音吸引，她们看到两个年轻女生在街上放肆地大笑，笑声叮当作响，像清澈的溪水潺潺流过，又像是熊熊燃烧的柴火发出脆脆的噼啪声。那是一种温暖人心的，充满活力的自然的状态。"你还记得你觉得自己很厉害的那次吗？实际上你弱爆了！"一个人喊道。"是吧？真疯狂。"另一个人回应道。她们发的"r"音很圆润，看来是美国人。然后，两个人又陷入了无法阻挡的咯咯笑声，完全没有意识到女人们的领导者正在审视她们。上年纪的女人不以为然地上下打量着这两个疯癫癫的女孩，很难知道她不满意的是两个美国女生的行为、国籍、迷你裙，还是擦糊了的烟熏眼影，也许四者都是。"这年头的年轻人。"领导者叹了口气，妇女团的其他成员立刻表示默许，也跟着叹了口气，她们中间只有一个红头发的女人，看着两个女孩露出了一丝微笑。

这种对年轻的蔑视是如何在这些年长的女性心中产生的呢？经验的积累是否取代了她们曾经拥有的、而现在却只属于美国女生们的好奇感？我13岁的时候，一家冰淇淋店的收银员无缘无故地对我和我的朋友特别刻薄，当我的朋友委屈地告诉了她的母亲时，她的母亲半开玩笑地告诉我们，如果有年长的女人对我们刻薄，那是因为她们嫉妒我们光滑的皮肤和丰满的脸颊。但我以为不止如此。生理上的年轻是一个非常表面的因素，所谓嫉妒也只是一种表面现象。中年女人们对这些女孩的不以为然，也许有更深层次的，哲学的、思维的原因。我相信有一种更可靠的解释是，伴随着年龄的增长与经验的增多，随之而来的是对世界和生活的好奇感的消失，而好奇感、新鲜感又是激发年轻人的活力和勇气的关键因素。这些中年妇女的态度中，包含着一种对生活的倦怠和麻木，大部分女人活到这样的年龄，"每一天都是新的一天"对她们来说已经毫无意义了，她们的每一天都过得像似曾相识，她们眼中唯一的新鲜事是脸上长出的新皱纹。

这群女人中间，只有那个红头发的女人似乎还保留着某种好奇心，她的青春并没有被日复一日的庸常生活完全消磨掉。她没有像她的同代伙伴一样，忘记了她们也曾经拥有过的天真和自由不羁，她看上去被年轻人散发出的单纯的快乐感染，并分享了其中一部分的快乐。也许，青春之花在她的躯体上已经凋谢了，但那朵花在她的心里留下了一颗种子，这种子长出了另一棵树，隐秘的结实的树，仍然生机勃勃，让她能够继续热爱一切新鲜的人和事，保留对生活的好奇感和想象力。

*

我跟着这群女人来到了 Bac 街，发现原来她们都是去圣母显灵圣牌堂（Chapelle Notre-Dame de la Médaille Miraculeuse）的，我早该从她们严肃而庄重的衣着上猜到她们的目的地，没有什么标志比她们脖子上挂着的一模一样的显灵圣牌更明显的了。这是星期天的上午十点，抱着婴儿的女人也跟在后面，那个婴儿已经停止哭叫，很安静地睡着了。

女人们走进通往教堂的圆拱门，门的两边各坐着两名戴着头巾的乞讨的妇女，手里都挥舞着一个空纸杯。当这群人在教堂庭院的入口处停下来时，一名乞讨的妇女向领队伸出了她的杯子。领队看了看她挥动的手，然后抬头看着坐落在基座上的圣母玛丽亚雕像，"Monstra te esse matrem..." 她喃喃自语，读着圣母像周围的丝带上的拉丁句子，"展示给我们看你是我们的母亲"。她静静地站了一会儿，一副若有所思的样子，然后从那个乞讨的女人身边走过，没忘记在门口和看门人打招呼。其他的女人们也跟随着她走进了通往教堂的院子。乞讨的女人绝望地放下了胳膊，将膝盖抵在胸前，蜷缩成了一团。她的脚在移动中碰翻了一块潦草的纸板，上面写着：三个饥饿孩子的母亲，给点零钱，任何东西都能帮忙。

抱着婴儿的女人也在同一地点停了下来。像刚刚走过的那些女人一样，她抬头看了看雕像，然后又低头看了看那个在地上蜷缩着身子的女人和她那湿漉漉的牌子，乞讨的女子似乎沮丧到已经摇不动杯子了。这位母亲静静地俯下身，一只手哄着孩子，一只手从她的羽绒服口袋里拿出几欧元和一袋苹果酱。她把一张五欧元的钞票放回口袋，然后把剩下的东西都放进了女人的杯子里。乞讨的女人抬起头，轻轻点了点头，再次将自己在地上缩成一团。那位母亲站了起来，跟随着妇女团队走进了院子。

管风琴悠长的音符已经从教堂的门口传出来，

10点05分，早晨的弥撒就要开始了。女人们纷纷在教堂的长凳上坐好，她们都坐在第一排，那个矮个领队坐在正中间。在她们后面，一个坐在长凳边上男人站了起来，用手势让那位母亲坐到他的座位上，而他自己走到更远一点的地方坐下。那位母亲感激地向他道了谢，坐了下来，用手捂住了孩子的头。

大教堂这样的圣所给人一种强烈的安慰感，它不是来自于上帝本身的存在——我是一个无神论者，甚至无法感知上帝。安慰感来自于群体力量，一群相信共同信仰的人聚集在一起，构成了一个完整、完美的精神圆环。亚洲女人，中年男人，瘦弱的少年，还有带着四个蹒跚学步的孩子的金发夫妇……所有这些人，每个人都有自己的空虚需要填补，每个人都带着各自的焦虑、悲伤和欢乐，每周聚集在这里一次，通过祈祷和福音团结在一起。即使是那个矮小的，眼里似乎只有自己的妇女团领袖，也屈从于这种集体精神，一种比个人更有力量的存在。

我想象他们开始吟唱圣歌的时候，他们的声音会充实彼此身体细胞里的空隙，那些平时生活里折磨他们的痛苦，意识里看不见的邪恶小鬼的尖叫声，会在这圣歌中一点点淡下去，一个神圣的痂会覆盖伤口。我不知道我是否相信帕斯卡说的"上帝是一个无限的球体，它的中心无处不在，圆周无处不在"，但我相信人们建立在上帝身上的共同信念使他们自己在做弥撒时成为一个无限而完美的圆，至少在弥撒的一个小时里是这样，他们在一个系统中，不那么孤单。

管风琴停止了，接下来的是两列在圣坛旁的修女的合唱。一位神父慢慢地走到了祭坛前面，把圣经放在了支架上，开始了他的弥散。作为一个无神论者，我坐在长凳上感觉不舒服，于是待在门边，靠在冰冷的石墙上。我担心因为我的缺乏信仰而导致教堂里漂浮的虔诚轻盈的精神，会掺进沉重的颗粒，同时我也很想知道，在我的心中，信仰是否有可能以某种形式寄存在哪里。

歌声停止了。

"因父、及子、及圣神之名……"神父开始了他的布道，听众齐声回应"阿们"。"愿和平与你们同在。"神父说，管风琴和修女们用类似副歌的合唱回应着他的圣歌，我听不清她们的歌词。神父又说："主啊，我们是你的子民。我们在这个星期天聚集在这里，欢迎上帝宽恕的恩典。让我们准备庆祝圣体的奥秘，承认我们犯了罪。"然后他开始了阅读经文，下面的听众也喃喃地加入他的朗读。我没有太注意阅读的内容，我的注意力被神父说的一个词带走了。他提到人类的"犯罪"，而"犯罪"和"钓鱼"在法语中是同一个词。这一发现促使我把去教堂的人想象成缅因州的一群捕虾人，在清晨出海之前，他们聚集在甲板上讨论海洋状况和天气。"这是个糟糕的早晨。"中年男人对着十几岁的瘦弱少年和亚洲女人喊道，而另外两人都穿着对他们来说太大的橙色橡胶工作服。"我希望今天不会有鲸鱼被我们的装备缠住。"中年男人继续说。"当然不，"树枝一样的小青年大声回道，"鲸鱼的死亡与我们无关。这是一起针对渔业的阴谋。""太对了，"亚洲女人回应道，"我们不会让他们这样把我们打倒的。"然后，他们的讨论被从船舱里出来的妇女领队打断了，她挥舞着一个空杯子，喊道："我的咖啡喝完了！谁给我倒杯咖啡！"然后，她转向穿着迷你橡胶工作服、在甲板上爬来爬去的婴儿，喊道："你！去给我拿杯咖啡来！"我想，捕虾人的交流也是一种聚在一起的仪式，只是没有哥特式建筑和天使壁画加持。

　　管风琴猛烈的敲击声把我从渔夫的场景中拉了

回来,我意识到我走了会儿神。巴黎教堂里的弥撒除了让我联想到缅因州的龙虾,我没有获得其他更深刻的领悟。管风琴手在弹奏时犯了一个错误,一个走调的音符混进了精心编曲的曲子里,他让不完美溜进了对上帝和完美的赞美中。我想,之前所有的音符都白白牺牲了,走调的音符毁了一切。

萨特让我相信音乐是由音符的死亡构成的。要形成一段音乐,每个音符都必须通过呼吸的能量或手指的力量投射到空气中,然后坠入深渊,它们的生命比苍蝇的生命还短。音符们的短暂跳跃是光荣的,它们目标明确,齐心合力,就像神风特攻队一样,他们致力于一个使命,一个任务:创造出干净、清晰、有凝聚力的美丽的声音,每一个音符都应该是完美的。正因为如此,管风琴那个走调的声音听上去是一个音符最悲惨和最无意义的死亡,它不仅没能完成它自己唯一瞬间的发光,还让其他同伴的完美飞跃蒙上了阴影,毕竟,美妙的音乐是所有音符的共同努力。

"愿主与你同在……"神父继续念诵道,除了我,似乎没人注意到音符走调了。"也与你的心灵……"人群回应道。管风琴又一次响起来了,这一次没有出错,人们开始一起吟唱。当这么多人的声音融合在一个回音响亮的空间里时，每个歌唱者都脱离了他个人的特质，他们每唱一个音，就有一部分他自己离开了他们的身体，消失在空气里。在我眼里，他们正在模糊成相同的容器，接收着一种相似的集体崇拜的东西。我突然感到有什么东西正试图顺着我的食道，从我的胃深处爬出来。要么是我早餐吃的吐司长出了腿，爬上了我的喉咙，要么或许是我也被集体崇拜刺激到了，尽管我完全没有理解这种崇拜的意义。

"信仰的奥秘是伟大的，"神父唱道，"我们宣布你的死亡，主耶稣。我们宣告你的复活，我们等待你荣耀的到来……"我明白每一个词单独的意思："信仰"是对某事根深蒂固的相信，"死亡"让生命成为可能，"复活"是电子游戏角色死后发生的事情；但所有这些词加在一起，对我来说就失去了意义。我无法想象耶稣闪耀着他所有的荣耀，从地上复活的场面，我只能想象神父的话是白纸黑字地印在神父的圣书上。

唱诵的声音越来越响，管风琴的声音也越来越大，几乎变成了打雷般的轰响，好像管风琴在责备我的走神和胡思乱想。因为我纠结在一个音符的错误上，现在它要把它发出的每一个音符都深深地塞进我的耳膜。我开始头痛，头晕，开始恶心。原本和谐的乐声现在扭曲变形成了一种令人不快的噪音，好像人们在鸡尾酒会上的喋喋不休，互相交谈，不断窃笑。他们在笑什么？我吗？有什么好笑的？他们能看到我吗？可我在这里，躲在角落里。我环顾教堂，试图弄清楚发生了什么。在仔细查看了教堂的每一张脸和每一幅壁画后，我的目光终于落在了圣母玛利亚的巨大雕像上。她俯视着她的儿子耶稣，头被一圈星星包围着，她张开双臂，在混乱中显得那么宁静，又那么温暖。一条写着铭文的丝带在她的头上飘着："啊，无罪的玛利亚，为我们这些求助于你的人祈祷吧。"又一次，这些话对我来说毫无意义。我无法将圣母这个意象从她那座庄重威严的巨大雕塑里抽离出来，更无法想象她为穿着橙色工作服的捕虾人祈祷的情景。这个塑像和自由女神像还有那个社交焦虑的作家像有什么不同？是什么赋予了它具有其他雕像所没有的神圣力量？如果是尺寸大小的话，自由女神小姐肯定胜过了圣母玛利亚。自由女神小姐和圣母玛利亚又与一块未被雕刻的大理石有什么不同？就材质而言，他们是一样的。我甚至认为大理石也许更有质感，将大理石雕刻成雕塑会减少材料的质量和体积，因此，一块原始的大理石更有实质。

各种疑问像缠绕在圣母头上的星星一样缠绕着我，只是星星照亮了她的脸，而我的迷惑却把我拖进了一个没有出口的黑暗兔子洞。唯一的出口就在我身边，通往教堂外面的巨大木门。于是我向前一推，离开了教堂。我没有信仰可以留给那个地方，我也没有祈祷，我唯一留在教堂里的是我身体的余温，有那么一小会儿，我依靠的石墙不再那么冷了。

*

教堂外面的天似乎格外明亮。我还能听到没完没了的布道声和祈祷声，隔着一扇厚厚的木门，声浪减少了许多，它们被压缩成一种低语，就像隐约的铃声，给周围的环境增加了几乎难以察觉的复杂性。我转过身来，再一次看看教堂，想搞清楚在我心里这样一个地方有什么意义，一个代表信仰和人们寻找信仰的地方。对于我，任何一种被神圣化的东西，不管是是阴谋论还是 UFO 目击事件，我都不在乎。我希望能找到一个比我自己更大的，能够在更高的宇宙空间里俯瞰我这样一个生命的视角来看清楚我到底是谁，这样我就不必徒劳地在异国他乡寻找自己的本质了。我羡慕自由女神像、社交焦虑的作家雕像和圣母玛利亚雕像，因为他们永远都被固定在一块石头里。他们摆脱了哲学家希拉里·普特南所说的"缸中之脑"的状态，即如何模糊不清地游走于虚拟现实和真实现实的状态。这些雕像，他们的思想，他们的个性，他们的故事，他们的脾气，都被固定在静止的形态中，没有模糊性，也没有变化的可能性，它们的存在是一个确凿的事实，一目了然。

我走出院子，回到我来的那条街，Sèvres街。要是时间能回溯，我宁愿抹去我刚才的经历，倒不是说我所感受的有多么糟糕，但它确实让我有点不舒服。这时，尽管天气仍然寒冷，街上已经增添了很多年轻人的身影，他们看上去生机勃勃，充满希望，毫不在意寒风刮着他们裸露的脖子和脚踝，若无所事地走在街上。我回到了拐到教堂前的那条路，名字不熟悉的精品店一个接一个地出现了，它们的门还是紧闭着，星期天很多商店不开门，除了杂货店和面包店。

一个女人在我前面穿过马路，走进了一家面包店。我跟着她走到了商店的橱窗前，停下来看那些看上去美味诱人的羊角面包和费南雪。透过窗户，我能看到面包师正在帮那个女人挑选糕点，她买了杏仁塔和乡村面包。一位从店里走出来的顾客看到我，主动帮我拉开了门，示意我走进去。我犹豫了一下，点头感谢了他的热情，走进了店里。门在我身后关上，同时响起了清脆的提示铃声，面包师抬头看着我，热情地说了句"早上好"。我低声回应了他的招呼，担心他会像公园管理员一样开始更加热情的寒暄，于是赶紧排进了等着买面包的队伍，把目光落到各式蛋糕上，好像我刚才没有在外面想好选择哪种蛋糕似的。我买了散发着黄油香气的羊角面包，又选了热量很高的巧克力面包卷，我想："如果我不能把自己变成一块确定的大理石，那么就让我吃很多的小蛋糕，变得跟大理石一样重吧。"

然后我走出面包店，走向了下一个路口。

Chloé Chloe Chluoyi LuoYi

Unrooted

My roots are scattered all over the place. As a sprout, I often envisioned myself as a centennial oak tree with roots reaching as deep as the Earth's bedrock and a trunk wider than a hug, but it turns out that I grow like a weed.

Whenever my roots get comfortable seeping into the soil, learn to absorb the matter and fluid of that specific ground, and cuddle up with the native organisms, I'm eventually unrooted and plopped into another soil before I have time to grow thick and strong. Bits and pieces of that almost familiar dirt stick to my roots as they're unrooted and replanted, but that's all that it is—bits and pieces that are swallowed by newer soil sooner or later.

And then, the cycle starts again. I settle in, learn to get comfortable in the new dirt, absorb unfamiliar matter and fluid in new lands, and cuddle up with new organisms. But besides a looming hole in the ground that another plant will soon refill, do I leave anything to the old soil? I'd like to think that I do.

Perhaps weed isn't the right plant for this analogy. Perhaps I'm more of a raspberry bush, a grapevine, or any climber plant. My roots are cemented where they begin, but my leaves and branches twirl far and tight on endless plant sticks that expand into foreign lands.

I bear fruits along the way, and when they ripen, they fall to the ground, decompose, and seep into the soil they hover over. Whether they grow into plants of their own or turn into nutrients that nourish other roots is out of my control, but I'm simply comforted by the idea that at least some parts of me remain where I traveled and keep on giving in the local circle of life.

Linguistic Schizophrenia

When I first started reading Salman Rushdie's *The Satanic Verses*, I was baffled by some of his word uses—not so much by how crude they were, but by their spelling. "Amrika." "Chweetie-pie." He spelled them like the characters pronounced them. He printed their accents on paper.

Phonetic spelling is an assured way to bring depth and personality to a character, just like using colloquial language in dialogues. But self-conscious as I am, that spelling made me reflect upon my own tongue. What if I wrote out how I speak? How much of it would come out as standard American speech? How much of it would come out in a Franco-Chinese accent?

If it were five years ago, 80% of my words would have a dictionary crying. "Girls" would be spelled "gueurelz," "world" would be spelled "weureld." But I've now reached a state where I sound American enough to fool the British in "Ellowen Deeowen" (as Rushdie would write) into thinking that I'm from the States, and to fool Americans into thinking that I'm from California, or at least Canada.

However, despite a close-to-native accent, speaking English remains awkward, not because I am forcing sounds that my tongue and throat can't pronounce, but because I speak English by speaking French with English words. I learned to respond "not much" to "what's up" soon after I came to the US, but outside of memorized formalities, I still very much apply French linguistic logic when forming my sentence structures. This is why I'm constantly torturing you with lengthy sentences; you may thank Baudelaire and Flaubert for that.

English has started to take over the space that French occupies in my head, but I don't think I'd ever be able to get rid of how I speak. It's rooted too deeply in my childhood and education. It's a foundation that can't be unbuilt.

Different language systems inscribe different thinking patterns, and I am split into several languages, different incarnations.

True Ought, Told Ought

Travel always has notes of escapism: escaping an environment we know too well, escaping people we can't stand, escaping days that are starting to look the same, and responsibilities that weigh us down.

But traveling is also an opportunity to scrutinize our actions and decisions. It gives us some distance from our lives to reevaluate what we have at hand. Seeing lives different from your own is the best reminder always to doubt your beliefs and realize that nothing is certain. You recognize which elements in your life are acquired tastes and which aren't.

In the United States, especially among young people, many balance their lives by partying and binge drinking one day, then sweating it out at SoulCycle the next day. Swedes, conversely, don't go from one extreme to another but prefer to maintain balance within a golden range. They cycle to work daily and enjoy a glass of wine with coworkers over pleasant conversation after work. Rather than extreme excitement, it's a purer, simpler form of happiness, more sustainable too.

So, consider all the so-called "oughts" we believe in and obey. Which of these "oughts" are natural, which are constructs? Which are essential, and why? How many of these "oughts" occupy much of our time and energy but don't have intrinsic value?

And once you figure all that out, the enigma I have yet to solve is: how can you live with others, if not as an isolated, atomized individual, when you unlearn what you have learned?

My Love Mine All Mine

I always keep the good of what hurt me to still love the world and not hate its pests.

What existed was true. I lived something. Me. Not my father. Not my brother. Not my friends. But I.

The sensations exalted in my body and senses belong to me: I have my sorrows and embellish them as I please. I felt. And even in the ugly, it was beautiful.

Cat the Bat

I noticed that none of my thoughts and attitude changes are radical. They always occur little by little, like the "c" in "cat" slowly growing a tail to make the "cat" a "bat." It's such a discreet and tempered process that by the time the changes occur, they don't even feel like changes. I suppose it's the same in other domains: relationships aren't nurtured overnight. An oil painting doesn't dry instantly. Fruits take time to grow unless they're Jack and the Beanstalk or genetically modified foods, but science has yet to get there.

Sometimes, this frustrates me. I grew up around speed. I'm used to the fast-paced life and might be addicted to the adrenaline of constant change. Spinoza wrote that we are never anything but our desires, and any change, any action is performed to accomplish those desires. So, where does that leave me? Am I addicted to changes because I desire too much?

I realize that having too many desires and being scatterbrained ultimately yields nothing, no substantial changes, as you spend all your energy building foundations that need more than you can offer to grow taller. You're always left with unfinished construction sites that you'll toss in a corner to gather dust.

I can only pick my strongest and broadest desire, that is, to make something out of myself while doing what I like and focus all my efforts on building on top of it. What I can't nurture, I'll find in someone else, and admire it in them. That's the wonder of meeting people with different backgrounds; you get to walk in the shadow of their path and get answers for what could have been.

Daydreaming

Cookie Jar

My head is filled with cookies. Chocolate ones, bitter gourd ones, hope-flavored ones, big ones, small ones, smooth ones... there are of all types.

Somewhere along the line, the cookies jammed up my head. They kept jostling, each trying to get my undivided attention, forcing my skull to the brink of explosion.

There is no other way: the older cookies must go. The newcomer cookies, thus crush the old ones, turning the poor stale wafers into layers of dust that sink to the bottom of my head. Although the crushed cookies have lost their initial shapes, they still taste the same. Just a little kneading is all it takes to roll them back into who I used to be.

The Twilight Zone

There is an instant that occurs every night, which I call the Twilight Zone. It is the moment when I'm dragged from fading wakefulness to sleep. In less poetic terms, it is the brink of entering non-rapid eye movement stage 1 sleep.

Most of my most unhinged ideas emerge during that instant. As my brain waves slow down, I loosen my grip on logic and reality. In fact, boundaries between real and unreal completely blur, and the absurd fiction that my brain constructs appears just as likely as everyday tasks.

Once my brain starts weaving words and images into surprisingly coherent narratives, I have two choices: I can either make the active decision to wake up and jot down what the passage to the other realm infused in me at the cost of losing sleep, or tell myself that I'll remember the idea when I wake up and let myself pass out. From experience, these bedtime stories always evaporate the following day, so I open my eyes, grab my phone, and hectically write down images and words as I catch them, neglecting proper grammar.

The mornings after are reserved for revising these notes. Sometimes, my writing makes perfect sense. Other times, I'm reading cursive. But no matter the legibility, the Twilight Zone remains my favorite moment of the day, as I get to escape the daily state of complete awareness and full lucidity, which I find incompatible with the chaotic essence of life.

Son of Void, He is Boredom

Sometimes, when too many things go through my head, I don't think about anything.

Imagine the instrumentals of *Light My Fire* playing a thousand times in canon and constantly resonating in your head. Everything and anything accumulates and collides like agitated atoms to form, in the end, a cacophony that explodes into a mushroom cloud.

Those are clouds of heterogeneous thoughts. No matter how much I want to nuance and blend them, they don't. They bump, bounce, and quiver but refuse to form a mist, a homogeneous whole.

And the mushroom cloud's fruit is the worst. Son of void, he is Boredom.

Fragments

I sometimes imagine that if I close my eyes, I shall open them at the same time on the same day but in another place.

When I see people crossing the street at intersections, Yellow Submarine plays in my head.

Never think that you know everything. Never be certain about anything. When you think that you are certain, are you certain about being certain?

The plane is a capsule that reboots and prepares you for a different setting. A different lifestyle. A new start.

If Time is Eternal

I'm afraid that everything starts with no end, that the concepts of hours, minutes, and seconds are fictional, and that time is eternal, like space. I freeze when I picture space and time; they are too abstract for my comprehension, and I get stuck when I fail to simulate. I lose signal.

Every day, I wonder what story hides behind each face. It's no accident that I cross paths with one. Why am I passing you? Why are we on the same street?

Photos captured by cameras are never the images we want. The second we press the shutter, it's already too late. Only by becoming a prophet and anticipating the arrival of a magical moment can you capture it. It's like swinging a baseball bat; you must be able to see the ball's trajectory to hit it accurately.

Marlon Brandos

I find myself most at peace wandering in bookstores, most specifically secondhand bookstores. Feeling old crumbling pages against my fingertips is comforting. I enjoy the woody scent of the yellowed pages tickling my nostrils as I lose myself among piles and shelves of abandoned literature. The musky dirt and the greasy stains embedded in the damaged books do not disgust me—on the contrary, they lure me to touch. Whenever I'm stressed, all I need is to grab an old used book and sniff it as I run my fingers through the pages. No drug can beat that feeling. The leather-covered ones are my favorite ones. They diffuse a strong, distinguishable, almost animal-like smell. I call them Marlon Brandos.

I like to imagine who the books' previous owners were. Who would take notes of Jean-Francois Lyotard's writing for fun? Clearly, someone who reads Voltaire for fun. Why would someone sell *A Day Book of Montaigne*? After reading an extract a day for N number of days, there were probably no more days left. How many people have held this book before me, and where do they call home?

I'll never find the exact answers, but the simple thought that every book was once a personal valuable warms my heart. The stories behind storybooks are just as intriguing as the books themselves, and we call them "lives."

Closeted

My room's cleanliness reflects how I deal with problems.

Emotional problem? Just throw it in the closet. It's there, but nobody sees it.

So I stuff it and stuff it until there is too much stuff to be stuffed and the closet explodes.

Oops.

Homesick

Why do I feel like this? "Because I miss home. I'm homesick. " But why am I homesick? What do I miss about home that I can't find here? My room. The sun. A space of my own. Mom, Dad, someone who doesn't neglect me for video games. Someone who understands what I feel without me having to find the words to say.

I am not good with words. I feel and think but fail to instantly verbally translate them. I can only write them down, clean them up, trim my sentences, and review my words. They must be carefully arranged to reflect exactly how I feel. I cannot do that when I speak, not instantaneously. The words are congested.

I am a tire. A deflated tire. I am tired. I am tired of being tired and making people around me tired because I am tired. Homesickness is a disease, and sadness and boredom are its symptoms.

Farewell 2B-215

Moving out of my freshman dorm room, May 2019.

It's time for me to leave this room, the silence of the morning, the key in the door, the apprehension of monotonous colors.

Among the various slices of time that flew away like wild pigeons, the ground has never been so polished as this very moment.

Glancing at the mirror, I suddenly remember that my face is only one of the many it has seen. I wonder what grief and goodness endowed these everchanging landscapes as they peaked and melted. The loneliness of lovers there breathed, and the fatigue, the drought of hope, and the never-ending boredom bowed the head of their young souls.

But the features that shaped them were not all sadness. Their youth rose like waves that crossed a rock too high for their return. Their puddle now languishes there, imprisoned, an intense youth condensed in crystallized salt.

When the gentle fires of summer lead the next soul to its lifeless, dull bed of ashes, the waves shall rise again, and youth, crystallize again in the looking glass.

Existence and Disappearance

Existence and Disappearance

I like snowflakes melting on my face as if trying to bury me in the white landscape, layer after layer, snowflake after snowflake. It's a gentle and subtle disappearing, just like how certain people and memories gradually fade from our heads, new neural connections taking over old ones.

Every collision between snowflakes and skin is a tiny explosion. What seems to be silent and gentle crashes are thousands of crystals disintegrating upon contact with the body's heat, creating a microcosm of meteorites slamming into the Earth.

There's a loneliness to the sound of boots pressing onto the crunching snow, leaving temporary traces that'll disappear in an hour or two. Each footprint signals that I came and was present, but it is a discreet presence that disappears with the slightest wind blow.

This idea of walking and being while being constantly erased is why I like wandering in the snow alone so much. All my thoughts—like these random rambles and words—promptly disappear, leaving no trace, no evidence behind, unless I write them down. I'm walking on a tabula rasa.

I start from zero in thinking matters, climb to perhaps one or two, sometimes a thousand, then reset as if nothing happened once I regain the warmth of the indoors and the constraints of walls.

Horses and Cows

- I've never been so close to nature. Because I've always lived in cities, animals are reduced to cats and dogs, and even then, I think about them relative to humans. They are pets. They wander around us and depend on us. They live in a small apartment in *le Marais* and sleep on plump pillows with tassels we gifted them for their third birthday.

- And have you seen many of them—real animals—here in Jackson?

- Yes, some. More than I thought possible. Yesterday we went biking. If you take a left, carry on straight, and follow the road, you'll find a lodge ten kilometers in. And if you cross the road, you'll see splendid stallions taller than I am. We petted them. They were very gentle for animals of their size. They loved pats on the snout. We then walked across the road to see cows, but they were terrified.

They took a step back for every step that we took forward.

It's funny, the stallions seemed comfortably alone while the cows gathered. It's as if the stallions were content with their voluntary loneliness while the cows, unable to remain alone, tried to find happiness in a community, yet to no avail.

- And you? Are you a horse or a cow?

- A stallion, of course. Better to enjoy alone than to perish in a group... but hey, look! It's not every day that deer come graze your garden. Perhaps they do here...

Happy New Year

If there is a universal time when happiness should peak, it is the end of the year as the holidays kick in and festivities follow one after the other. But often, an inexplicable sense of loneliness arises instead, accompanied by doubts: why isn't my family reunited? Why is my uncle fighting my dad? Why do I have to stand the judgment of people I don't even like? Why don't I feel happy? Does happiness even exist?

Perhaps this sense of dissociation comes with an erroneous definition of happiness in the first place. The illusion of happiness lies not in its existence but in its definition. Kant defines happiness as satisfying all our desires, in extension, intensity, and duration. But such a definition of happiness may be the exact cause of our unhappiness since it always takes more to achieve the satisfaction that will never come.

True happiness is an engagement with life, committing for better or worse. Absolute happiness is a pipe dream, an innate mistake, and incompleteness is unsurpassable; it is consubstantial with existence. Happiness is assuming the confrontation with the inevitability, suffering, and uncertainty inherent to life. Men die, cry, and suffer, but they can also be happy, not in the brief moments where pain gives up, but despite pain, even with pain.

San Francisco-Shanghai Express

A white room is alive. It isn't empty but a monochrome and infinite space that overflows with meaning. It renews itself and always says more. It is Kandinsky's *White on White*, a cosmos with inexhaustive interpretations of the support, pigment, and frame while always retaining its essence, a white monochrome ingenuity.

A white room is a strange spiritual utopia. I wouldn't know what to do in a yellow, purple, or red room, but four white walls open to infinite space; a microcosm opens to a macrocosm.

I transport myself in my white cube. I tore off the colored lining from the outside world and wove it into threads I now twist and manipulate to recreate my universe, a flat yet voluminous universe where one sinks in and does not come out. My ideas become free objects; they unfurl out of my palms and become a light that transforms perception—an aimless matter in a dynamic search for thought activation.

I cannot quite grasp it.

It escapes me.

My universe is no longer mine.

It has never been mine.

In this white space, I hope for a subway from San Francisco to Shanghai.

To be a Kite

An airplane's window opens onto a fairy-tale landscape that transports us away from the everyday life that we know too well, too dull.

If standing at the foot of a building jungle humbles us, flying over them, taking an omniscient look at the earth chaining our feet and pulling us towards its bubbling heart like an overly passionate lover—Hades infatuated with Persephone—elevates us to the status of God, as the altitude accelerates our heart rate and the thrill of power. But once grounded, we find ourselves again reduced to the feet of the world.

The crown of mountains entwines Man in a vast lace of greenery overhung by a blue velvet cut by powdery peaks. Pearls of purple flowers form a capricious trellis as if a painter had arranged them in the most ornamental way. It is a fragile jewel, as the flower will not see dawn if the human hand skims it. We must, therefore, be content with contemplating it from a distance, so that this museum can be built and rebuilt on its own, unlike artificial vessels exhibiting artificial works lit by artificial lights.

This far too beautiful canvas makes us believe ourselves free, but a man in a beautiful painting remains trapped in a painting, regardless of how pleasant. This world walks us like a kite. The wire gets longer, and the kite flies higher ... look! It's almost reaching the heavens! But eventually, the thread stops, the spool stops turning, and that's it, Man is trapped. Only the destruction of the canvas shall make him free.

Vacant Vacations

Vacations are "empty time void of any pre-established function and use. They belong neither to God nor to daily, professional, social, and family life necessities. They belong to us. They are generally joyful property, but can sometimes be distressing, undermined by a fear of void," writes Jean Viard.

Vacations are a deserted time, a space free of structures. In this space-time, we can either use our temporary freedom to create another frame or entertain the possibility of living without shores to reach, without beginning or end, without history, norms, and events.

This is where habits appear as a positive stabilizing force. Habits are frameworks that challenge the tyranny of deserted time by excessively populating it with events, rites, gestures, objects, and ceremonies.

Even on vacation, I come up with repetitive rites and actions that serve as a temporal marker in the void, structures that cover existence's elementary flatness. I do not submit to the incontestable authority of order but make a choice that maintains my happiness and peace. It is perhaps an expression of my desire to create, define, and perpetuate my own universe, one that I rule and is destined to resist all others.

Life Itself

Autumn is a Second Spring

Fall is my favorite season. When grapes start blushing, and there are enough fallen pears to make you trip, I know fall is here.

It's odd. I'm aware that seasons come and go yearly, yet I always find myself pleasantly surprised by the sight of the first falling leaves.

Nothing's new. Certainly, I get a little older every year, but the tenderness of the autumn light, the austere last burst of nature's beauty, and the smell of cider in the air is a chorus that doesn't callus my ears. It's as if repetition isn't a cyclical daunt or one of the torments in Dante's *Inferno*, but a recurring pleasure that comes back and back again when the time is ripe.

Perhaps repetition isn't dull but gleaming because I know that each season is finite, and there may be a day when fall won't return. The anticipation of such disappearance makes repetition a brave continuity of life that resists destruction. As such, for every fall that dawns upon us, what we celebrate isn't newness or a new season but the resistance of life in the face of death.

Morning, Stranger!

How lovely to start a morning by chatting with gregarious strangers to the smell of crispy bacon and the sound of sizzling eggs!

This morning, I headed to the café and waited for my bagel, an apple in one hand and a coffee in the other. The barista was in a jovial mood and joked around. I didn't get the jokes, but he was indubitably nice. A man came in with a construction hat, radiating the same joy and energy. To my introverted surprise, he greeted me, and I greeted him back.

"How are you today?" he said.

"It's windy," I replied.

"Yeah, it's chilly, but I like it!" he exclaimed. "Are you a model?" he continued.

How did he know?

"You have a lovely pose and look," he added,

reading my mind.

I laughed and thanked him.

I would've talked a little more, but a bagel and an 8 AM class were calling for me. I thus rushed out the door and ran into the wind. On mornings like these, chilly wind gusts only blow you out of bed faster to embrace a new day.

A Word in History is an Entire Life

We walk along the San Francisco Bay. It's the beginning of May. The temperature has risen a few degrees over the past week or two. We stroll on the dry sidewalk as couples appear hand in hand amid crowds of runners, a familiar and serene scene.

It would be difficult to distinguish between this summer and the past few summers if not for the masks that cover passersby's lower faces. The fauna seems indifferent to the return of our kind, and the exotic flora, both domestic and wild, gleams brightly under the honeyed sun, unconcerned about the human condition.

We walk a long, long time. We walk sheltered from the sun, in the shade of eucalyptus trees, by the sea near bathers, and on the hills. The touristy pier leads to an elevated park, and the park to a coastal avenue towards Golden Gate Bridge. The landscape unravels uninterrupted, in accordance with time.

When historians look back to chop down time and reduce the world into events, everything seems so simple. "This or that period is characterized by this and that. Between such date and such date, this happened." But many branches that grow from "this" and "that" are omitted: the good weather, the return of nature, and a child that plays on the beach.

These are shards of happiness that we don't see in textbooks. These are tales to tell by word of mouth. These are the breath of humanity, traces that constitute an entire life.

Isolation Island

Human connections are affirmations of our own existence. To see and to be seen, to hear and to be heard, to resonate and to be resonated with. As humans, we are interdependent on each other. We seek to be cared for and loved and to pass it on. But what happens when we suddenly find ourselves isolated?

My eyes crossed paths with a man in the building next door. He stood there, glancing at me with my face against the glass. I wondered, did he share the same longing for a gasp of fresh air?

After that muted interaction, I became thirsty for more human connections through blue layers of tainted glass: I watched a college student sent back home wander around, not knowing what to do. I wanted to help the man staring at his computer screen for hours while I stared at him. I tried to catch their attention, but it was in vain. This isn't a fairy tale; people don't just talk to strangers.

So, I turned to those who I knew, those who I couldn't see through tainted glass, those who were oceans away, but those who, in the rare moments where screens aren't screens between people, felt the same way I did.

Womanhood

All Will Form A Common Frost

I was walking between you and this other person who was you, also. You led me in the front, and I followed in your shadow.

Despite the breeze that blew in from the window into the room deafened by a long absence, the odor of wood remains, breathing.

Something absent is evidently present.

Just like constellations of classic novels offer a romanticism hard to find in modern books, the density of this room developed great spaces of travel, a given freedom, a swan on a wound.

Silence, wind, and dust, all will end up forming a common frost.

Womanly

I remember seeing my face become rounder, my hips wider, and my bust puffing up a little bit every day, slight but noticeable changes.

These changes were beyond my control. I felt possessed by dark forces that acted inside my body, saddening me with constant anxiety.

Yet, simultaneously, I felt a little closer to the women, actresses, and models I saw on billboards and magazines, goddesses that boys talked about.

Some parts of me appreciated the newly found attention, but mostly, I felt awkward and confused about my changing body. I wore oversized t-shirts to hide my shape and tried to hide unfitting bras that showed even under loose clothing.

It was years later, once my angles and curves found a new orchestration that I came to accept my new figure.

I am not the most sumptuous nor the most sinuous.

I am even the most serious.

With my tall forehead and my sharp cheekbones,

I look like a pretty boy, some would say Alain Delon.

But what's the point of saying I don't love myself?

"Don't," a negation that isolates "I" from "love," burning with condescension.

Behind my falsely naive attitude, my mischievous air of woman-child, and the many nonsenses that I keep committing, I am a woman, pure and genuine. Through the voluptuous envelope that nature has given me, I aspire to a magnificent design: to perfect myself. It is a violent desire, more violent than all the others, although unrealistic. It lives and transcends me constantly. Yes, I want to give back to life the gift it gave me, this sublime gift that some still consider a scourge: to be a woman and to be proud of it.

Around the World

Anatomy of a Subway

Subways are public and private at the same time. They are public in that they gather hundreds of people in the same vehicle, each susceptible to the scrutiny of others. They are private in that everyone usually minds their business and respects other riders' personal spaces.

Its dual property makes it a fascinating space where you can glimpse into someone else's life and mental space while maintaining sufficient distance. It's a safe space where I feel like part of something communal without intruding too much, and reciprocally, the boundaries of my private life are respected.

Subways are a window into observing lives other than my own. These are people that I might never see elsewhere, people who have nothing to do with me but with whom I share something momentarily: a look, a handrail, a seat.

Psychic Planetarium

I came back to Boston, bracing for the start of classes. It's my first time back in the city since the pandemic hit. I've missed walking along the brownstones, being blown away by unexpected wind tunnels, stepping on fallen leaves soaked in melted snow puddles, and following solemn passersby's tight and hurried steps.

Wherever I go, I like to study and adopt local habits. I am a mosaic of the people surrounding me; I am what they say, do, and think. I adopted Silicon Valley's tech bros' productivity obsession, the Shanghainese's unbreakable regularity, and the French folks' joie de vivre.

We all have a psychic planetarium with stars that shine or dim depending on the input they receive. What characterizes us is not one trait or another but the complex puzzle that changes along our experiences, skill set, and influences.

An Impressionist Blizzard

I have this egocentric urge that makes me want to feel like I am the only person in this world, like I could scream as loud as I want and nobody would hear me, like I own the streets that I walk on, and nobody could cross my way.

Although walking is difficult, a blizzard offers the perfect conditions to feel like that. The city becomes a total white-out; it is silent through the flatness of the light but loud through the constant howling of the wind and the murmur of snow falling off trees.

When it's negative 11 Celsius outside, your skin flushes like it's clenching on to be the last remaining breath of warmth and life in this belligerent and disordered space. In fact, does the concept of order even exist here and now? With no vision, constant white noise, and temperatures preventing proper brain function, logic seems out of this world.

This pointillist landscape has an element of mystery because each flake—although ephemeral—is clearly distinct by its weight and humidity index. It reminds me of Debussy's compositions: both possess an impressionist character. Debussy's notes reveal themselves like the branches and windows discernible behind troubled snowflakes.

It wasn't long before I lost the sentience of my fingers. I thus removed myself from the painting, leaving Monet's magpie alone, and hid in the comfort of the interior, like the 600,000 other people in the city.

I wanted to tame nature, or at least ride its wave, but I couldn't, and it started swallowing me like a frog in boiling water. I can't imagine where I would stand without a roof over my head, a heater, and cooking utensils to get me through the storm. Without technology, where would we stand?

On the Beach

A gloomy beach is summer snow, nocturnal sunshine, and a carefree mother; an oxymoron that messes with common sense but completely renews your perception of reality and rewires your sensory experience of the world when you encounter it.

Half Moon Bay is my first experience of a not-so-touristy beach town, perhaps just a typical NorCal beach town. I was so accustomed to beaches like Venice Beach, where people outnumber sand grains, that it felt odd to see similar commercial street layouts and bubbly storefronts minus the sun and the people on Half Moon Bay's Main Street. Without the crowd's brouhaha, you could almost eavesdrop on the conversations between the bookstore and the small city hall that the wind carries through trees and fences. They are quite a gossiping pair.

Finding access to the beach is a bit of a leap of faith. You must follow a dirt path on a cliff without a clear destination and can only hope to find a narrow opening between the rocks that would let you dip your toes in the sand.

An impatient dog performs the real leap of faith. Frustrated by the waves' calling and its inaptitude to bark back at proximity, it jumps off the cliff and crashes into the sand while its owners busily converse. The distracted pair eventually hears distant whimpering and, panickily, starts looking for the dog. The dog is victorious.

The only ones who can find their way around are teenage girls walking around in pairs in hoodies and sweatpants. The beach is their hangout spot. They don't meet up to do or to talk about anything specific. They are simply there to watch the ocean wash time away and to tell stories they've told a hundred times before. For every story they tell, they tweak their wording and intonation so the listening party stays engaged upon hearing an all-too-familiar tale.

Of course, it's also possible that they have forgotten how familiar these stories are. Here, every bit of life is buried in the sand and blown away by the wind.

Art and Aesthetics

Art and Beauty

I distinctly remember writing a philosophical dissertation in high school on "Should art be beautiful?" Our class was divided into two camps: those who believed art to be ornamental and thus beautiful and those who thought that art is art if it expresses an idea.

A couple of exhibitions at How Museum reminded me of this divide. The first floor displayed Sorayama and MR.'s work, and the second floor displayed Beuys's work. Sorayama's sensual robots and MR.'s colorful pieces were visual feasts to the eye, while Beuys's work consisted of a mix of faded posters with faint handwriting and long and slow films. People rushed to take pictures of and with the first floor's stimulating work, yet none pointed a camera at Beuys' work. From the photography frequency, it was clear which was more ornamental, and which was more philosophical.

The final verdict we came to in class escapes me, but I always argue that art is what expresses an idea. In some ways, even the most decorative drawings and sculptures express ideas, albeit aesthetic. After all, beauty itself remains a concept. Given how easy it is to satisfy this criterion, it is no wonder that, as Beuys said, everyone is an artist.

Midday Thought

"Midday thought" is a philosophical term coined by Nietzsche and adopted by Camus. It refers to a beaming thought forged by the blazing Mediterranean sun at noon, which shines so much that it lights up the depths of absurdity. It is the spear that Liberty holds in Delacroix's painting, leading the people to riot against the renunciation of life, a spear so sharp that it punctures even the most cynical of philosophers.

Despite the absurd nature of his writing, Camus never renounced the pleasures of the Mediterranean coast. He recognized the turquoise tides as a passionate waltz, reenacting the highs and lows of the human condition, and heard an ode to life in the rustling of olive trees, gentle beings raised by sky and sea, which in turn nourish us. "There's only one culture," he wrote. "Not one which thrives on abstractions and capital letters. Not one that condemns. But one that lives in trees, hills, and men..."

Picasso in Madrid

I spent most of my time in Madrid in my hotel room. With flight delays and insufferable jetlag, I only explored the city for an hour before New York's moon reached across the Atlantic Ocean to lull me to sleep.

I didn't even check out the museums like I usually do anytime I visit somewhere new. I barely had enough energy to process the current time and day, let alone an entire city's culture and history condensed in a temple-like structure.

Despite being unable to contemplate Spanish masterpieces at the Prado, as I sipped coffee on the balcony, battling the tiredness weighing down on me, I noticed that the chair I used to rest my feet looked awfully familiar. Yes, the caning. I saw it in Picasso's painting.

Still Life with Chair Caning and a couple of

Braques' paintings were THE paintings my middle school art teacher used to introduce us to cubism. No matter how my teacher broke down the images, I never could distinguish concrete objects and faces in distorted renderings. But I do remember being impressed by the shard of realism that the caning brought to Picasso's otherwise symbolic piece. Though the caning meant to question the relationship between technical skills and art, I thought that it narrowed the gap between abstract art and reality, reminding the viewer that even the most abstract pieces stem from everyday life.

Thus, it makes sense that I, a stranger from the next century, unconsciously reproduced the scene from the painting in Picasso's home country. I took Picasso's lemon rind to flavor my sparkling water, cut my croquettes with his knife, and wiped my mouth with his scalloped napkin.

We all eat, sleep, dream, play. We all perform similar actions. But the difference lies in our approaches, perceptions, and what we make of the mundane.

Some turn a meal into abstract art, others simply flush it down the toilet.

A Subjective Scene

A cat has been circling our garden. We don't know where it's from or where it's going, but it often comes around to sunbathe or hide from the rain. I've tried approaching it once, but I scared it away. I can only talk to it through the glass, like this.

I find myself looking through glass and windows a lot. I often see things happen but never take part. I'm out of the frame, looking into the frame. I enjoy being the subject, not the object of observation. But then again, by painting and writing what I see, I'm inevitably putting myself in the subject matter. I distort the visible through intimate sensations that I can't shake and modify being and colors through an interior eye dominated by my state of mind.

The woman on my canvas isn't herself but how I perceive her. The tension in the hand that I paint and the glimmer in the eyes that I draw are but impressions and deductions. She may very well feel something else, and my perception of her may very well not translate perfectly through your eyes. You may even see a whole other woman.

After all, the artist's role is to become the other. We have mirrors instead of faces. Our role is to make what's most personal the most collective. Specific instances and emotions are magnified and distorted into sceneries everyone can relate to.

Less is More

I brought Wittgenstein with me on my trip to New York, so I've spent a good amount of time thinking about language and how it affects our experience of the world. Words are powerful tools. Thought is composed of words, so to some extent, the more words you know, the more ideas you can form and the "richer" you are. However, the real power lies not in memorizing the most extensive collection of complicated words but in neatly using concise language to convey the strongest emotions and clearest thoughts. In other words, less is more.

Wordsmith masters surely have complexities in their repertoire, but I doubt they use it for show. Instead, like cubist painters who mastered figurative paintings but stripped down their expressions to child-like drawings, every brushstroke and every word is purposeful.

I still find myself using words for the way they click on my tongue and their rhythmic decadence, but I am learning to put substance over form and find lyricism in the minimal.

If You Don't Understand the Rules, Then There Are No Rules

Verbal expression is limited, so we turn to visuals and music to convey the indescribable. Animation, opera, and cinema are perhaps the wealthiest artistic mediums to currently exist, as sound, movement, and words all come into play to render complex layers of emotions, meanings, and ideas.

Though I've toyed around with words and brushes long enough to be able to draw the contours of my thoughts, my expression remains handicapped due to my lack of musical background. How I would love to scream and smile with a violin and give a bird its wings with a piccolo.

Being restricted to visual arts and writing is knowing enough of a language to make it through the day-to-day but not knowing it well enough to develop a personality and articulate unique thoughts. It causes tremendous mental traffic jams, and the only way to mildly dredge them is to cast the shadow of a thought with a channel I'm already familiar with.

But the upside of such ignorance is that when I do pick up an instrument, I'm never restricted by a "correct approach." To have no foundation means that I can think outside of the box. In fact, the box doesn't even exist.

This is the blessing and the curse of the inexperienced rogue artist. You'd never compare to the conventional maestros, but you can always create your own playing field.

Music is a Filter

Music is the most powerful filter for life. When you're walking down the street, what's playing in your ears sets your mood and your energy. It even changes how your surroundings appear to you. Is the girl walking out of the store about to have a meet-cute moment, or is she at an all-time low? It depends on whether you're listening to the Smashing Pumpkins or Patrick Watson. What about the skaters? Are they angst-skating or just vibing? Depends on if Mac Demarco is playing.

I've curated a niche collection of songs because I wear earphones constantly. But lately, I've realized that this habit may stem from an attempt to escape from silence in my head, a silence that would push me to face some fearful thoughts that I try to avoid.

Music silences my thoughts when they are too agitated, and the more anxious I am, the noisier and the more complex the music. High-tempo and complex compositions are gatekeepers that prevent unwanted thoughts from crossing the mind-and-trouble barrier.

But I've realized that doing so doesn't inherently appease any sorrows. In fact, they only build up more. What's more helpful is to process the roots of whatever's bothering me, and to do so, my mind must be completely available, that is, silenced.

Lately, I've been trying to go on my daily walks without background music other than the ticking sound of traffic lights and occasional car honks. Surprisingly, by making myself available to my thoughts, I also made myself available to the world. Without the intense strutting to the pressing beats of the Talking Heads, strangers started talking to me.

Music might make you feel like the main character, but I've had all my main character moments when I'm present, music-less.

The Next Crossroad

Sunday morning, Paris was still asleep. The sky had lost the summer lightness, and heavy clouds wallowed above the gray zinc roofs, blurring the distinction between the heavens and the ground.

I walked along the cobblestones of the Quartier Latin, towards the firmly shut doors of the Sorbonne. The cafés, usually filled with glass clinking and loud chatters, were awfully quiet. The only traces of the night before's lively chaos were cigarette butts floating in turbid rain puddles. They looked like miniature boats sailing in a pond, like the ones that children pushed around at the Jardin du Luxembourg.

Autumn had settled in. Cracked tree trunks let out mossy moisture that dripped on fallen leaves. My boots landed heavily on the drowsing leaves, without making a sound. The moisture muted their crisp cries, tenderizing their crackling breakdowns. It was the first time in a while that I had felt this calm.

The last time I was in Paris, I was a different person. In fact, I'm not even sure that I could qualify as a person. I had no real identity, and only existed within relationships with others; my professors, classmates, and a loose-knit friend group that extended from classmates, and perhaps, also the Creole lady behind the college café counter, whom I briefly chatted with every morning when waiting for my coffee, before heading to class.

I never sought after any of these relationships; they all came to me passively. They always started with eye contact that I couldn't avoid, a "hello" that I couldn't ignore, or, in the most forced scenarios, a group assignment e-mail that I couldn't decline. And when the simple greetings turned into questions, I turned them back to the questioner instead of answering, launching my interlocutor into unilateral tirades on their sorrows and likes. By then, I would have plated myself with reflective shards and melted the amorphous blob that I am into anything that would fit the shape of the receptacle. My identity was so sparse and malleable that I could slide into the mold of anything. Romane. "Rome-Anne." Even my name wasn't mine, but a hybrid of the city where my parents met and my grandmother's name. I couldn't exist on my own. I was always defined by others, be it those who came before me or my environment.

*

I walked along Rue Soufflot, heading towards the Jardin du Luxembourg. The cigarette ships made me want to see real sailing ships. A woman stood by a bakery on the Rue Saint-Jacques. The occasional breeze blew whiffs of buttery sweetness out of the vent, signaling the imminent opening of the store. "Opening Hours: Monday through Saturday, 7:00–19:00. Sunday, 8:00–13:30," the sign on the door read. It was 6:40, and the baker transferred sheets of baked goods to the window display, to the faint beat of reggae that escaped through the door crack. In the darkness of the morning, the flaky crusts glistened under a warm lamplight, like treasures in a long-lost underwater chest. Today, he'd only be a baker for a bit. He'd have the whole afternoon to be a father, to visit his kids, and, maybe, if he had seen the woman at the door, to take her out for coffee.

I've often been tempted to walk into one of these bakeries since I got here, but every time I was about to step in, after studying the sugar pattern on the croquettes and the syrup drizzle on the raspberry tarts, I never worked up the courage to push through the art-deco front door. I was afraid of relapsing into the vortex of identity confusion, where a simple "bonjour" would extend into a "how's your day?" which in turn would trigger my old habit of returning the questions and molding myself according to the responses. Those were manners from another time, another phase, that I hoped to leave behind. I came to Paris precisely to observe a world different from mine, and where I stand within it, or outside of it. No matter the framing, I wanted to paint myself as a stable picture that stayed the same regardless of the perspective. I wanted a stable sense of self. And to find that, I had to avoid any engagement that could scramble the picture.

The closest time I came to finding myself was my junior year of college, in a campus lift. One October morning—one warmer and brighter than the Parisian autumn daybreak—my 9 AM class ended early, and the professor released us ahead of time. As always, my bag had been packed 5 minutes before the class wrapped up, so that I could avoid the goodbye chitchats, get an elevator to myself, and avoid an eternity of awkward silences and stiff exchange of smiles. My long strides and fast pace often meant that my calculated attempts to secure personal space were successful. In the event of failure, say, I see someone approach as the doors closed, I'd hold it open for them and start to decide which wall to look at during the minutes of silence sprinkled with occasional "dings!" that were about to come. I didn't know who I was, but I knew that I didn't want to be rude.

That October morning, as always, I rushed out of class and headed straight toward the elevator. I walked close to the wall on which side the elevators were, because, like a racetrack, the distance traveled closer to the wall is always the shortest and fastest. My rush was worth it. I was the only one waiting for the lifts. I pressed the elevator button and started rejoicing at the free hour that just appeared in my day. I didn't really have any activities or tasks to fill it with, but the simple thought of gaining more time, thus more freedom, to subject my body to whatever thought, action, or inaction that pleased me was a delight. But as my mind fluttered to thoughts of occupying the newfound freedom with a game of online chess or mindless media consumption, footsteps grew louder and closer. A tall feminine figure soon appeared in the frame, heading straight toward my privatized vehicle. The doors started closing, but she didn't seem to accelerate. She kept on slowly but loudly breaking the tiles with her block heels as if she was sure that the door would stay open for her. And it did. I held it for her. She didn't know who I was, but she knew that I wouldn't be rude.

She looked up from the ledge of her cap, revealing half of an eye covered by a wispy blond fringe, and extended her narrow lips into a faint smile in lieu of thanks before turning to face the door. The elevator buzzed and started its fiddly descent. I stood in the corner, contemplating the buttons, but also her cloudy reflection on the copper panel behind the buttons. Her washed-out jeans and white tank top were stretched by quite an athletic build. Her arms had a slight dent below her shoulder caps, casting a sharp shadow that only marble statues have. And although her tilted cap darkened her upper face, her narrow eyes glistened under the ledge, perpendicularly framing her prominent nose with a slight bump, and her square jaw lightly clenched under the overhead light.

She struck me, and I didn't know why. I have always found androgynous looks to be particularly dazzling, but there was something else about her.

She wasn't just beautiful; there was something uncanny, slightly uneasy about her beauty.

It was only when I watched her figure disappear in the ground-level crowd that I realized the uncanniness stemmed from the axiom that we were the same. We were anatomically the same; we had the same height, same build, same angularity. But she shone like the sun, and I beamed like the moon. Her blonde hair and grey-blue eyes must have made the difference; both my hair and eyes were brown. Or, perhaps, her assertiveness and calmness contrasted with my turbulent and avoidant demeanor. She'd be what I'd be if I stood up straight: a question mark stretched into an exclamation point.

I later found out that she had been studying me too, because days later, after the encounter, she would send me a social media follow request, the modern way to signal, "You caught my eye." And on my birthday, her best friend (my group project partner from a billion years ago) posted photos to celebrate her coming of age. Sharing a birthday only further cemented my belief that we were two sides of the same coin.

Despite never speaking to her or crossing her path ever again, I still thought of her and trusted that she thought of me too. After all, despite running on different orbits, the sun and the moon remain fundamentally connected by the forces of gravity. And once in a while, when the time is right, their path organically aligns, projecting magical eclipses in campus elevators.

*

When I got to the Luxembourg Gardens' gates, which saw dozens of morning joggers coming in and out on weekdays, only a few elderly men rested on the benches across the street. Billions of raindrops and wind gusts cut through the benches' dark green paint, revealing light brown wood patches, much like the brown spots that time left on the men's hands. Later in the day, when the city would have woken up from its hangover, the benches would be packed with students reading, friends chitchatting, and parents watching their younglings shrieking and kicking the gravel on the ground.

But meanwhile, the chilly dawns belonged to lonesome elders, their daybreak promenades, and the whispers of the soft breeze that caressed their hair. It was the only time of the day when they could visualize the Paris that they knew; the Paris with sidewalks polished by leather shoes, not sneakers. The Paris where the Notre-Dame needle still stood as erected as their younger selves at student protests. In an empty city, it wasn't hard to be transported back in time.

Storefront panels might have changed—a shoe repair shop might have been converted into a designer boutique here, a bookstore into an architecture studio there—but the outermost shell, the Haussmann architecture, stayed the same. In the window displays, the unchanging limestone guarded dioramas of memories that reflected in the men's eyes, frozen like the dancing faun statue that led to the gardens' sail ship pond.

I walked past the men towards the gates quietly, throwing a discreet glimpse here and there from the corner of my eye. None of them looked up. I was like a specter to them, the projection of a future they tried so hard to keep away, but that carved through their hands, up their arms, all the way to their neck, and down their eyes. Eventually, it would leak inside and reach their soul, triggering a sudden and painful awakening of their mortality and the sweet but illusory nature of living in the past. My generation was a sunspot that tarnished the sun that was their "belle époque," a dust speck that is well and truly there, but that disappears with a slight squint of eyes, or during dawn, on the weekends in Paris.

I pressed on the side gate, only to find that it made a startling noise and wouldn't budge. "October Opening Hours: 7h45–18h45." I was too early. I thought about turning back and going down to Montparnasse, but I felt short of breath, and was enthralled by the near-meditative states of the men on the benches. Their faces were mostly inexpressive, if not with a soft hint of sorrow between their brows, yet so at peace. I wondered if I could submit myself to such a state with so little life experience. If I sat on a bench and contemplated what I've seen and where I've been, could I reach the same level of tranquility? What if I did the opposite, and contemplated what was to come? So, I crossed the street and walked along the row of green benches, until I found an unoccupied one to sit at.

As I sat down, an elder man with a wool peacoat and leather gloves one bench down turned and glanced at me. I felt awful, as if I just scratched a painting that I wasn't supposed to touch, or even see. I glanced back and squeezed out an upside-down smile as a sign of apology, to which he responded with a faint smile. We both turned back to face the park and sat in silence.

The sky was starting to lighten into a steel blue above the spade tips of the gates. Other than a few birds chirping and my neighbor's occasional throat-clearing, nothing could be heard. It wasn't until what seemed like an eternity later that a quiet but deep and raspy voice pierced through the monotony of sounds. "I often get coffees there, the staff is very nice." I got drawn out of my reverie and turned toward the provenance of the sound, my next-bench neighbor pointing at the store behind my bench. I looked behind at the modest terrace and said, "Oh, yes, it seems like a nice spot." He turned back to face the park, and so did I.

Silence reigned again for a minute or so. I looked at the piles of fallen, rotten leaves and watched as the wind painfully pushed their bodies against the ground, leaving a faint trace of moisture behind. They moved slowly, arduously. The moisture leaked into tiny cracks in the concrete, imprinting a fractal of the leaves' shadow. Afar, a man in a yellow vest approached with a trolley, a broomstick clenched between his fingers. He swiped away the leaves as he moved, compiling them into scattered little hills along the street. With every swipe, he blurred the moisture's pattern with his broom, connecting the traces of distinct leaves, and merging them into a dark, shapeless blob. With a few simple gestures, he obscured the individual messages that the leaves painfully drew with their blood. And in a few hours, when the sun would come out, even the senseless blob that remained of their living would have been dried to nonexistence.

The tragic dance of the leaves would never stop, so I turned to my neighbor to stop the show.

"Do you come here often?" I said, lightly turning my cheek toward him.

"I live just a few alleys away," he said, "so I come here for some morning air every so often."

"It is a nice spot," I replied, realizing that I repeated myself.

"What are you doing out so early?", he asked, taking the reins of the questions. "I can only assume that you stayed up all night."

"No, I'm just an early riser. I can't sleep past 6," I said, shriveling back into brevity.

"You're too young to be that old. At your age, I never woke up before 8h30. And when I woke up, I'd spend an hour getting coffee with my friends. We all lived close — nearby here actually — and would talk our time away on terraces." He paused, then looked at the leaf swiper. "Dreams are too enthralling to be broken at 6. You should relish them carefully, while you still can."

"Do you not dream as much anymore?" I asked.

"I do, but I don't remember them as much as I did," he said.

"Why relish in fiction when you can live in reality?" I pressed on.

"Fiction?" he repeated, with a hint of surprise. It struck me that my question may have come across as insensitive, but he chuckled with childish enthusiasm and carried on. "Dreams are just as real as reality. You dream with the same senses that you experience the world with. You still see, smell, hear, and touch, only with much more vibrancy. Your senses are enhanced."

He raised his hand and, lightly pointing his index, started drawing the contour of the trees in front of him. "You see movements that you could never see awake, you encounter colors that have no name. You can even smell them and see fragrances."

"Aren't they lonely though?" I said. "Dreams are strictly your own, they're not a shared experience. You can't invite people into your dreams. And when people do appear, they disappear in a flash. You might experience a beautiful world, but it's a beauty that only you can access, one that you can't share."

"They are, but it's no different from this world where you and I meet. This is a lonely world where faces blur and disappear too. Only in this world, they take a couple of years to disappear" he replied. "The faces that I knew 30, 40 years ago, they're just as blurry as the faces in my dreams; I find myself struggling to remember my own mother's face. I can only vaguely recall her smile, and the mole sitting on top of her right eyelash. I suppose," he said, knocking the wood, "these benches also remind me of her angled shoulders. Heck, she was a tough woman. But I can't picture anything else. Her face is a blur."

He removed his gloves and put his hands in his pockets.

"I suppose that faces blur faster in dreams because dreams have an accelerated timeline. You live a whole life within a night. You experience everything harder, faster, stronger — a little like you guys with your phones — but they also fade harder, faster, and stronger." He tilted his head and looked straight into my eyes. "You should take a good look at me and see if you can draw my portrait in 10 years!"

I quickly diverted and looked away, before discreetly going back to his face to outline his jaw, his cheeks, his forehead, his mouth, his nose — every feature but his eyes. Even without looking at them, I could feel that they'd devour me. They scrutinized every inch of my being from left to right, inside and out, like a blinding flashlight with no visible light beam.

Seeing my (lack of) reaction, he continued.

"You know, in physics, much of the unknown is described through darkness. 'Dark matter. Dark flows. Black holes.' Anything that we can't shed a light on is dark. But I no longer want to force light where it should be dark," he proceeded. "I've spent much of my years trying to understand why the world is the way it is. Where do we come from, where are we going? What is this planet that we live on? Why are we glued to the ground while birds fly in the sky? How expensive is the whole universe? I've been on a perpetual quest to rationalize and explain the world. But as soon as I assert an explanation with reason, reason negates itself. We overturn old paradigms to instill new ones, only to overturn the new ones with even newer ones. All these efforts and so-called eurekas only to find ourselves back at the beginning, only this time, with wrinkled hands and aching joints."

He took his hands out of his pockets, lightly rubbed his left knuckles with his right hand and put his gloves back on. "So, after dedicating my entire life to answering whys and hows, I came to the conclusion that whatever light we cast on truth is distorting, and the only way to even get close to it is through darkness. This darkness is the one that we see in our dreams. That senseless, ephemeral, and ever-changing space holds more truth than any law of physics or cell diagrams. In the end, scientific diagrams are no different from Hilma af Klint's paintings or a witch's grimoire—just symbols that are sometimes logical, sometimes mythical."

On that note, he ploddingly buttoned his coat, turned to the side to put his weight on the washed-out backrest, and strenuously stood up.

"Well, I've latched enough on you today. Make sure to get enough sleep, and remember my face," he said humorously, pointing his index and middle fingers in a V and gesturing at his face, before walking away.

I watched as his shriveled figure slowly progressed down the street, like fallen leaves pushed by the wind. He walked past the street sweeper and greeted him with a nod. By then, the sweeper had swept all the leaves into piles and started collecting them into a container. Half the street was already leafless, regaining its neutral state of bare slab of concrete, of an untouched piece of paper.

Eventually, my bench-mate made a right and

disappeared from my sight.

What color were his eyes again?

I couldn't recall.

*

After the man left, I sat a little longer on the bench, contemplating the things that he said. His words reverberated in the silence of the morning long after his silhouette disappeared, wrapping around branches, slithering in and out of tree holes. He seemed to sustain that the world had not one truth but many truths, be it in terms of laws of gravity of individual stories. Did he conflate the notion of truth with possibility? Or hypothesis? Perhaps even the facade, of things, how things appear? Because the prerequisite of truth is that there can only be one, universal and unchanging. Truth is not channeled through our senses and perceptions, which, them, can be diverse. Truth is what lies beneath it all, what our sensory receptors can't hack, and therefore what our intellect can't process. It is the state of things beneath illusions, the tree that falls even when we can't hear it.

Then, a terrible thought struck me. If I was right and there was only one truth, a truth inaccessible to us beyond the illusory shadow cast by our senses, that meant that if I did have a real, immaleable self, I would never be able to access it. My eyes, my ears, my touch— all my senses corrupt the clarity of data that compose the real me. And no matter how brilliant a brain I have, like an efficient math formula equipped with the wrong input, it would never yield the correct output.

I supposed I could gather data from a second or third party, but their data-gathering process would be just as corrupted as mine. They, too, used their ears, their eyes, their touch to interact with the world, including the object that I am in their world. They, too, would provide corrupted data that would only draw vague— if not inaccurate— contours of my identity. Bacon and Velazquez both painted Pope Innocent X, but which portrait was he really? None. In fact, both portraits portray different versions of

Pope Innocent X, but the man beneath the cloak, Giovanni Battista Pamphilj, remains unknown.

*

The sky brightened enough for the gates' spikes to clearly cut through its patch of blue, and a pair of park rangers languidly got off a vehicle to open the park. The purring of the ranger's car and their vernacular chitchat officially signaled the end of Paris' travel back in time. The old men started getting up from the benches, and unhurriedly crossed the street to go through the park. The younger one of the park rangers, a slender dark-haired man with a patchy 5 o'clock shadow beard, stood by a newly opened gate, while his coworker strolled back to the still-purring car. Leaning against the fence bars, he greeted every man that passed by with a cordial, semi-rehearsed "bonjour." Sometimes, he said it when the passer-by stepped in front of him. Other times, it was a pre-anticipated greeting that he threw at the target while they were still a few steps away. On rare occasions, he projected it to the back of the passers-by, long after they'd stepped into the park, forcing them to turn around and acknowledge him.

I studied his curious display for a few minutes and deduced that he didn't time his greetings according to the park visitors' positions, but according to a rigid, fixed time interval, something along the lines of 1 "bonjour" every 8 seconds. Why? I didn't know. I could only assume that he'd been on the job for too long and had said one too many greetings to mean them. I tried to picture him, on his first day on the job, carefully learning the ropes and meaning every word that he said. But as his fingers grew more dexterous around the chains, tying and untying them like second nature, he lost his warmth. It was as if every contact with the cold iron gates neutralized his temperament, giving him rheumatism of the heart. Now, he was left with nothing else but the shell of a word, which he systematically repeated in intervals, like the bars of the fence.

I watched him for a little longer, and once I was satisfactorily confident of my hypothesis, I decided to put it to test, and joined the sparse line of bench flaneurs going through the park.

I crossed the street like the ones who walked before me, paced toward the gates, and slowed down when I got close enough to the greeter. Calculating each of my footsteps, I waited for the ranger to release his latest "bonjour," then projected myself forward at a pace that guaranteed that I would stand right in front of him in exactly 8 seconds.

"1…2…3…" I counted in my head, carefully adjusting the size and landing of my strides. "4…5…6…" My gait must have looked a little funny because, while he barely looked at the other passers-by, he looked right at me as I approached. "7…and…8." Perfect. My foot landed next to his as I finished the count. "Bonjour," we projected at the same time, his tenor voice echoing my contralto. "Bonjour," he said again, this time with a vocal inflection, refusing to give the last word.

I didn't look back and walked right past him.

"That second 'bonjour' messed up his intervals," I thought. "Now, he'll have to start again."

It wasn't long before the ranger resumed his greetings at the same old pace, with the same old tone, but the fact that I disrupted his lethargy and beat him at his own game — even if just for a minute — made me euphoric.

Did messing with his mind really make me happy? Did I enjoy wreaking havoc? Not really. But I did enjoy seeing through hidden patterns disseminated into the world and breaking them. When you're unaware of those patterns, they may easily dictate your life and consume you like a tidal wave, without you even realizing it. But as soon as you bring your head above water and notice the logic and rules that run the world, it's easy to crack the code and take control, like I took control of the ranger's game and shook him of his subconscious. That was, of course, a harmless example, but the same rules apply to scenarios of much higher magnitude.

*

As I approached the crown jewel of the garden and the reason for my visit — the sail ship pond — the joy brought about by the little stunt that I pulled dissipated. Any sparks that it brought to my eyes were quickly dimmed by the weight of the cold and dusky morning. I found myself falling back into the state of neutrality that accompanied me since dawn. The patterns I disrupted had regained their momentum, like a sharp wound that somehow healed instantly.

The sail ship trolley wasn't out yet. The water was calm. The only boat on the horizon was a ship with a crushed mast, lying at the feet of one of those ubiquitous green metal chairs in the park. I've always thought that these chairs were a much better choice than static benches. They are charming yet light to carry, enabling flexible dispositions. Large parties could gather them in a circle so that everyone could look at everybody and have a place to sit. Loners could also grab a chair and dash into the shade of a tree. They'd be able to people-watch from their chosen perspective, without compromising their comfortable solitude.

I wondered if, having spent all this time in the park, the ranger noticed the ingenuity behind the chairs. I wondered if he noticed anything else that was secret to me.

I picked up the ship with a broken mast and wrapped the mainsail around the mast bit that remained attached to the deck. The fabric was black. It was a broken pirate ship, the only one in a batch of colored national sail ships, the black sheep of the bunch. Children either loved it for its uniqueness or hated it for what it stood for. Only a few kids loved it for what it stood for; kids who'd grow up to support villains in Marvel movies. Which one of them broke it? An overeager pirate lover? Or an ankle-biting superhero?

I examined the ship's body, no cracks or significant damage. It should have still been able to float, as long as the weight was evenly distributed. What remained of the mast severely leaned to the right, so I kneeled on the ground and picked up a handful of gravel to scatter on the left side of the deck. I placed the boat in the water with one hand, and with the other, dropped the gravel one by one, being careful not to overload it. 6 gravels seemed to have done the trick: the ship detached from the support of my hand and stood on its own. Any sudden movement could have destabilized it, thus I refrained from pushing it. I got it standing again, I thought, yet I couldn't fully reinstate its function.

I made it stand again but it was crippled. I pushed it above and beyond its limits, but maybe it wasn't my place to do so. Maybe it was tired and wanted to be left alone. Maybe it was the end of its journey as a sail ship, and it had embraced the fate of being forever displayed on a shelf or getting a second life as a recycled wood pencil. Yet, I forced it on the water, made it stationarily float above a dark pond of water. If the mainsail unraveled or the wind blew a little too strong, all chances of a second life would have dissipated. But so was life. You must pick yourself up no matter how broken you were.

As long as you have a breath left in you, you have to lock it in you, and keep grasp on the material world. That was what Jimmy told me.

Jimmy and I went to the same high school. He'd sit next to me on the school bus when it was full, but we never talked. That was until he broke his foot and couldn't play soccer with his mates during lunch breaks anymore. Then, he started joining me on the steps of our school entrance as we'd chew on our prepacked sandwiches.

Jimmy would go on and on about his life with no restraints. His mouth made up for the decreased activity of his foot. He told me everything from his sister's wannabe boyfriend and his hamster's tragic fall down the stairs, to his parents' obsession with Christian decor and his love for Manchester United. He even spilled his best friends' deepest darkest secrets, though he had sworn to keep his lips sealed. I wasn't too worried about him spilling mine because he never asked me anything. Our relationship entirely entailed him talking, and me listening.

One night, as we rode the bus home, he kept rambling on and on while staring at his fingers. It was unlike him; he always spoke with utmost confidence while looking straight at his interlocutor. "That's how you get people to take you seriously," he said. But that night, he didn't look that assured. "Every day," he said, "I wake up to nail my skin and bones together, or my vitality leaks out. But the leakage never stops. Every time I mend a patch of my skin, another inch rips apart. My life is a permanent effort of mending and patching, and I'm waiting for the day the leak would stop. Maybe, once my skin is fully covered by layers and layers of thick patches, I'll finally be leak-proof. But then, will I still be myself again? I guess I'll find out when I'll be old."

Jimmy would never find out. 2 years after graduation, 18 miles into a race, his heart gave up.

I never went to his funeral, it felt out of place. I knew all about the people in his life, yet never felt like part of it. Besides, I moved across the country for college, and wouldn't have been able to make it. I only symbolically said goodbye when Jimmy's best friend, the only one who noticed my tree hole of a function in his life, asked me to send some soil from where I was for his burial. It was a collective effort that his friends around the world partook in. I grabbed a fistful of dirt from a houseplant that I brought from home and mailed it anonymously. I knew that Jimmy wouldn't need my name to recognize that it was from me. Each mineral particle in the soil breathed the stories that he told me. Unlike the park's thin white dirt which kicked up into clouds with every step that I took, the soil imbibed with Jimmy's stories was dark and heavy, and emitted a rich mossy scent that reminded me of dark forest hearts untouched by human hands. The olive twig that grew in it was also astoundingly sturdy; it had a thick stem for a tiny tree. One thing was for sure, its vitality would never leak— at least not until I'd transfer it out of the sheltered pot, into an unknown, perhaps hazardous soil, where it would have to fight for minerals against stronger, thicker trees.

*

A miniature replica of the Statue of Liberty guarded the northeastern entrance of the park, near the Rue Guynemer entrance. It stood hidden between oak trees, nestled on a square pedestal of carefully trimmed hedges. What a minuscule, almost ridiculous-looking pedestal compared to its American sister's gigantic, climbable throne. One is a stairway to heaven that lifts people up, a container that allows millions of faces to peek out of its crown yearly and gaze upon an entire city. A paradisiac elevator. The other is just another bronze statue that blends in with the other ones in the park. An average cloaked bronze woman rendered tiny by the buildings that stand behind it. And keep in mind, Parisian buildings aren't even that tall: to preserve the city's signature landscape, buildings aren't allowed to be more than 5 stories tall. The Montparnasse Tower being an experimental exception, a creation that unified the cross-generational definition of an eyesore.

If Miss Liberty of the Park got off her pedestal, we would have been the same height, we would have seen eye to eye. It's astonishing how the size of a hand and a foot and a crown changes your entire perception of the figure. Without her towering height and oversized features, she resembled but another student roaming the park after class, carrying her class notes and hourly cigarette.

*

My shadow merged with the shadow of the buildings crowning the park. I dipped into it like a glacial lake. The straight, aligned rows of buildings closed over me, forcing my feet to step on a pre-assigned path, a narrow uphill cobblestone street that extended far away. "Charcuterie." "Monoprix." "Librairie." All sorts of words ornated the lower levels' storefronts. Serif, sans-serif, all caps, no caps, black words with white outlines, white words with black outlines, italicized golden words without outlines... These big and small scribbles were the only differentiating factors between rows of identical buildings. But despite aesthetic differences, the words insinuated the same: "You can walk wherever you want in this alley as long as you stayed in the alley." They instated a false sense of free will, much like the teachers that I submitted to throughout my schooling years. Grade after grade, different versions of the same authoritative voice repeated the same phrase, "Write whatever you want, as long as it's within the prompt." Every one of them tried to curb my tendency to grow my ideas out of the frame; they didn't like how my words grew like carnivorous plants that shattered the support pole they were supposed to hold on to. Big red "Farfetched" and "off topic" became regular markers on my copies, scarlet letters which I wore with pride. I never relented. My teachers' words meant nothing next to my father's. He was a stellar writer in his youth, the type that got his compositions read out loud in front of the class every Monday. My teachers all wished I was him, yet he approved of my weeds. "You don't get anywhere by playing it safe," he'd tell me. "Better stand out with inconsistent extraordinary than blend in with consistent mediocrity. You're on the right track. Your own track."

I took these words to heart in all my exploits, rejecting conformism and paving my own way in every aspect of my life. Every endeavor that I took on had to be carefully thought through, and only then chosen. Before jumping off a cliff because my peers did, I carefully calculated the gain-to-loss ratio, then decided whether I wanted to follow along, or climb a cliff by my own. I quickly concluded that most cliffs were not worth jumping off, as I had no interest in being just another body from the corpse pile to soften the next person's fall. As a result, I kept to myself and climbed my own cliffs. When there were no more cliffs to climb, I built a tower on the tallest cliff. And when I needed a break from laying bricks and cementing the structure that would fulfill my purpose once completed, I looked out from the embrasures that I left in the walls and contemplated the world below me. When the tower was still a meager foundation, I could see my peers jump off cliffs one by one, and happily mingle over the carnal mattress that they formed upon landing, before the next batch landed on their faces. But as the tower took height, the hedonistic smiles on their faces blurred into an indistinguishable blob, as if their features sunk into their skin, and they were turned inside out. Now, when I looked down, I couldn't even distinguish the contours of human bodies anymore. Thousands of bodies stacked over each other looked like wildflowers in spring.

High above the clouds, the skies were a permanent neutral shade of blue.

There was no rain, no sunshine, no ups, no downs.

Distance washed out the cacophonic sound waves from below.

Silence reigned.

I wondered if the permanent hustle bustle on earth persists.

I wondered what it was like to experience severe weather down low.

Rue d'Assas finally ended at the Alphonse Deville Plaza, a small triangular concrete island outlined by a few tree bushes and a toilet. In the center of the island hid a small angular lot, where three benches turned towards the statue of a shriveled man standing in the bushes. Behind the man stood two bronze slabs as tall as him, with wobbly inscriptions carved on their uneven surface. I paused at the curious display; they were short segments of words separated by a point. The man must have been a writer of some sort, and behind him stood his lifetime of work.

He had bristly brows like a paintbrush that farcically contrasted with his bald head. His expression, however, was stern, his lips tightly sealed. A long and prominent nose dominated his face; if I were to imagine what the personified Nose in Gogol's literature looked like, this would be it. Below his narrow shoulders, he had one hand in his pocket, the other out and slightly curved, with fingers under tension, as if he was trying to hold onto something. An expressionless yet alert face seated on a body under tension; his entire body language indicated discomfort. He reminded me of the awkward kids that stood in the corner at college parties and kept to themselves, their entire body language screaming that they didn't want to be there. He reminded me of myself.

Truth is that my social discomfort was never misanthropy. It lied in the despair of not knowing how to exist within the same space as others. It was rooted in feeling like my body, my presence and my existence were extra entities, dead weights that couldn't float with the conversation flow, nor the movement of light bodies that drifted across the room, from one group to another.

In a room where chitchat and laughter fused with music and the clinking of glasses, I could only anchor myself within my own body and harden my shell, so as not to drown in the rising tide of exchanges and questions.

From within my shell, I could hear people loud

and clear. I could see their expressions, notice their intonations, and strip down the fancy packaging of their words to what they really meant. But the tragedy lied in that after I stripped them down, I couldn't package my own response in a way that matched my interlocutor's tone. This disability made anything that came out of my mouth either extremely harsh or incredibly forced. I became hyperaware of my speech and engaging in small talk felt like trying to talk without a tongue and vocal cords. I gasped for air and tried to project sounds from the depth of my lungs and throat, but no matter how much force I put into it, all that came out was a shapeless blob, a structureless mumble, a goose's honk.

Mr. Writer here, with his forward neck, tense fists, and sober gaze, looked exactly like me each time I contemplated whether to approach a group at a party or to leave the premises. And each time, I left the premises. I decided that it wasn't a cliff worth jumping off from and went back to building my tower.

*

I crossed the street and stepped into another park, Boucicaut Square. That one I knew well. I frequently frequented it. I ventured there for the first time after buying overpriced honey and taramasalata at Le Bon Marché.

Usually, after shopping, I would head directly to the Sèvres-Babylon station to join the underground crowd and re-emerge ten minutes later on the other side of the Seine, at my temporary home. But that one day, as I exited the store, a sudden stillness seized me, followed by an inordinate sense of vertigo. The crowd around me started walking in circles, and the midday sun shot ice javelins instead of warm sun rays. The zebra crossings guiding clients into the store ballooned into gigantic animals. One of the two creatures then opened its muzzle, turning into a cavernous mouth, and closed itself on me, swallowing me whole. I started to shiver and stagger and let go of my taramasalata tube and honey jar to hold onto a street pole. A few eyes grazed at me, in the cold and unbothered "seen it all" way that Parisians do so well, until one pair of big brown eyes, sparkling and kind, bent down to pick up what I came here for and handed it to me. "Are you okay?" the big brown eyes asked, pursing its lips together, accentuating the "you." "I'm fine, thank you," I responded, looking around and blinking my eyes, adjusting to the sunlight that reappeared. I regained balance and let go of the pole. The ice javelins were gone. The animals crawled back into the ground. People started walking straight again. The big brown eyes, which turned out to be a short, stubby girl with wild brown curls, smiled at me, let out a "good" (emphasis on the "oo"), and walked into the store.

I was afraid of vertigo catching up again, so I headed into the square and sat down on a bench deep in the park, near the fence, where the crowd was scarce. I've had enough scornful eyes stare at me for the year and would rather faint in peace than under scrutiny. Luckily for me, my body temperature was normal, my blood circulation was fluid, and the animals didn't come back for me. My stale, eventless reality was back: it was just me, my taramasalata, and my overpriced honey jar. "Thank god overpriced honey uses sturdy jars," I thought, examining the fall victims in my bag, "otherwise 24 euros would have gone down the drain." The jar somehow justified the price.

I put the jar back in my bag and braced to get up. It was then that I saw, there, sitting at the opposite bench, a tall, lanky young man gracefully scrolling through his phone, his narrow eyes fixated on the content. His untamed brown hair signaled that he just rolled out of bed, yet his carefully layered outfit—a blue open shirt over a white t-shirt and beige slacks—suggested that he cared a minimum about his looks. "Certainly, he's going for the effortless French boy look," I thought, "or maybe, he is an effortless French boy. Hard to tell which it is." The wind then blew open his shirt, revealing a "MoMa" print at the upper left corner of his t-shirt, right where the heart is. "An effortless, or seemingly effortless French boy with American

Modern Art on his heart. Sounds like a dream," I thought.

I then left my bench as planned but, have set on many unplanned visits to the square ever since. I told myself that it was to enjoy the company of nature — nature in a blue shirt and beige trousers — and I did stumble upon the beautiful sight of nature a few times, usually during the week, around 3 or 4 pm. But one day, as nature sat on his usual bench, a delicate, sweet-looking girl approached and asked him if he knew where she could buy cigarettes. He gestured towards a street, but the girl didn't understand. So, he stood up and walked her over.

After that, I've never seen nature-in-a-blue-shirt-and-beige-trousers again.

As I exited the park, the sudden urge to revisit the location of its first sighting took over me. So, I turned around, went back into the depth of the park, and headed to the familiar bench.

I sat on the bench for a few minutes, before ultimately deciding that it was a stupid gesture and that I was wasting my time.

Afar, church bells started ringing. I counted ten times. A faint sound of angelic vocalizing rose in the air.

It seemed like the few minutes I spent on the bench were a few hours.

*

I rose from the bench and felt blood once again flushing through my legs. My jeans grew cold and hard and wrapped my legs tightly like a stiff, wet canvas. The morning sun rose through the sky like a runny egg yolk that burst its juice onto rooftops, tainting the grey ledges in a bright shade of orange. The city looked like a tropical paradise. I stayed wary. The National Weather Service issued a morning frost alert, signaling low temperatures in the early hours, a first glimpse of winter. It was as if the sun and the cold made a deal: the sun baited unknowing people out with its peacock tail so that the cold could bite onto the first pair of cheeks that dared to peep through the door.

I walked out of the square and discovered that a slow-moving crowd accumulated along Rue de Sèvres and turned into Rue du Bac. Elderly and middle-aged women with short, tousled hair walked in pairs, forming a herd of silhouettes in austere long coats, wool gloves, and leather handbags. "What a chilly morning," one said, her shoulders raised to her ears to protect her neck from the cold. "It is, and it's only the beginning," her shorter neighbor sneered. An infant started crying behind them. Its mother, a young, fleshy woman with brown skin and charcoal brows held it closer in her puffer, and let out a long string of "shhh," trying to appease the baby. The shorter woman turned around to look at the crying infant, then the mother, prompting the rest of the herd to do the same. "She must have been the leader of the pack," I thought, "always saying the last word and commanding the actions of the group."

The woman's attention was then grabbed by a pair of young, leaping voices, laughing their lungs out in the streets. Their laughs tinkled like clear water graveling down a brook, or the crisp cracklings of a blazing wood fire — a vivacious spirit of nature that warmed you up. They came from the opposite direction of where the crowd was headed. "Do you remember when you thought you were the shit? You were definitely not the shit," one voice exclaimed. "I know right? Crazy," the other voice responded. They spoke English with very rounded "r"s. Hmm, fellow Americans. Both voices then fell back into unstoppable giggling, completely unaware of the pack leader's scrutiny. She looked them up and down disapprovingly, though it was hard to know if she disapproved of their behavior, nationality, or their bodycon mini dresses and smudged eyeshadow. Perhaps all four. "Youth these days," she sighed. The others promptly acquiesced and joined in the sighing — all but a woman with red hair, who looked at the two girls and let out a faint smile.

How did such disdain for youth emerge in these women's hearts? Did the accumulation of experience replace the sense of wonder they once possessed, and that now migrated onto the

American girls' faces? When I was 13, the cashier at an ice cream parlor was particularly mean to my friend and me for no reason. My friend reported back to her mother, and her mother half-jokingly told us that if any older women were mean to us, it was because they were jealous of our smooth skin and plump cheeks. But I thought that there was more than that. Biological youth was a very surface-level element and could only inspire very surface-level envy. These women's scorn was anchored on a deeper, philosophical, existential level. The only theory that I found susceptible was that with age came experience, and with experience came the death of newness, the ubiquitous feeling that fueled the vitality and boldness of the youth. These women mourned their ability to see newness. Each of their days was lived as deja-vus. "Every day is a new day" meant nothing to them anymore. The only newness in their eyes were new wrinkles on their faces.

The woman with the red hair, however, seemed to have retained somewhat of the ability to wonder. Her youth hadn't dissipated in a blitzkrieg of nausea toward life. She didn't look struck by the delay that existed between her girlfriends, the world, and the cries of innocence and complete freedom that they thought they would have forever. She was still sensitive to the joy that exuded from a new generation of youth and felt connected to it. When the flower of biological youth withered within her, it left a seed that sprouted into a pair of unwavering eyes that could notice the new and exciting every day. That is why she could look at the girls and smile. Habit kills imagination, but hers lingered on like a stubborn sprout.

*

I followed the herd of women into Rue du Bac. They were all heading to church, to the Chapel of Our Lady of the Miraculous Medal. I should have known by their sober attires. It was a Sunday, at ten in the morning, and nothing was more telling than the identical gold medals around their neck.

The woman with the infant followed behind.

The baby had stopped cooing and fell asleep.

The women approached the arched door that led to the chapel, where two women with headscarves sat on their suitcases, one at each side of the door, brandishing empty paper cups in their hands. As the group stopped at the entrance, one of the women on the ground reached out her cup to the pack leader. The pack leader looked at her waving hand, then looked up at the statue of the Virgin Mary nestled on a pedestal. "Monstra te essem matrem…" she muttered, reading the ribbon of Latin words around her nest, "Show yourself to be a Mother." She stood still for a minute, looking thoughtful, then walked past the begging woman, greeted the officiate at the door, and ballooned into the courtyard that led to the praying chapel, followed by her minions. The woman lowered her arm in despair, brought her knees to her chest, and curled into a ball. Her foot knocked over a piece of scribbled cardboard during the movement. "Mother of three hungry children. Spare a change. Anything helps," it read.

The woman with the baby stopped at the same spot soon after. Like the pack leader, she looked up at the statue, then looked down at the curled-up woman and her dampened sign. She seemed too defeated to shake her cup again. Quietly, one hand still lulling her baby, the mother bent down and took out a few euros and a bag of applesauce from her puffer's pocket. She put a five euros bill back into her pocket and dropped the rest of the items into the woman's cup. The begging woman raised her head, gently nodded, and curled back into a ball. The mother rose and followed the women into the courtyard.

Sustained notes on the organ started to ring from the chapel's door. It was 10:05 and the morning mess was about to start. I followed the mother into the chapel and saw that the women's pack had already taken their seats on the church benches: front row, center seats, the short woman sitting in the middle. A man sitting at the edge of a bench got up and gestured for the mother to take his seat, while he made his way further down the bench.

She kindly thanked him and sat down, covering the baby's head.

There was something comforting about being in the vicinity of the holy. It wasn't the presence of God itself that was soothing; I was too much of an atheist to even conceptualize that. Rather, it was the gathering of people who believed in a common faith that created a completeness, a perfect circle. This Asian woman, that voluptuous man, that twig of a teenager, and this blond couple with their four toddlers… All these people, who each have their voids to fill, gathered here once a week with their separate anxieties, sorrows, and joy, and came together as one through prayers and gospels. Even that short woman who seemed to hold no one in higher esteem than herself submitted herself to this common experience.

I imagined their voices filling the gaps in one another's bodies as they chanted, muffling the screams of the evil imp tormenting their thoughts on the daily. I didn't know if I believed Pascal when he asserted that "God was an infinite sphere, the center of which is everywhere and the circumference nowhere," but I believed that the common faith that people harvested in him rendered themselves an infinite and perfect circle, at least for an hour, during Mass.

The organ stopped ringing. What filled the silence instead were two rows of nuns humming at each side of the altar. A priest then slowly advanced to the front of the scene, placing the bible on elevated support. The Mass was about to start. I didn't feel comfortable sitting on the benches, so I decided to stay put by the door and leaned against the cold stone wall. I did not want to weigh down the incoming levitation of faithful voices with my lack of faith—though I did wonder, what rested in my heart where faith could have been? Anyway, I would have hated to be the odd particle stuck to the bench like an old chewing gum while the rest of the audience transcended somewhere else.

The singing stopped.

"In the name of the Father, and of the Son, and of the Holy Spirit..." the Priest started, prompting an "amen" from the audience in unison, "may peace be with you," he sang. The organ and the nuns echoed his chant with a similar chorus, and words indiscernible to my ears. "We are your people, Lord," the priest continued. "Here we are gathered on this Sunday to welcome the grace of the Lord's forgiveness. Let us prepare to celebrate the mystery of the Eucharist by recognizing that we have sinned." He then started to read some sacred scripture from his book, prompting the audience to join their voice to his. I didn't pay much attention to the content of the reading, because the only thing that I could think about, was how "to sin" and "to fish" were the same words in French. This discovery prompted my mind to imagine the churchgoers as a group of lobstermen in Maine, gathered on deck to discuss the state of the sea and the weather, early in the morning, before heading out to sea. "It's a rough morning," the voluptuous man hollered at the teenage twig and the Asian woman, both swimming in orange rubber overalls way too big for them. "I hope no whales will get caught up in our gear today." "Hell no," the twig yelled back. "The deaths of the whales have nothing to do with us. This is a conspiracy targeting the fishing industry." "Damn right," the Asian woman added, "we ain't gonna let them bring us down like this." Their discussion then got interrupted by the pack leader coming out of the boat's cabin, brandishing an empty cup, yelling, "I'm out of coffee! Somebody get me some coffee!" She then turns to the baby crawling on the deck in its mini rubber overalls, and cries, "You! Go fetch me some coffee!" The communion of lobstermen— I supposed that was a form of coming together as well, just without the gothic architecture and cherubic murals.

A sudden bang on the organ drew me out of my fishermen's dream and plunged me back into the reality of being in a Parisian church, listening to scriptures that evoked nothing but Maine lobsters in me. The organ player had made a mistake; he let a false note slip into a carefully composed partition. He let imperfection slip into the celebration of God, of perfection. All the previous notes died perfectly for nothing, I thought. That one note ruined everything.

Sartre convinced me that music was made of the death of notes. To form a piece of music, each note had to project itself into the air through the momentum of a breath or the strength of a finger, then crash into the abyss. Their lives were shorter than the life of a fly, but unlike my peers who threw themselves off cliffs, their leaps were glorious as they had a purpose. Like kamikazes, they dedicated their entire existence to one mission, one and only: to produce a clean, clear, and cohesive sound for the enchantment of the ears of men. For this, the false note that leaped from the organ knew the most tragic and aimless death. Not only did it fail its one moment to shine, but also tarnished its peers' perfect leaps. After all, making music is a team effort.

"The Lord be with you…" the Priest continued chanting. It seemed like nobody noticed the false note but me. "And with your spirit…" the crowd responded. "It is the church, body of Christ, and the temple of the spirit. We praise you in your joy."

The organ rang again, this time without mistakes, bringing the attendees into a chant. The voice of the disciples merged into a blob, half muted by the potent sound of the organ. When that many voices merge and blend in an echoing space, the concept of individuality was drawn out of every singer. With each word that they chanted, a little bit of themselves exited their body; they became vessels that embraced collective idolatry. I suddenly felt something trying to crawl out of my body, down my esophagus, from the depth of my stomach. Either the toast that I had for breakfast grew legs and was climbing my throat, or I was drawn into the collective idolatry, despite ignoring the meaning of any of it.

"The mystery of faith is great," sang the priest. "We announce your death, Lord Jesus. We proclaim your resurrection; we await your coming in glory…" I knew what each of the words meant individually: "Faith" was a deep-rooted belief in something. "Death" was what made life possible. "Resurrection" was what happened when your video game character died. But all together, they made no sense at all. I could not picture Jesus' rising from the earth, glowing in all his glory. I could only visualize the words in black and white, imprinted on the priest's sacred book. A lack of imagination on my part.

The chanting voices echoed more and more, and the organ grew louder and louder, into thunder. It was as if the organ was avenging my disdain towards the false note by screwing every single note that ensued deeply into my eardrums. It gave me a headache, and I felt dizzy and nauseous too. The harmonizing voices then started to morph into an unpleasant cacophony, like people blabbering at a cocktail party, talking over each other while sniggering unceasingly. What were they laughing at? Me? What was there to laugh about? Could they even see me? I was there, hiding in a corner. I scanned the chapel, trying to make sense of what was happening, and after scrutinizing every face and every mural, my eyes finally fell on the giant statue of Mary, overlooking her son Jesus, surrounded by a halo of stars. She seemed so peaceful amidst the chaos, so welcoming, with her arms wide open. A ribbon of inscription shot over her head: "O Mary conceived without sin pray for us who have recourse to you." Again, the words meant nothing to me. I could not conceive Mary beyond the giant sculpture that was meant to sublimize her, even less picture her praying for fishermen with orange overalls. And how was that sculpture different from the statue of liberty, or the socially anxious writer? What gave it the sanctity and godly powers that those statues didn't have? If it was the size, then Miss Liberty certainly overpowered Mary. And how were Miss Liberty and Mother Mary different from an untouched block of marble? Substance-wise, they were the same. I'd even say that the marble had more substance; chiseling marble into sculpture reduced the mass and volume of the material, therefore, a raw block of marble would weigh more.

Questions wrapped around my head like stars wrapped around Mary's head, only the stars brightened her face, while questions dragged me deeper into a dark rabbit hole with no exit. The only exit lied beside me: the massive wooden door out of the chapel. I thus pushed myself forward and slid out of the entry. I didn't have faith to offer. I didn't have prayers. The only thing that I left to that place was residual body warmth. At least the stone wall wouldn't catch a cold now.

*

The day seemed excessively bright outside. I could still hear the endless chanting and praying, but behind a thick wooden door, they weren't as loud anymore. They shrunk into a whisper, like a ringtone that added auricular complexity to the surroundings, but barely noticeable. I turned around to examine the chapel one more time and wondered what it would have been to have a place like that in my heart. A place dedicated to faith and belief, any kind of belief. It could have been conspiracy theories or UFO sightings; I couldn't care less. I just wanted something bigger than myself to occupy that space, so that I didn't have to fill it by finding a stable picture of myself in a foreign country. I envied the statue of liberty, the writer, and Mary for finding themselves paralyzed in a block of rock. They've escaped the state of being a brain in a vat, a self-aware abstract concept. Their thoughts, their personality, their story, and their temper, were all immobilized within a static representation of themselves, without ambiguity or the possibility of change.

I walked out of the courtyard and turned back to the street I came from, Rue de Sèvres. If only walking backward could erase the experience I just had. It wasn't particularly dreadful, nevertheless still a little off-putting. The youngsters were now out, despite the freezing weather. They seemed unoccupied by the wind slashing their exposed neck and ankles, and leisurely strolled along the sidewalk. I continued down the street and followed the path that I would have taken if I didn't turn Rue du Bac. Boutique stores with unfamiliar names popped up one by one. Their doors were tightly sealed; stores didn't open on Sundays, but grocery stores and bakeries have been inviting clientele in for a couple of hours already.

A woman crossed the street in front of me and headed into a bakery. I followed her silhouette to the store's window display and stopped my course to examine the croissants and financiers. My attention drifted from the food to the people inside, and I watched as the baker assisted the woman with her choice of pastries. She got an almond tart and a country loaf. Having scrutinized everything that I could scrutinize, I set foot to regain my route. But just as I walked past the bakery's door, an exiting customer held the door and gestured for me to go in. I hesitated for a second, then nodded to thank him, as the mother with the baby did at church. I stepped into the store, triggered a bell to ring, and was greeted by an energetic "Bonjour." I greeted the baker back with half his energy and got in line. "Now look who's becoming the park ranger," I thought. I glanced at the pastries as if I hadn't already hypothetically made my choice outside and waited for my turn to order. "If I can't turn myself into a block of marble, I might as well inhale three dozen chouquettes and weigh like one," I thought.

图书在版编目（CIP）数据

在中间 /（法）罗衣著. -- 上海：上海文艺出版社，
2024. -- ISBN 978-7-5321-9051-5

Ⅰ. I565.65

中国国家版本馆CIP数据核字第20247NP408号

发 行 人：毕　胜
责任编辑：肖海鸥　叶梦瑶
封面设计：尚燕平
内文制作：常　亭

书　　名：在中间
作　　者：[法] 罗衣
出　　版：上海世纪出版集团　上海文艺出版社
地　　址：上海市闵行区号景路159弄A座2楼 201101
发　　行：上海文艺出版社发行中心
　　　　　上海市闵行区号景路159弄A座2楼206室 201101 www.ewen.co
印　　刷：苏州市越洋印刷有限公司
开　　本：1092×787 1/32
印　　张：12.875
插　　页：10
字　　数：206,000
印　　次：2024年7月第1版 2024年7月第1次印刷
Ｉ Ｓ Ｂ Ｎ：978-7-5321-9051-5/I.7124
定　　价：59.00元
告 读 者：如发现本书有质量问题请与印刷厂质量科联系　T：0512-68180628